MIDNIGHT
CRAVINGS

ALSO BY ALLISON HOBBS
Brick
Scandalicious
Put a Ring On It
Lipstick Hustla
Stealing Candy
The Sorceress
Pure Paradise
Disciplined
One Taste
Big Juicy Lips
The Climax
A Bona Fide Gold Digger
The Enchantress
Double Dippin'
Dangerously in Love
Insatiable
Pandora's Box

Joelle Sterling

MIDNIGHT CRAVINGS

SBI

STREBOR BOOKS

NEW YORK LONDON TORONTO SYDNEY

Strebor Books
P.O. Box 6505
Largo, MD 20792
http://www.streborbooks.com

© 2012 by Joelle Sterling

ISBN 978-1-59309-419-5
ISBN 978-1-4516-5588-9 (ebook)
LCCN 2012933939

First Strebor Books trade paperback edition October 2012

Cover design: www.mariondesigns.com
Cover photograph: © Keith Saunders/Marion Designs

10 9 8 7 6 5 4 3 2 1

Manufactured in the United States of America

For information regarding special discounts for bulk purchases, please contact Simon & Schuster Special Sales at 1-866-506-1949 or business@simonandschuster.com

The Simon & Schuster Speakers Bureau can bring authors to your live event. For more information or to book an event, contact the Simon & Schuster Speakers Bureau at 1-866-248-3049 or visit our website at www.simonspeakers.com.

This novel is dedicated to my niece, Jordan Arianna Sealy

CHAPTER 1

Holland Manning's hand wandered to the nape of her neck. She cringed as she touched the area where her newly shorn hair came to a point. She felt utterly naked—completely vulnerable with short hair. Hair that once hung to her shoulders now abruptly stopped at her jawline on one side. The other side had been raggedly hacked at the top of her ear.

She'd asked for a layered cut—an asymmetrical bob.

"No problem," the stylist had reassured her when Holland gave her a picture of singer, Rihanna. The stylist did a hack job. A first-grader using a pair of safety scissors could have done a better job than that so-called professional.

Staring in the mirror, Holland winced as she analyzed her reflection. She tried to focus on her good points. Her skin was smooth and flawless, showing no signs of her long battle with acne. And with her braces finally off, straight teeth were a major improvement. Sadly, neither of these enhancements could deflect attention away from her scraggly hair. Allowing her hair to be hideously butchered like this was total self-sabotage.

Holland zoomed in on her nose, which had always been a problem area, and her nostrils seemed more pronounced, flaring unattractively. Her chin looked particularly elongated and pointy.

Oh, God! Angst-ridden, she closed her eyes. She envisioned stream-lined nostrils and at least an inch of chin surgically removed.

Chaela Vasquez and lots of other girls at school had gone under the knife to enhance their looks. If Holland's mom could afford it, she'd get some work done on her nose. Not a full nose job—more like a mini-procedure. A few tiny snips to her nostrils would make a huge difference.

Glancing in the mirror, she turned her face to a different angle. There was no improvement; she still looked gross! Getting her hair cut was the worst decision she'd ever made. This horrendous style magnified her poorest features. Heartsick, she fought the urge to cry. There was no time for tears; summer break would be over in less than a month, and she needed to come up with a solution.

Frustrated, she grabbed the swath of hair that hung limply in her face. This piece of hair held no purpose. She grabbed a pair of scissors and considered cutting it. With lots of gel and hairspray, perhaps she could give herself a mini-mohawk. *Bad idea.* Creative hairstyling was not one of her strengths. Imagining a far shoddier hair disaster, she put down the scissors, and released the handful of hair.

Trying to blend in with the popular girls...the cool kids with perfect hair and impeccable fashion sense, Holland had attempted to step up her game, but now she wished she'd never bothered. She should have been content staying under the radar. Now, with such a noticeably bad hair cut, she could count on lots of negative attention.

Holland wouldn't be able to handle kids pointing fingers and laughing at her. To become the butt of cruel jokes would totally destroy her.

Her best friend, Naomi, was taunted every day. For some unknown reason, she never went to her parents or asked any authority figure at school to intervene. She bravely endured the heckling and jeering and withstood all the cruel pranks that were played on her. Now Naomi's off the hook. Somehow, her parents found out what was going on, and had her transferred to an all girls' academy.

It was painful to think about how cruelly Naomi was treated at school. No one should have to live like that. Thankfully, Naomi's new school had a zero tolerance for bullying.

Holland returned her attention to the mirror. Hoping to find some redeeming qualities, she scrutinized her hair once again. Nothing had changed, and it was terrifying to imagine how Chaela Vasquez and her groupies would react to her on the first day of school. *God, I wish I could crawl into a hole and hide there forever.*

All of her problems would be solved if she could go to the academy with Naomi. But that was out of the question; her mom could barely afford their regular monthly bills. Private school tuition was out of the question. *Maybe she'd consider the idea of homeschooling me—at least until my hair grows back.*

Way to go, loser, she chided herself as she imagined her heart-throb, Jarrett Sloan's, appalled expression when he took a glance at her stupid hair.

Holland noticed her mother, Phoebe, standing in the doorway, observing her. Her expression was hard to read, but Holland could feel her emotions: a mixture of pity and concern. To no avail, Phoebe had tried to talk Holland out of cutting her hair.

"I thought I'd look edgy," Holland said in an apologetic tone.

"It's not that bad, Holland," Phoebe replied, wearing a weak smile that failed to reassure. "It's not like you lost a limb. It's only hair…it'll grow back." Her words were followed with a headshake, which Holland interpreted as an unspoken, 'I told you so.'

"Do you know any hair-growing spells? Something that works really fast?" Holland giggled as if she was joking, but the desperation in her voice spoke volumes.

"Well…I suppose I could do some research. Or I could ask one of my coven sisters," Phoebe said as she turned to go to her work area that was once the family dining room.

Her mother belonged to an online witch's coven. She spent more money than she should on occult paraphernalia. Their modest home was overrun with candles, weird herbs, crystals, vintage jewelry, and all sorts of witchery tools. She'd recently launched a website, offering love and money attraction spells. Business was not exactly booming, but Holland's mother was confident that word of mouth buzz would eventually direct traffic to her site.

For as long as Holland could remember, her mother had dabbled in the occult, boasting that she and her daughter were the last descendants of a long line of witches. Holland had never taken Phoebe's claims seriously. There was no proof that either of them had any special powers.

Last year, her mother was into astrology and numerology. Before that, she was reading auras and tealeaves. Her mother was such an embarrassment with her various New Age interests, and lately she'd been getting a lot worse. Her interest in witchcraft was becoming an obsession—an expensive obsession. Phoebe was spending so much money on the tools of her trade, she was neglecting important bills.

Still, in her desperation to get her hair back, Holland was willing to try anything—even one of her mother's half-baked spells.

While Phoebe researched spells, Holland mixed a potion of her own: L'Oreal, copper-blonde hair color. Grabbing the long hank of dark brown hair that hung in her eyes and down to her cheek, she squirted the contents of the plastic squeeze bottle.

The end result was streaked hair that didn't look too bad. After flat-ironing the front of her hair and applying gobs of gel to closely cropped parts on the back and the right side, she miraculously ended up with spiked hair that looked sort of awesome.

Impressed with the results, she beamed at her reflection.

After a couple more approving glances in the mirror, she galloped off to show her mother her stunning hairdo.

In the dining–slash–work room, Holland was greeted by the sight of Phoebe sitting cross-legged on the dark tile floor. The table and chairs were pushed against the wall. She sat in the center of a chalk-drawn circle.

It was on the tip of Holland's tongue to blurt out that she didn't need the spell anymore, but Phoebe was already mumbling a chant—something repetitive and indecipherable. Her eyes were closed while four white candles burned inside the circle.

Holland gave a little sigh.

Geeze, Mom! This is seriously overkill, she wanted to say, but her mother was so deep into the spell, she didn't have the heart to tell her that she no longer required her witchcraft services.

In a moment of panic, Holland's eyes darted to the curtains. She was instantly relieved to find them closed. The neighbors didn't need to witness this embarrassing spectacle. They'd be freaked out if they could see her mother right now.

It was bad enough that whenever Phoebe went out to the grocery store, the dry cleaners, or wherever, she'd walk up to total strangers and pass out her card, attempting to drum up business. It was so embarrassing the way people recoiled after her mother announced that she was a witch, and she could cast love and money spells. People sort of automatically assumed that being a witch was synonymous with being a devil worshipper.

She hoped that her mother's witchcraft obsession would end soon. Holland would be ridiculed endlessly if the kids at school found out that Phoebe was a witch for hire.

Holland gazed at Phoebe again, and decided that it was only fair to respect her efforts. She was, after all, acting on her daughter's behalf. Giving her mother some space and privacy, Holland quietly slipped out of the front door.

At the end of the block, she veered off the main street, and zipped onto the dirt path, taking the shortcut to Naomi's house.

Naomi and Holland used to share the same social status at school: unimportant and invisible. Holland and Naomi had both always been more interested in having their noses stuck in a book than keeping abreast of the latest fashion trends. They were both on the D list as far as popularity went. But at some point during ninth grade, Naomi had dropped down to the F list. For no apparent reason other than the fact that she was a super smart, straight-A student, she had become a target for bullies.

With Naomi going to a new school, Holland would be utterly alone. It was clearly time for her to make an attempt to fit in with other students—the cool crowd. Though she hated to admit it, Holland was seriously considering dumbing down this year.

CHAPTER 2

Jerked from sleep and unearthed from his resting place by an invisible force, he grudgingly gave in to awareness. Back among the living, his clothing in tatters, he was disoriented and hungry. A ghastly sight, he stumbled out of the woods.

Shielding his eyes from the blinding bright sun with a dirt-encrusted arm, he took a few faltering steps. Limbs stiffened from lack of movement, he could barely stand upright. Acting on instinct, the haggard boy staggered back into the woods, intent on obscuring himself from view. Leaning against the trunk of a tree, he gazed down at his feet. The scars were troubling and mystifying.

A sharp and agonizing hunger pang drew his attention away from the mystery of the wounds. Bent over and clutching his stomach, it seemed that his very soul was crying out for sustenance.

From the corner of his eye, he saw something move through the grass. His stiff muscles did not deter him. Swift as lightning, he dove downward. Clawing at the ground viciously, he captured a small squirrel before it could scamper up the tree.

Ravenous, his teeth ripped through fur and skin. Biting into a live animal was disturbing. With blood dripping from his lips and down the front of his ragged shirt, he glanced around the woodsy environment. A million questions filled his mind as he ravaged his meal.

His hunger satiated for the moment, he dropped the squirrel's carcass and looked at his bloody hands in disgust. Filled with self-loathing, he wiped the blood onto the soiled fabric of his ragged pants.

Sitting with his back pressed against the sturdy tree trunk, his wandering eyes took in the surroundings, and then his gaze settled on a hole in the earth—his former grave. A flash of memory: dirt hitting his prone body. Panic. Terror. Darkness. And finally, acceptance and peace.

How long was I in the ground? He dragged red-stained fingers along his jawline as he frantically searched his memory for answers.

In his mind's eye, he saw a boat—a sailboat overcrowded with anxious people. Haitian people—hoping to find a better life in America.

He'd boarded the boat with a satchel filled with extra clothing, slung over his shoulders. He remembered his mother's voice calling to him, "Safe travels, Jonas!"

The boat was cursed and all the passengers were doomed. Ah, Mother, you had no idea that you were sending me on a voyage to hell.

Vivid memories began to resurface. Before the hurricane, he had been receiving a good education, paid for by a charitable organization. He'd been taught English in his school, and he spoke the language fluently. His mother yearned for him to one day attend college and become a man of importance, preferably a physician. But like everything around him, his school had been demolished.

In America, he was supposed to continue his high school education, go to college, and eventually provide a better life for his family back in Haiti.

Jonas worried about his mother and little sisters having to carry the five-gallon bucket of water from the water depot to their crumbling home. Did his mother know that the money she'd borrowed for his passage to the United States had been wasted?

Of course, she knew. By now, relatives in America had informed her that Jonas had never arrived. Lenders back in Haiti would be demanding repayment. Harassing and threatening his mother.

I'm so sorry, Mother.

It was best that she believed that Jonas's body was at the bottom of the ocean. The truth of his fate would destroy her. What mother could endure the knowledge that her child had been changed into something unnatural—a soulless monster.

A bird fluttered overhead, reminding Jonas of his persistent hunger. As if preparing to snatch the bird from the sky, he stiffened in a predatory manner, his grasping hands reaching upward. But the bird was out of his reach. Back in Haiti, he'd suffered through long stretches without food and very little water, but this kind of hunger was unlike anything he'd ever experienced. Being impoverished and living on the garbage-strewn streets of Port-au-Prince was better than eternal damnation.

For what purpose had he been awakened? He looked around, wondering what had happened to the others from the boat. Were they still under the influence of the poison or had they been buried, too?

Yearning companionship, he looked around. Aside from the hole that he'd crawled out of, the earth was undisturbed. There was no one else here in the woods. He was utterly alone. Disappointment crumpled his strong features. Woefully, he dropped his forehead on his dirt-caked arm. Why had he been pulled from sleep to wander alone in this strange land? He was doomed. Surviving from one moment to the next, scavenging for food. What had he ever done in his young life to deserve this wretched existence?

⊕ ⊕ ⊕

The shortcut to Naomi's house was peaceful. No traffic. No people. Lots of trees and birds chirping…like a mini-oasis away from normal life. Walking along the dirt path, she lapsed into a quick fantasy about her dream boy, Jarrett Sloane. In her fantasy, Jarrett had finally noticed her. His eyes were smoldering with passion when he told her that he thought she was hot.

Practically swooning at the inner vision of Jarrett undressing her with his eyes, Holland found herself blushing at the very thought. Her gaze dropped downward and she noticed a set of strange footprints.

A confused frown formed on her face. They weren't shoe prints; they were prints of bare feet. All five toes were visible, but oddly, the soles of the feet had deeply grooved, bizarre etchings that reminded Holland of Egyptian hieroglyphics, only these etchings looked sinister. They looked otherworldly. No human being had a cluster of intricate drawings etched into the bottom of his feet.

Bending over, she looked closer at the markings. She didn't know what to make of them. Using her phone, she took a picture of what appeared to be alien footprints. This was the kind of mystery that her mom and her coven sisters would enjoy researching and trying to solve.

With more pressing matters on her mind, Holland took off running, eager to show Naomi her haircut.

She rang Naomi's bell and Naomi stood in her doorframe, gaping at Holland.

The way she was gawking was a little off-putting. Maybe she wasn't as hot as she'd thought. Self-consciously, Holland pushed her hair away from her eyes. "What do you think?"

"Wow."

"Wow, what?" Holland nervously bit her bottom lip.

"You cut your hair! That's like...so drastic."

"What do you think?" Holland asked anxiously.

"It looks amazing. I mean...seriously. You look like a totally different person."

Holland flashed a relieved smile. "I'm trying to get Jarrett's attention. I hope this works."

Naomi looked her over with appraising eyes. "Your hair is great, but you need a little more pizzazz."

Holland's smile vanished. "I do?"

"Yeah, you need some flashy jewelry. Smokey eye makeup. Dark lipstick and fingernails."

Holland frowned at her suggestions. "I'm not into makeup. It's so fake, and it's not who I am."

"You're glamming up your image, so why stop with a haircut? Why not go all out?"

"I'm not into fashion trends and neither are you," Holland tersely pointed out. "No offense but you're a bookworm. When did you become a beauty expert?"

"I've been playing around with makeup. And fashion," Naomi added sheepishly. "Do you want a makeover?"

Holland almost laughed in Naomi's face. But Naomi looked so serious, she respectfully held back her giggles. She'd known Naomi since third grade and Naomi was a science geek. In all their years of friendship, Holland had never known Naomi to even mention makeup.

"Come on, it'll be fun," Naomi encouraged.

Merely humoring her, Holland followed Naomi through the family room and up the stairs. Moments later, Naomi pulled a plastic container from under her bed.

Holland was stunned when Naomi popped the lid, revealing a huge assortment of makeup and beauty products. "What are you doing with all this stuff?"

"I've been thinking…like…instead of college, I might go to a beauty school. A career as a makeup artist would be hot. I could work with celebrities. Work on movie sets and TV shows."

"What happened to being a microbiologist?"

Naomi shrugged. "Changed my mind."

"Why?"

"My parents had to take out a second mortgage on the house to pay tuition to private school. They may not be able to afford college."

"You're like a genius…you'll get a scholarship."

"I hope."

With her grades, Naomi would definitely get a full scholarship. She had to know that. Figuring that Naomi was secretly experimenting with makeup to revamp her look before starting the new school, Holland tactfully dropped the subject.

Oddly, as close and Naomi and Holland were, they'd never discussed Naomi's innermost feelings about being bullied.

Back in ninth grade, Holland had watched in horror from her lunch table as mean girl, Chaela Vasquez, pretended to accidentally spill chocolate milk on Naomi's white sweater. The laughter in the school cafeteria was raucous and deafening. While chocolate milk saturated her sweater and drizzled down her beige skirt, Naomi continued filling her lunch tray as if nothing had happened.

Amidst spiteful boos and catcalls, Naomi was expressionless as she crossed the cafeteria and then joined Holland at the lunch table they shared, acting as though nothing had happened.

"Naomi, don't you think you should report Chaela to the principal?" Holland had whispered.

"No, I'm fine," Naomi had said in a disturbingly calm voice.

"I have a hoodie in my locker," Holland persisted, staring in horror at the brown stains on her friend's sweater.

"I don't want your hoodie," Naomi said sharply.

Naomi had gone throughout the rest of the day wearing that soiled sweater—like a martyr. Kids made fun of her, saying that her sweater was covered with poop stains. Someone started a rumor that Naomi had had a diarrhea explosion during lunch. It was a God-awful day.

And that's when Naomi had first put up the wall of silence. That's when the two friends had begun their unspoken agreement not to discuss what was happening to Naomi.

Toward the end of tenth grade, Holland decided that Naomi needed an intervention. Naomi's way of handling being bullied clearly hadn't been working. She acted aloof and above it all, but deep inside, she had to be hurting. Finally breaking her silence, Holland told Phoebe about Naomi's troubles.

Holland had expected her mom to have a secret meeting with the school counselor or Naomi's parents, but of course, Phoebe had another idea. She worked a spell of protection for Naomi. She burned white candles and spoke some mumble jumble, explaining later that she had surrounded Naomi in peaceful white light. Holland's mother had been certain that Chaela and the mean girls wouldn't bother Naomi anymore.

Soon after the spell was cast, Naomi announced that she was transferring to a new school. Merely a coincidence, Holland had told herself.

With Naomi off to a new school, Holland wouldn't have a friend in a world. Naomi brushed an assortment of colors on Holland's eyelids; Holland's mind was filling up with fearful thoughts. Psychoanalyzing herself, she was forced to admit that a part of her feared that Naomi's departure at school would put a target on her back.

She cringed at the thought of getting picked on every day. In retrospect, languishing on the D list wasn't so bad. Obscurity was preferable to being ridiculed and scorned on a daily basis.

Naomi snapped Holland out of her reverie. "Open your eyes," she said, and held out a hand mirror.

Braced for a frightening clown face, Holland hesitantly opened her eyes. "Is that really me! Oh, my God! I don't even recognize myself," she said in an awestruck voice.

Naomi smiled at her handiwork.

"How'd you learn to do this? It's perfect. Like makeup artistry."

"YouTube videos," Naomi said, matter-of-fact. "Ready for your nails?"

Unable to tear her eyes away from the mirror, Holland nodded. "I had no idea that makeup could change my whole identity. I'm like…really pretty," Holland blurted.

"Yeah, makeup does wonders," Naomi replied. She sorted through bottles of nail polish. "What color? Pewter or dark chocolate?"

Holland glanced away from her reflection long enough to look at the nail polish, and selected pewter.

With her lips pinched in concentration, Naomi painted Holland's nails. After she finished, she added some fancy, black squiggly lines in the middle of each nail.

Holland was impressed. "Wow! What's come over you, Naomi? How do you suddenly know all these beauty tricks?"

"Fashion magazines and how-to videos." Naomi finished the manicure with a clear topcoat, and then clicked on a small fan.

Cautious not to smudge her nails, Holland held her hands in front of the fan. "Wouldn't it be fabulous if you and I went on a double date with Jarrett and one of his teammates?"

"That'll never happen, Holland. At least not in this lifetime," Naomi said solemnly.

"Why not? I heard that Jarrett and Chaela Vasquez broke up."

"Where'd you hear that?"

"I snooped on his Facebook page. He changed his status to single."

"Jarrett and Chaela are always breaking up. Don't get your hopes up, Holland."

"But Chaela has a new boyfriend. She has a new profile pic of her and a boy, Willow Hill. "

"I guess anything's possible," Naomi conceded. "You and Jarrett would make a cute couple."

"And what about you and one of his friends? We could double date...wouldn't that be fun, Naomi?"

"Even if I got asked out on a date, which is *highly* unlikely, my parents wouldn't allow it. You know how they are. I can't date until I'm eighteen."

Holland gave a solemn head nod. Naomi's parents were super strict.

"Let's do something about those jeans," Naomi said, changing the subject.

"What do you mean?" Holland asked skeptically.

Naomi held up a razor. "Let's give your jeans a more current look."

Holland frowned. "These are my fave jeans. They're really comfortable—nice and worn in the knees."

"Holland, your wardrobe is tired; it needs a remix. I can jazz up those jeans with a few rips and some pulled threads."

"Okaaay!" Holland said with a sigh, and then stood perfectly still while Naomi made stylish slashes in the front of her faded jeans.

CHAPTER 3

The hunger intensified with the darkening sky. Jonas immediately imagined a steaming bowl of lambi a la Creole, but instead of salivating at the thought of such a delicious meal, he felt nauseous. Unfortunately, none of his favorite dishes could satisfy this new hunger.

He heard footsteps in the distance. His heightened sense of hearing was a painful reminder of what he'd become. *Undead.* Yes, that was the term. *Undead...trapped between life and death.*

Jonas sifted through the rubble of his memory and recalled the elaborate ceremony that had taken place before the boat's departure. The ceremony honoring Met Agwe (the god of the sea) was tradition among some Haitian people; it guaranteed that all passengers on the boat would arrive at the destination safely.

Glorious weather promised a peaceful journey. Everyone was smiling and happy. And though a few people were dressed in casual, everyday clothes, most were wearing their Sunday best.

People were crammed together. Some were seated on a hard, wooden bench. Others sat on overturned buckets, crates—any available spot. Most of the passengers used their knapsacks for a cushion and were packed together on the floor of the boat. Feeling optimistic, the passengers kicked off their shoes, making themselves as comfortable as possible for the eight hundred-mile journey.

After a few hours at sea, the sky suddenly darkened. Howling winds and mountainous waves warned that an unforeseen storm was brewing. In the midst of a raging sea, the man-made boat became rocky and unstable.

"Met Agwe must be fed," the captain shouted frantically.

Jonas wrinkled his forehead in confusion and turned toward an older man sitting next to him. Dressed comfortably in an old blue T-shirt, embossed with the cracked and faded Pepsi logo, the man had seemed to be a cheerful type, with his mouth turned up into a perpetual smile. But now his lips were sloped downward as he peered at Jonas through world-weary eyes.

"A human sacrifice has to be made," the man explained grimly.

"I don't understand."

"Captain Henri will choose someone. After the sea is fed, our journey will be much smoother."

Jonas scowled. "Does the captain intend to throw someone into the water?"

The man nodded solemnly.

"You can't be serious; you're making a joke," Jonas said in disbelief.

"I'm very serious. Lower your voice," he whispered sternly. Not wanting to draw attention to himself, the man didn't allow his eyes to wander. Looking down, he concentrated on the leathery hands that were clasped upon his lap.

Jonas followed suit, dropping his gaze and folding his own hands.

Captain Henri paced slowly, the heels of his boots clacking against the wooden floorboard. A rotund man with scarred, pockmarked skin, the captain's narrowed eyes roved ominously over the shuddering passengers as he assessed the various choices.

Acting as guards, the captain's two-man crew stood at the ready, prepared to seize the misfortunate person that the captain selected.

As the vessel rocked unsteadily in the turbulent Caribbean water, a chorus of weeping and moaning erupted in the crowded boat, as no one wanted to be cast into the dark, shark-infested water.

"Quiet down! This boat will capsize and sink if we don't feed Met Agwe!" Captain Henri shouted impatiently. He then pointed to a woman that was wearing a red straw hat and a red dress with white lace around the neckline and the hem.

The woman's eyes became wide with alarm. Recoiling, she frowned and shook her head rapidly.

Among the passengers, tongues clicked in sympathy for the unlucky woman.

"What a pity," a few people murmured.

"It is a shame, but the sea must be fed," others rationalized.

Jonas made eye contact with the man wearing the Pepsi shirt. "This is outrageous. We can't allow that woman to be thrown off the boat," Jonas said in an astonished voice that beseeched his new friend to join him in coming to the woman's aid.

With a dark, sun-weathered hand that resembled worn leather, the man gave Jonas a comforting pat on his shoulder. "There's nothing we can do. It's out of our hands, son." He then made a hasty sign of the cross, and lowered his head as if in prayer.

Using a soft, cajoling tone, Captain Henri spoke to the unfortunate woman. "I'm a reasonable person, and I have to be fair. All these people have paid the price for a seat on my boat," he said, waving a thick hand through the air. "But you have not paid one dollar."

She cursed and insulted Captain Henri in rapid patois. Shouting in outrage, she sprang to her feet so quickly, her straw hat was knocked askew. "You made private arrangements with me," she cried out, her eyes filled with fiery anger. "You told me that I could pay after I find work in America."

The murmurings from the crowd took on a less sympathetic tone upon realizing that the woman who was to be sacrificed had not paid her fare. Looking upon the woman with self-righteous indignation, some spoke of the hardships that they had endured to pay for the voyage. Others disclosed that their families would be harassed by the lenders they'd borrowed from if they didn't get to America and earn enough money to pay back the loan.

In a lulling voice, Captain Henri appealed to the woman's sense of reason. "You must understand, this boat will sink if Met Agwe is not fed. I'm sorry; I have no choice. Come now..." He reached out his hand, as if expecting the woman to comply in quiet resignation.

"No!" she bellowed. "You can't do this to me! I don't want to die! Someone, help me!"

Captain Henri mopped his sweat-drenched brow and then beckoned his henchmen. Both men were odd sorts. One had a long, scraggly beard; the other wore a patch over his right eye.

Though it took all of his resolve not to defend a helpless woman, Jonas feared he'd be expected to exchange places with the ill-fated woman if he spoke up for her or attempted to come to her aid.

Filled with shame, Jonas turned a deaf ear to the woman's desperate plea and briefly closed his eyes. Then, stealing a guilty glance at the melee that was unfolding, Jonas witnessed the guards taking hold of the struggling woman. Two men roughly grabbed her by each arm.

Boring her eyes into Jonas's, the woman pleaded. "Help me."

Jonas looked away from her and focused on his bare feet.

"Coward," the woman shouted, drawing Jonas's gaze away from his feet to her angry face.

Forgive me. With an apologetic expression, Jonas looked the doomed woman in the eye.

She sneered at him, twisting her lips in hatred. Then, quick as a snake, she stuck her hand inside the satchel that was slung over her shoulder.

Assuming that she was reaching for a pistol, Jonas and the other terrified passengers ducked for cover. But instead of being riddled with gunshots, the travelers that were within the woman's reach were sprinkled with a grainy, white powder.

Screaming out a bitter incantation in rapid-fire, patois, the woman shook out the contents of her satchel, vengefully hexing the boat before the guards cast her into the abyss of the raging water.

Before settling on the floor of the boat, the mysterious powder swirled about through the air, causing a cacophony of choking and gasping among the passengers.

Blood trickled from the noses of those that had inhaled the powder. One by one, people were slumping over—gagging and vomiting before succumbing to death.

The captain demanded that the dead be removed immediately. "They're bewitched! Throw them overboard before they wake up!"

Jonas had heard tales of the undead, but had always considered it Haitian legend. He'd never personally encountered anyone that had been awakened by magic, and didn't believe it possible for someone to return from the dead.

For a brief moment, Jonas was frozen in his seat—immobilized by the ensuing chaos that surrounded him. The man in the Pepsi shirt elbowed Jonas. "Gather yourself together, son; you have to pitch in."

"I can't." Jonas shuddered at the thought of feeding people to the sharks.

"My name is Emille. I'm your friend," the man said. "As a

friend, I must inform you that you will be thrown into the water as the second live offering if you don't do what Captain Henri demands."

Jonas obediently jumped to his feet and began pitching in.

Women wailed and lamented as Jonas and the other male survivors shouldered the grim responsibility of burying the dead at sea. Tracking barefoot through the poisonous powder, Jonas dutifully assisted in picking up dead bodies and tossing them to the sharks.

Jonas and the other men worked without pause for what seemed like hours. It was a gruesome task. Flinging human beings into the sea was the most despicable act of his young life. When his work was finally over, Jonas walked numbly to his seat.

Twenty-nine passengers had dwindled down to thirteen. Depressed, confused, and ashamed, Jonas buried his face in his hands and discreetly wiped moisture from his eyes.

His tears stopped falling when he became distracted by a burning sensation on the soles of his feet. He pulled a foot upon his thigh, bent over and examined the bottom of his right foot. He scowled at the strange markings that had formed. His left foot bore identical marks.

Jonas looked around the boat and noticed other men and women frowning in bewilderment as they inspected the bottoms of their feet. All those that had the misfortune of being barefoot bore mysterious scars.

Captain Henri and his cronies were all wearing boots and were unscathed by the poisonous powder.

"Why are we marked like this?" Jonas queried Emille, speaking in a hushed voice.

"Don't let the captain find out," the man cautioned. "Put your shoes on. When you arrive in America, tell your family that you need to see a doctor. American medicine is very powerful." He patted Jonas's hand. "Everything will be all right, son."

But everything had not been all right.

⊕ ⊕ ⊕

Slumping miserably against a tree trunk, Jonas groaned at the recollection of the ordeal on the boat. Ravenous hunger demanded that he let go of painful memories, gather his wits and hunt for supper.

But clawing and killing was vile, a behavior that was more animal than human. Yet, he was neither. He was a cursed soul. An evil abomination.

His senses, reflexes, and strength had been sharpened beyond reason. Sounds that should have been inaudible were disturbingly noisy. He could hear everything…insects crawling; even the soft slither of worms produced an audible sound.

Sniffing the air, an inestimable mixture of smells swirled about. Breathing in and out, Jonas found that when he concentrated, he was able to differentiate between plant life, insects, birds, and beasts. Flaring his nostrils, he inhaled and recognized the smell of a raccoon. Following the scent, Jonas's dark brown eyes zoomed in on the animal, which was approximately fifteen yards away and contentedly feasting.

With his keen night vision, Jonas quickly discerned that the raccoon was eating a fallen bird. Jonas's mouth watered involuntarily. With a devastating sense of gloom, he accepted that the raccoon would be his next meal.

As he repositioned his body, readying himself to attack, it occurred to him to fight the urge to feed. It anguished him to take the life of another living thing.

It had been distressful feeling the squirrel's heart beating in rapid fear before he'd taken the killing bite.

Determinedly, Jonas vowed to starve himself before killing again. He refused to go through life like a ferocious animal, mauling and mangling helpless creatures so that he could survive. Starvation would bring death. Perhaps a permanent death this time. And, ultimately, peace.

Immense loneliness rivaled his urge to feed. He yearned for the familiarity of home and for the comfort of his family. The family he'd never see again. Even if he managed the impossible and made it back to Haiti, his mother and sisters wouldn't welcome him. They'd fear him—shun him. And rightfully so. He was an atrocity…a monster. A mutant form of life that was sustained by flesh and blood.

In a fog of grief, Jonas collapsed onto a bed of twigs and dried leaves.

Collecting himself, he sat up and stretched his leaden muscles, and then searched for shelter—a resting place where he could conceal himself until death claimed him.

Approaching footsteps alerted him, halting his movement. Motionless, he was intent on blending in with the night.

Then he caught a tantalizing scent. Seized with an overpowering urge to feed, his earlier pledge to starve himself was instantly forgotten.

Instinctively, Jonas bent at the waist. Like an animal, he was preparing to lunge. The scent grew stronger—a unique blend that was indisputably human, but unlike anything he'd ever smelled.

Instead of pouncing and mercilessly ripping into flesh, he controlled himself and watched with intense fascination. Under the cover of night, Jonas hid in the bushes and observed the source of the delicious smell. A girl walked along the dirt path.

She appeared to be close to his age, approximately fifteen or sixteen. He breathed in her fragrance and became pleasantly light-headed.

Suddenly, the girl stopped walking. She looked down at the ground, studying it, as if trying to find something. Jonas was tempted to come out of his hiding place to offer assistance. But he didn't trust his ability to control the insatiable hunger that plagued him. And even if he could subdue his ravenous appetite, surely his bedraggled appearance would frighten the girl away. He dared not budge.

The girl looked up at the sky. Soft moonlight illuminated her face. She was beautiful. Jonas was irresistibly drawn to her. The warm sensation that flooded through him was proof that he was not completely soulless.

CHAPTER 4

The sun had gone down by the time Holland left Naomi's house. The path that led home was now dark and foreboding. The average person would have taken a more populated route, but Holland wasn't afraid. Desolate places stirred her imagination. Shadows cast by trees and low-hanging branches created interesting designs, reminding her of abstract art. As she scanned the shadowy designs on the ground, she remembered the weird footprints from earlier. She squinted as her eyes swept over the dismal path.

She gazed up at the sky. The sliver of moonlight that glinted through the trees didn't provide much illumination, and she couldn't find any trace of those bizarre imprints. But there was proof on her cell phone.

Off the path now, bright streetlights and the roaring sound of traffic announced her return to civilization. Thanks to the beauty makeover, Holland felt ultra feminine. She stood taller. Prouder.

Wondering if others would notice her transformation, she headed in the opposite direction of home. High school kids usually hung out at the Wal-Mart shopping plaza. Going to Wal-Mart to pick up some makeup essentials was a good excuse to get noticed.

Walking along the busy avenue, she saw a group of boys loitering outside a convenience store. She frowned in disappointment;

they were middle school age—too young for their opinions to matter.

Some of the boys moved about clumsily in their lean, gangly bodies, the result of a sudden growth spurt. As she grew nearer, she avoided looking in their direction. She didn't want any attention from those young kids. Pretending to be distracted by an incoming text, she pulled out her phone and peered at the screen.

Then curiosity got the best of her. Wondering if there were any reactions to her improved look, she observed the boys on the sly. Quite a few heads turned in her direction. Gauging their expressions, Holland noticed several pairs of eyes lighting up as they assessed her.

A tough-looking boy with a small silver earring in his eyebrow stepped forward. He was huskier than the others, and he seemed to be the leader. "She's hot. Does she live around here?" he asked his buddies.

"Yeah, she's my neighbor," said an awkward kid that Holland recognized as the shy kid that lived across the street.

"I'd like to smash that!" The tough kid broke out in malicious laughter and made a crude gesture, making it clear that he regarded Holland as an object.

She picked up her pace. It was somewhat laughable that a defiant eighth grader with raging hormones was the first person to call her hot. Though he wasn't speaking in complimentary terms, it was a start, she supposed. Hopefully, her next encounter with the opposite sex would be with a more evolved person.

The parking lot at Wal-Mart was always super busy. Impatient motorists vying for parking spaces created traffic jams, and had little regard for pedestrians.

While cars were temporarily stopped at the multi-stop signs, Holland raced across the walkway toward the entrance. Out of nowhere, a white Dodge Durango zoomed forward. Fearing that she was about to be plowed over, Holland uttered a frightened sound. The driver hit the brakes barely in the nick of time.

Righteous indignation washed over her. She shot a hot glance at the driver. When she noticed Jarrett Sloan sitting behind the wheel, her aggravation instantly vanished.

He opened and closed his eyes, as if trying to sharpen his focus. "Is that you, Holland?"

Blushing, she shrugged her shoulders like a moron. *Ugh!* She hated that she was acting like a blithering idiot, but hadn't expected to bump into Jarrett for at least another month when school reopened.

"You look different... I hardly recognized you...you look so awesome!" Jarrett's eyes roved from her face down to her jazzed-up jeans.

It was the way he'd looked at her so many times before...in her fantasies. But right now, in real time, his heated gaze was completely unnerving. She had never spoken a full sentence to Jarrett—ever. In a state of shock, she'd drifted off into the dumb zone, and couldn't think of anything cool or clever. Desperate to come up with a witty reply, she blurted out the first thing that came to mind. Pointing to the 15 miles per hour sign, Holland said sarcastically, "Who gave you a driver's license, Jarrett?"

"I got connections. I know somebody who knows somebody," Jarrett quipped, laughing as he played along.

Holland was bantering and making verbal barbs with seeming ease, but inside, her heart was racing rapidly. She couldn't believe that Jarrett had noticed her, and that they were actually having a conversation.

Reality set in when a car horn honked, urging the Durango to move on.

"Need a ride?" Jarrett asked.

She wanted to swing the door open and jump in his ride, but her nerves got the best of her. "I can't. I...uh...I have to pick up a few things." She nudged her head toward the sliding doors of Wal-Mart.

"I can wait if you'd like." There was a tremor in Jarrett's voice that contradicted his confident smile. *Jarrett's nervous, too!*

She felt overwhelmed by Jarrett's offer, and shifted awkwardly from one foot to the other. "That's okay; you don't have to wait for me."

"I don't mind," he persisted. Several car horns blared in outrage as Jarrett held up mall traffic. "Hold your horses!" he yelled out his window.

This can't be happening. Jarrett is offering me a ride and he's willing to wait. I know I'm going to wake up and discover this was only a dream.

A smile tugged at the corners of her lips. She folded her arms and eyed him with mock suspicion. "You drive like a maniac, and I'm not sure it's safe to ride with you." Getting the hang of being witty and sarcastic, she gave Jarrett a wry smile.

"So, you're just gonna walk away and break my heart?" Jarrett made an exaggerated sad face. It was so adorable.

"You'll get over it." Holland sounded self-assured, but inside her heart was thumping. She wanted Jarrett more than anything, but she wasn't prepared. She needed to amp up her confidence a little more before trying to hold her own for the duration of the fifteen-minute ride home. She doubted if she could keep up her end of their clever banter for that long.

"Maybe we can hook up some other time?" Jarrett said, disappointment showing in his eyes.

"Sure. See you around." Holland gave Jarrett a smile and a wave, and then trotted over to the entrance of the store.

I just turned down a chance to be with my dream boy—how dumb was that?

CHAPTER 5

Wal-Mart was as eventful as usual. Shoppers whizzed past with carts filled with every conceivable item from cereal to flat-screen TVs.

Holland found her way to the makeup aisle, a part of the store that was totally foreign to her. But she couldn't sponge off Naomi forever. Gripping a blue shopping basket, she inspected the selections.

All the brands she'd seen in magazines were on display, and Holland didn't know where to begin. She moseyed over to the lip gloss display. A shimmering rose color caught her attention, and she tossed it in her basket. Next, she picked up a fuchsia blush, a duo of silver and black eyeshadow, and a bottle of mint green nail polish, and then made her way to the register.

Satisfied with her purchases, she walked out of Wal-Mart swinging the plastic bag. Holland was eager to get home and begin experimenting.

Halfway through the parking lot, she spotted Jarrett's truck. She couldn't believe he'd actually waited for her. He beeped the horn twice and gestured for Holland to come over. But she couldn't bring herself to walk in his direction. She wanted to, but feeling bashful, she pretended that she hadn't seen him.

She heard the engine as the Durango crept behind her.

"Hey, I waited for you for twenty minutes and now you're just gonna walk right past me?" Jarrett called out of his window.

Oh, my God, this is so embarrassing! Looking straight ahead as Jarrett rode beside her, Holland held her head down, her face flushed.

"Stop playing, Holland; you're making me look stupid." Jarrett laughed, but the sound held an embarrassed ring.

Holland stopped walking and looked at Jarrett. "I told you not to wait for me."

"Sorry, I have a problem retaining information."

She couldn't hold back a smile. "Well, that's your problem; not mine."

"I didn't know you were so cocky, Holland. I thought you were a nice girl."

"There's a lot you don't know about me, Jarrett Sloan. You've never said one word to me in your life," she said with a smirk on her face.

"Well, that's the past. I'm trying to get to know you now. Maybe I could find out what makes you tick if you'd stop treating me so mean. Hey, I'm trying to be a nice guy. All I want to do is give you a ride home. Hop in, Holland. I don't bite!"

His words sounded heartfelt. And though she loved the attention she was getting from him, she couldn't let him know. She looked over at Jarrett and sighed. Who would have thought that makeup and a new haircut could elevate her from a virtual nobody to an instant goddess?

"Holland, it's getting late; you shouldn't be out here walking alone. Let me take you home."

She gave a reluctant nod. "Okay, but you better drive carefully."

"I'll drive like a little old lady and make sure you get home safely," he said with laughter.

Holland walked around to the passenger side and felt his eyes on her as she climbed in.

"So what are you doing hanging out at Wal-Mart?" Holland asked, making small talk. She really wanted to ask him if he and Chaela were officially over, but she was hesitant to boldly pry into his personal life.

"I went to pick up something for my mom. They didn't have it so I was on my way home; then I saw you." Jarrett shrugged and gave a weak smile.

There was an awkward silence after Jarrett's response. Holland went into a mild panic, wondering what she should say next.

"And what brought you out to Wal-Mart tonight?" Jarrett asked, filling the gap in the conversation.

"Just checking out a few things."

"Oh, yeah? What'd you get?" He cut an eye at her bag.

"I bought some lip gloss and nail polish…you know, girlie things."

"You don't need that kind of stuff, Holland. You're pretty without it. I've always noticed you before, but tonight there was something different about you. It's like you have a glow."

Her makeover had given her the glow that Jarrett noticed, but Holland kept that to herself.

Small talk with Jarrett came surprisingly easy. They talked about school and teachers and some of their favorite TV shows. Time zoomed, and it seemed that the moment that Holland relaxed and let her defenses down, Jarrett had turned onto her street. She pointed to her house, and felt a stab of embarrassment. Her front door needed a paint job. The front yard looked unkempt. Her mother's herb garden had grown so wildly, it resembled tall weeds. The gardener that took care of the yard hadn't been around for a while, due to lack of pay. Holland made a mental note to get out the clippers and tackle the job of cutting hedges. How difficult could it be? And maybe she could find an instructional video on YouTube to teach her how to do exterior painting. She hadn't realized until now how severely neglected the front of her house looked.

Jarrett pulled over and parked at the curb. "Are you gonna give me your number?"

"Are you going to ask me for it?" Holland said saucily.

"Man, you're tough. May I have your number, please?" He held his hands together as if in prayer.

Holland laughed and recited her phone number.

Jarrett input the numbers in his cell. "Was that so bad?" he asked with a cocky smile.

"Not at all."

"Can we get together? You know...do something fun. Do you like to bowl?"

Holland frowned and shook her head. "I'm not much of an athlete."

"Bowling is easy. I'll teach you."

"I don't know."

"Come on. It'll be fun."

"Sure, why not?" she conceded. Then her heart started thudding and skidding around in her chest. The fact that he'd asked her out was confirmation that he and Chaela had called it quits. *Jarrett asked me to go out with him; my most cherished fantasy has finally come true.*

"How about Friday...around eight?"

"Okay," she said coolly. She looked out the window, hoping that Jarrett didn't see her blushing like crazy.

Taking her off-guard, he leaned over and pressed his lips against her cheek. Startled, she turned toward him and he immediately covered her mouth with his. Holland closed her eyes and tried to relax, but she was a bundle of nerves. She pulled back. "I have to go." She grabbed the door handle and opened the door.

"See you Friday, beautiful?" Jarrett gave her a flirty wink.

"Yeah, see you Friday. Oh, and thanks for the ride."

Behaving like a gentleman, Jarrett waited for her to get in the house before pulling off.

Holland couldn't wipe the smile off of her face. *I can't believe that Jarrett is interested in little ol' me!*

Holland's first kiss hadn't been exactly the fireworks she'd expected. She'd been too surprised and way too nervous to enjoy it. She'd try to loosen up and really get into the moment the next time Jarrett kissed her.

She couldn't wait to tell Naomi about her upcoming date. *Jarrett Sloan and me! Ohmigod, ohmigod, ohmigod!*

⊕ ⊕ ⊕

"Hi, Mom. I'm home," Holland yelled as she let herself in the house.

"I'm in the kitchen," Phoebe called out.

Walking through her mother's work area, she noticed that the creepy chalk circle had been removed. *Good!* How would she ever explain her mother's bizarre practices to Jarrett? She couldn't, and so there was no point in ever inviting him in. When he came by to pick her up for their official date, she planned to rush out the door before he had time to get out of his truck.

The kitchen table was cluttered with spell casting books, jars of herbs, an Ouija board, and other occult paraphernalia. Phoebe had cleared only enough space for her laptop, and a mug of tea.

"Mom, you'll never believe what happened?"

Phoebe looked up. "Wow, look at you, Holland! You look so pretty and all grown up." Her mother smiled broadly as she took in Holland's two-toned colored hair, her perfect makeup, and jazzed-up jeans.

Grinning, Holland turned in a complete circle, giving her mother a full view of her drastic makeover. "I don't know what you did, Mom, but it worked. I'm really happy with my hair." Holland ran her fingers through the blonde tresses that hung on one side.

"You asked me to cast a spell for hair growth, and since that didn't happen, I can't take the credit. You accomplished this all by yourself, hon." Phoebe looked at her with pride in her eyes.

"While you were chanting and working your magic, I suddenly got the bold idea to color the front of my hair. So don't you think your magic had something to do with it?" Holland said, humoring her mother.

"Maybe."

Holland had intended to tell Phoebe about Jarrett and their upcoming date, but she abruptly changed her mind. Knowing her mother, she'd want to cook up a love potion, and Holland didn't want to jinx the relationship with any of her mother's wacky spells.

"Naomi did my makeup. Can you believe it?" Holland added, careful to not mention a word about Jarrett Sloan. "She has this sudden interest in fashion and beauty, and she knows what she's doing."

"With Naomi's head for science and chemistry, I wouldn't be surprised if one day she developed her own line of beauty products."

"She's thinking about becoming a makeup artist, but developing cosmetics seems like a much better career choice for someone as smart as Naomi."

Nodding, Holland's mother took a sip of tea. "Oh, guess what? I got a call from a woman that I met in the grocery store. She booked a money attraction spell."

"Is she coming here?" Holland asked anxiously. It was bad enough that her mother dealt with kooks online, but bringing them to their home was a bit much.

"Yes, she's coming over at ten o'clock tonight."

"Tonight?"

"If business takes off the way I hope, I'll probably put up a wall and add a door. You, know, partition off a section of my workroom and use it as a private consultation area."

"Oh, great, now we're gonna have weirdoes showing up at our front door," Holland said sarcastically.

"Witchcraft is my passion, hon. Being able to make money while helping people is an extra bonus. Be happy for me."

Holland made an exaggerated, pained expression. She and her mother broke into peals of laughter. She kissed Phoebe on the cheek. "I'm happy for you, Mom."

"Thanks, hon." Phoebe returned her gaze to the computer screen. "Your dinner's in the microwave," she said absently.

"What's for dinner?"

"Your fave," her mother answered.

Holland glanced in the direction of the microwave. Without looking inside, she knew that she'd find pre-packed chicken strips and other frozen food that her mother had hastily slapped on a plate. Phoebe wasn't much in the cooking department. Holland hadn't actually considered chicken strips as her fave food since elementary school. But she didn't complain. Her mother meant well.

All of a sudden, the microwave began beep-beeping without pause. A series of random numbers began flashing on the display screen.

"What on earth?" Phoebe frowned in the direction of the microwave.

Holland shrugged. She pushed the END button, but the racket

continued as if an invisible finger were poking the number pad without cessation. She opened the microwave door, but that didn't stop the commotion.

"The microwave is going crazy—acting like it's possessed," Holland complained.

"Unplug it," Phoebe suggested.

Holland yanked the plug out of the socket. She waited a few seconds, and then plugged it back in.

The microwave was soundless. No longer alit with flashing numbers, the screen displayed the correct time.

Holland shook her head. "That was creepy."

"The spirit world loves to play around with electricity," her mother commented. "Someone's trying to get a message to you, Holland. Maybe it's your dad."

"Dad would never pull a prank like that. I think the microwave is on its last legs, and that malfunction was a warning that we need to start looking for a replacement," Holland said logically.

Phoebe nodded in acceptance, and returned her gaze to the computer screen. Then she looked up, her face taking on a troubled expression. "Something odd happened today...while I was chanting."

"Oh, yeah? What happened?" Holland asked as she examined the plate inside the microwave. She wrinkled her nose at the sad-looking meal: pallid-looking chicken strips, a few wilted broccoli spears, and congealed macaroni and cheese.

"Well, as you know, chanting puts me in a sort of trance-like state—a connection to spirits. I suddenly felt your presence in the room..."

"Oh! There's an explanation for that. I came in your workroom because I wanted to show you what I'd done with my hair, but when I saw that you were chanting, I decided not to disturb you."

"Uh-huh," her mother said with her brows furrowed thoughtfully. "But for those few moments that you were standing there, I literally felt and heard something click inside my head. It seemed like a passageway had opened."

Holland scowled. "What kind of passageway?"

"I don't know. I do know that something opened. A gateway to a higher state of consciousness, maybe?" Phoebe scrunched her face and shrugged.

"That's freaky, Mom. You just gave me the shivers."

"And the really odd part is that it didn't happen until you came into the room."

Holland scowled. "What are you implying?"

"Well...you're sixteen and I've read that that's the age most witches come into their power. Have you sensed any changes? Did anything strange happen today?"

"No! And I'm not a witch. Geeze, Mom." Holland thought about the bizarre footprints that she'd photographed and decided that she no longer wanted to discuss the weird images with her mother. In fact, she planned to promptly delete the picture as soon as she had some privacy.

"Your grandmother had special gifts," her mother said fondly. "She was a born healer and she communicated easily with the spirit world. I have to work hard and do a lot of studying to get my spells to work, but you may have inherited your grandmother's gifts. I hear it skips a generation."

"This conversation is way too creepy for me. Can we change the subject?" Holland pulled out a chair to sit at the cluttered table. Seeing something from her peripheral vision, she froze. The planchette that sat atop the Ouija board was inching its way from the center of the board, moving on its own accord.

Her mouth agape, Holland stared at the Ouija board. The

planchette picked up speed and suddenly scooted over to the letter F.

"M—Mom," she stammered. "Look!" Holland pointed at the Ouija board. "The Ouija board is spelling something—the planchette is sliding around the board!"

Holland's mother shot out of her seat and stood next to her daughter. Mother and daughter gawked at the planchette as it glided around the alphabet.

After spelling out the word, "footprints," the planchette became still.

"Oh, my God! I can't believe that freaking thing moved!" Holland blurted.

Perplexed, Phoebe squinted in thought. "Footprints? What could that mean?"

Knowing the exact meaning behind the singular word, Holland swallowed hard. "I don't know what it means and I don't care. It's nonsense! You should get rid of this thing. Or keep it boxed up somewhere. I'm sick of all this creepy, witchcraft stuff. Why can't you act like a normal mom?" Holland shouted, finally letting out her pent-up frustration over her mother's peculiar ways.

"The spirits are trying to communicate with you, hon. There's obviously been some kind of breakthrough. I can't interpret that message because it was specifically for you. You have untapped potential, and you should embrace your powers." She stroked the front of Holland's hair.

Holland edged away from her mother's touch. "I don't have any powers!" Carrying her dinner plate, she stormed off to her bedroom and slammed the door.

CHAPTER 6

During the pitch-black night, Jonas hunted. Animals couldn't hide from him. His olfactory sense told him their exact location. Pacifying the raging hunger, he fed on possum, snake, and wild rabbit. Devouring animals sustained him, but didn't take away his craving for the taste of human flesh and blood. It was a repulsive, fiendish longing and Jonas feared that he'd lose his last shred of humanity if he ever gave into his unnatural desires.

With his stomach full, Jonas returned to his resting place in the woods. Hidden from sight, behind bushes, and covered by a blanket of underbrush, he lay in the fetal position, wondering if he'd ever be able to reclaim his soul. It wasn't likely. He was literally lost, with no idea where he was or how far he was from his relatives in Miami.

A bug meandered across the sole of Jonas's foot. Jonas uncurled his body and sat up. Swatting at the insect, his fingers brushed across the odd-looking markings on his skin. In the velvet darkness, he could clearly see a series of circles, triangles and squiggly lines. The strange markings appeared to be branded into his skin.

Haunting recollections took him back to the boat. As if reliving the horror, Jonas let out a howling sound that was so loud, night birds fled from trees, squawking in fear as they flapped their wings and soared into the dark sky.

He tried to fight back the grotesque memories, but failed.

Jonas and the other "marked" passengers had slipped on their shoes to avoid detection. Throughout the night, Jonas had slept fitfully.

At sunrise, the captain's men walked amongst the passengers, scrutinizing their faces, searching for signs of anyone becoming ill from the poison.

While Jonas was able to maintain an unreadable expression, next to him, his friend, Emille, began to flinch and tremble violently.

"Emille! Are you okay?" Jonas gasped.

The scraggly-bearded crewman regarded Emille suspiciously and pointed at him. "What's wrong with that man?"

"He's upset by the tragedies we've witnessed," Jonas spoke up.

Emille's teeth chattered noisily as he shuddered and shook.

Attempting to comfort his friend, Jonas placed an arm around Emille's shoulder. "It's going to be okay. You'll get medicine in America. Hang on, Emille."

Emille jerked and jolted as if electricity were coursing through him.

"Grab him by his ankles," the henchman spat bitterly.

"But he's not dead," Jonas said desperately. "The sharks will eat him alive if we throw him in the water."

"Do as you're told; hold him!"

Following orders, Jonas grappled with Emille's quivering legs. During the tremors, Emille's scuffed shoes thumped together so harshly, one shoe fell off of his foot.

"Oh, God!" a woman shouted when she noticed the enflamed markings on the sole of Emille's foot. By now, the other crewman rushed over, pushing Jonas out of the way. Jonas watched helplessly as the two men grappled with Emille. After finally restraining him with chains, they lowered him to the floor of the boat.

Shackled and laid out on display, Emille's face was grotesquely distorted as he thrashed and writhed.

Shortly after Emille had been contained, two others—a man and a woman—that had unwittingly stepped in the powder fell ill and began to exhibit similar symptoms. The couple was constrained with rope. On the floor of the boat, three squirming human beings were lined in a row and fastened together like chattel.

The ghastly sounds that emanated from their throats expressed anguish and unbearable suffering.

It seemed as if Jonas was in the midst of a horrific dream. The few people that had not been overcome by the terrible illness were shrieking, moaning, and weeping like mourners at a funeral. The journey that had held so much hope and promise continued to worsen. It was indeed the voyage of the damned.

Finally, the groans of agony from the captive, sickly trio began to quiet down. Their bodies stiffened and became still, and Jonas was hopeful that their suffering had ended.

Captain Henri ordered his crew to take Emille and the couple below deck. Jonas was relieved that the captain didn't demand that they be thrown overboard. He was also perplexed. Were they actually dead? Feeling renewed hope, Jonas prayed that Captain Henri had a remedy below deck that would restore their good health.

Jonas anxiously waited for news of Emille's fate, but the crewmen dodged questions, and finally outright told him to mind his own business.

Trying to take his mind off of the three stiffened bodies that were shrouded in mystery, Jonas retrieved from his satchel a dog-eared copy of *The Invisible Man* by Ralph Ellison. He hoped to lose himself in the novel. Hopefully, by the time he finished the book, he'd be stepping onto American soil.

But his escape from the harsh reality of the dangerous journey he'd embarked on was short-lived. Alarmed by a sudden tingling sensation at the bottom of Jonas's feet, Jonas closed the book and began chanting a mantra: *There's nothing wrong with me. I'm healthy. I'm fine.* The tingling grew more urgent, traveling up his ankles and legs, causing Jonas to involuntarily twitch. *There's nothing wrong with me. I'm healthy. I'm fine,* he fervently repeated in his mind.

But something was horribly wrong. No longer able to control himself, facial tics and body spasms drew attention from the scant few passengers that had not been exposed to the poison. Jonas grunted. He twisted and turned, and thrashed. Regarding Jonas with their mouths agape, the onlookers began to ease away from him.

Jonas dreaded being chained down like Emille and the others. Instinct told him to run. There was nowhere to flee except the dreaded, shark-infested water; yet, in a haze of panic and confusion, escaping by any means was the only thing on Jonas's mind.

It took a painstakingly long time for him to pull himself to his feet, and by the time he'd managed to rise from his seat, the crewmen had been alerted. Before Jonas could put up any kind of struggle, he was gripped and dragged to the cramped area below deck.

He tried to speak. Tried to reason with his captors, but only garbled nonsense spilled from his lips. He was tied next to Emille, and a fleeting glimpse of his friend's wide open, unblinking eyes assured him that Emille was out of his misery and now lay dead. But why were they keeping Emille and the couple on the boat? Jonas could not think of any reasonable explanation.

Time passed slowly. Nights were cold and windy and days were scorching hot. Jonas had gone from violent trembling to a deathly still paralysis. He could hear, smell, and see, but he couldn't utter a sound or move a muscle. His tortured mind raced with fearful thoughts. Would Captain Henri mistakenly believe that like the others, Jonas had also succumbed to death? Would he be hurled into the unforgiving sea?

The loud motor of the boat died down. Lying on his side, Jonas couldn't get a clear visual of what was going on, but judging from the excited murmurs and the numerous pairs of ankles that scrambled past him, he surmised that at last, they were close to the American shore.

But this would be no ordinary arrival. This boat would not dock in a normal manner. Passengers wouldn't be welcomed by family and friends as they disembarked from a ramp.

Loud splashes could be heard as people began jumping from the boat, frantically swimming the few miles toward the land of opportunity.

Untie me! Jonas longed to jump into the water with the others.

His heart leapt with joy when he heard the sound of ropes being untied and chains being unlocked.

"Stand up! Do as I say," the captain commanded. Jonas's fallen companions began struggling clumsily to their feet.

"Take three steps," Captain Henri implored them.

In a mechanical manner, Emille and the couple took three sluggish footsteps.

"Too slow! Do it again. Take three swift steps," the captain said furiously.

Jonas was elated that Emille and the couple had survived the poison, but he was appalled by Captain Henri's lack of sensitivity. Only a few moments ago, Emille and the couple had been on the brink of death. Captain Henri hadn't so much as offered them a sip of water before he'd begun ordering them to demonstrate their physical abilities. What would the heartless man demand next—an arm-wrestling match?

"What is your name?" Captain Henri barked, testing their verbal skills.

Emille and the couple spoke their names in coarse, discordant voices that were low-toned and incomprehensible.

It didn't matter, he told himself. Despite Jonas's annoyance with the captain, he was elated that they were alive. The nightmare was over! Soon they'd be back to their normal selves.

Anxiously, Jonas waited to be untied. He was still unable to move or speak, but he assumed that at any moment the poison would wear off and his limbs would begin to function properly. He also assumed that he, too, would soon be swimming to shore.

Jonas was eager to begin his new life. His relatives had a job waiting for him. He'd work every day after school and all day on the weekends. He'd work tirelessly to pay back the money that his mother had borrowed to give him a better life.

"Alain!" Captain Henri clapped his hands impatiently.

From his position on the floor, Jonas could see the scraggly bearded crewman hurrying toward the captain.

"Yes, sir, captain," Alain said respectfully.

"I'm keeping the woman for myself, but I want you to take the two men to Madame Collette in Little Haiti. Tell her that she can have ten-percent commission if she puts you in touch with buyers that are looking for free labor."

"Sure thing, Captain," Alain replied. Then in an uncertain tone, he asked, "Are they able to swim?"

"The poison took away their will. They cannot make decisions anymore. If you order them to swim, they'll do exactly as they're told."

That his fellow passengers had no will of their own was outrageous and very sad. He was grateful that he didn't share their fate. Though he remained paralyzed and mute, his mind was intact, and he still possessed opinions and intelligence. He'd be back to his old self after the white powder released its paralyzing grip on his muscles.

"Emille," the captain called out sharply. "There isn't much time. You must follow my instructions to the letter."

Emille groaned a sound that wasn't quite a word, but indicated that he understood.

"Terrence," the captain said to the other bewitched man. "I'm taking your pretty wife; you don't need her anymore. She'll be in good hands with me." Captain Henri chuckled spitefully. His two crewmen laughed along with him.

"Listen carefully, Emille and Terrence. You must follow my men and obey them. Swim swiftly, and stay by their sides when you get to shore. Do you understand, Terrence?"

Terrence and Emille both gurgled in assent. Spellbound, they would have agreed to set themselves on fire if they had been ordered to do so.

What a scoundrel and an opportunist Captain Henri had turned out to be. It was unconscionable that he was willing to profit from the free labor of helplessly bewitched people.

"What about him?" one of the crewmen asked, nudging the toe of his shoe into Jonas's side.

"Leave him. He won't wake up. Hurry, now; let's go!

Don't leave me. I'm awake! I can hear you. Please don't leave me. Jonas attempted to wiggle and squirm. He struggled to blink his eyes, but couldn't move a muscle.

Jonas watched helplessly as six pairs of legs moved out of his view. When he heard the creak of the wobbly steps that led above deck, he went into a panic. *I'm alive; I'm alive,* he shouted in his mind while his voice remained mute.

He heard the sounds of multiple splashes of water as the

captain, crewmen, Emille, Terrance, and his now ex-wife abandoned ship, leaving Jonas behind.

Lying on his side, Jonas listened to the silence. The unmanned boat floated aimlessly. Sooner or later, someone would take notice of a boat adrift in the ocean. The Coast Guard would most likely respond. Being rescued meant that immigration officials would be involved. Like a criminal, Jonas would be sent to a detention center, and then deported back to Haiti.

Jonas would rather lie on the bottom of the boat and die than be sent back to a life where he had no means of earning a living. No way to pay off the huge debt to the lenders that had financed his trip.

Jonas needed to stay in America to earn money. Once the spell wore off, he'd be as good as new. Willing himself to believe that a bright future was possible, Jonas made plans. Instead of enrolling in school, he'd work night and day. He'd send his earnings to his mother, keeping only a minimal amount to get by. He'd continue his education only after the debt for his passage to America was paid in full.

CHAPTER 7

Time passed. Minutes. Hours. If only he could get off the godforsaken boat.

Jonas prayed that a kind soul would find him and take him to his relatives. If medicine didn't work, perhaps his family knew of a witch doctor that was experienced in dealing with voodoo and dark magic.

The silent night was suddenly filled with the roaring engine of a speedboat, and Jonas was certain that his prayers had been answered. He was overjoyed when moments later, he heard voices and felt the vibration of footsteps directly overhead. But joy quickly dissipated when he recognized Alain's dirty, scuffed boots descending the steps. Alain was followed by a man wearing a shiny, new pair of light brown boots.

Alain stood over Jonas as the other man knelt down and examined him, shining a flashlight in his face, and smacking his cheek to get a response.

Jonas's wide-open stare was fixated on the man that scrutinized him. He was a white man, and he spoke in an authoritative tone. Was he an immigration official? Jonas was puzzled as to why Alain would bring someone from immigration to a discarded boat that had brought in refugees?

"That boy is dead; he's no use to me," said the white man.

"He only appears that way. He'll wake up," Alain said encouragingly.

"I don't know..." The white man gave Jonas another look and then stood up straight.

"I'm giving you the boy at a good price," Alain said in nervous, broken English.

"Boy! What boy?" the white man scoffed. "All I see is a corpse."

"I've seen this many times. The boy will wake up in a few hours. He'll come back to life, ready to work harder than any of your other workers. I guarantee it."

"That's a crock of shit."

"It's true. I'll drop my price down to two hundred if you take the boy. You'll get more than your money's worth after he comes out of the spell. You have my word of honor."

"You Haitians and your voodoo crap; you're all full of it," the white man said mockingly. "Madam Collette promised me two free laborers; I left the farmer's convention and drove to her place as fast as I could. I get there and she tells me that another farmer beat me to it."

"Free labor is a hot commodity. Another buyer picked up Terrence and Emille."

"Yeah, looks like I ended up with the shitty end of the stick."

"You got me, boss man."

"You ain't no prize. You got a lot of gall, wanting me to pay top dollar for your services when you never picked a Vidalia onion in your life," the farmer complained.

"I learn fast," Alain replied with a wide smile. "No worries, boss man. You're getting a good bargain with this boy. He's young and strong. He'll do the work of four men."

"This boy ain't worth a plug nickel if he doesn't get up on his feet and get to moving. I can't linger around in Florida, waiting for some damn voodoo spell to break."

"Give me fifty dollars for him, boss man," Alain said urgently.

"Fifty? Well, that sounds fair enough. If he doesn't wake up, I can use him as compost for my crops." Laughing hard, the farmer slapped his thigh.

"Thanks, boss; you won't regret it. Once this boy is up and about, he'll pick onions from sunup to sundown."

⊕ ⊕ ⊕

Lying on the back of a pickup truck and covered with tarp, Jonas was wedged between large bags of onions and metal objects. Oddly, he wasn't afraid. He was greatly relieved to be off of the boat and on American soil. He'd overheard Alain and the farmer, and was aware that they were taking him to Georgia. He could see a map of the United States in his mind, and was thankful that Georgia wasn't too far away from his aunt and uncle in Florida.

Alain turned out to be as conniving as Captain Henri. Poverty, Jonas surmised, sometimes brought out the worst in human nature.

There was no doubt in his mind that the moment that the poison wore off, he was going to take off running. He'd hitch a ride to Florida. He'd walk all the way if he had to. His relatives were expecting him. They had a job lined up for him—a paying job, and he didn't want to miss one day's work if he didn't have to.

The truck exited the smooth highway and rolled onto a bumpy back road. Suddenly, one of the back tires began to wobble. The truck slowed and came to a stop. A door opened and slammed shut. Jonas heard the farmer gripe, "Goddamn tire; what the hell did I run over?"

Boots crunched against gravel as the farmer briskly made his way to the rear of the truck.

"Hey, Alain! Get your lazy ass out of the truck and help me change this tire."

Alain made ambling footsteps to the back of the truck.

Jonas heard clanking and clanging as the car jack and other items were being moved around. For the first time since he'd stepped in the poisonous powder, he felt pangs of hunger. A gnawing, terrible hunger!

The farmer pulled back the tarp, and this time when he shined the beam of light in Jonas's face, Jonas blinked rapidly.

"Well, what do you know? Somebody decided to wake up from his nice, long nap."

Jonas was as surprised as the farmer. Not only could he blink his eyes, he could also wiggle his fingers and toes.

Scratching his scraggly beard, Alain peered down at Jonas. He broke into a huge grin. "Hey, welcome back to the living!"

The farmer presented a reptilian smile, and broke into laughter. "You woke up right in the nick of time. I was going to dig a hole for you—use you to fertilize my crops."

Jonas winced from a wave of pain that felt similar to a punch in the stomach.

"Hey, I'm only joking. You're coming to work for me on my farm. What's your name, boy?"

Jonas spoke his full name, but the sound that came out of his mouth was similar to static—scratchy, unintelligible noise. His inability to articulate was unsettling. He licked his lips and tried again. More static.

"What's wrong with your voice? Need some water, son?"

Jonas nodded. He wasn't thirsty, but hoped that a sip of water would help activate his vocal chords. He had to let this farmer know that he didn't intend to pick onions without pay. If the farmer offered fair wages, he'd work a few weeks or as long as it took to earn enough money to pay for a bus ride to his family in Florida.

Concerned about the well-being of his free laborer, the farmer bellowed at Alain, "Grab that bottle of water from the cup holder."

Alain quickly followed the farmer's orders and handed him the plastic container that was half filled with water.

"Get busy changing that tire, Alain. I have to see what I can do to bring this boy back to good health." The farmer lifted Jonas's head and carefully placed the mouth of the bottle at his lips.

As Alain jacked up the truck, the farmer tended to Jonas as if he were a prized calf. Jonas tried to take in a sip of water, but hit with another attack of unbearable hunger, he quivered violently. Water dribbled down his chin. The hunger was outrageous. Like his insides were being twisting into knots. Staving off the severe pain, Jonas grimaced and drew his legs up to his chest.

"Whoa!" The farmer backed up a little. "Alain! To hell with that tire; come take a look at this boy."

Alain dropped the tire iron and stood over Jonas.

"Why is he squirming and carrying on? Is that typical behavior?"

"I think so."

"You think so? I thought you were an authority on voodoo. If this boy kicks the bucket, I'm not taking him on my property. I'm dumping him over there in those woods over yonder, and I want my fifty bucks back."

"The boy's all right, boss. Look, he's calming down." Alain pointed at Jonas, who was pulling himself into a sitting position. "He'll be walking and talking and ready to work first thing in the morning," Alain said sheepishly.

As Jonas listened to the exchange between Alain and the farmer, a base and primitive instinct was overwhelming him. Jonas battled to control wild and dangerous impulses that overpowered all rational thought. Consumed by an agonizing hunger, he gave up his internal battle. Relinquishing every shred of normal human behavior, he lunged for the farmer. Growling like an animal, he appeased his ravenous appetite with a bite out of the farmer's shoulder.

The farmer screamed painfully and grabbed at his wounded shoulder. Startled, Alain hollered even louder.

The stunned farmer watched in disbelief as Jonas spat out a piece of bloodied shirt, and chewed hungrily on a hunk of his flesh.

Jonas was appalled by his action, but the hunger was stronger than his will. He swallowed the human meat, and the taste of blood lingered on his tongue. He wanted more. With spittle and blood trickling out of the corners of his mouth, Jonas pounced again.

Teeth bared, Jonas gripped the farmer by the ripped shirtsleeve as he aimed for a muscular bicep.

Tussling with Jonas, the farmer howled in distress and implored Alain to help him. Alain swung the tire iron, but instead of hitting Jonas, he hit the side of the truck. Alain's second blow landed on Jonas's forearm, loosening his grip on the farmer.

Acting swiftly, the farmer reached for the pistol that was tucked in the back of his pants. When Jonas sprang at him, he fired a single shot.

With a bullet lodged in the center of his chest, Jonas tumbled backward. Filled with a mixture of relief and sorrow, Jonas closed his eyes. He'd been turned into some kind of amoral beast, and he didn't want to live that way. On the other hand, he regretted letting down his family. His mother and his little sisters were all depending on him.

The moisture of tears dampened his lashes as he felt life slowly slipping away. The farmer's irate voice became distant.

"Dammit to hell; that sonofabitch bit me," the farmer hissed.

Stretching out the collar of his shirt, he examined his injury, but the glow of the moon didn't provide adequate lighting.

"Get over here, Alain. Shine that flashlight on my shoulder, goddamnit!"

With his eyes shifting from the farmer to Jonas's prone body, Alain crept forward with the flashlight in hand. "Is he dead?"

"If he ain't, I'ma kill him again," the farmer said illogically as Alain flashed the light on his injury.

His mouth twisted to the side, the farmer examined his shoulder. "Good thing I put that rabid fucker down before I brought him onto my property. No telling how many migrant workers he would have snacked on in the course of a day."

He pulled a bandana from his back pocket and tied it around his shoulder, covering the wound. "I got scratch marks on my back from those convention hookers...now this! I don't know how I'm gonna explain all this mangled flesh to the wife!" The farmer spat on the ground in disgust.

He pulled a shovel from the back of his truck. "Get to shoveling. We gotta bury this boy."

Death was taking its time, and once again, Jonas was unable to move or speak. Though his sight was blurry, he was vaguely aware of his surroundings. Through eyes that were slit open, he saw the silhouettes of trees and the flash of twinkling stars. His hearing, however, was amazingly sharp as he listened to the unmistakable sound of a hole being dug. He heard a shovel hitting the ground, the thud of dirt landing in a heap, and the intermittent scrapes of metal against rock.

Jonas was dropped into the gaping hole like a rag doll. Though he welcomed death, Jonas was terrified of being buried alive. In his mind, he screamed for mercy as each heaping of dirt was piled on him.

Finally, it was over. He was embedded in the earth and completely covered with soil. Surprisingly, there was no struggle for breath. The end didn't come in a fit of strangled gasps and choking. Instead, there was absolute darkness.

And peace, at last.

CHAPTER 8

In her bedroom, Holland swiped her finger across the screen of her phone, scrolling through pictures. When she came upon the image of the alien footprints, she grimaced. Unaccountably cold, she felt a sudden chill running up her spine. The footprints looked otherworldly and peculiar. It didn't help that the Ouija board had taken it upon itself to bring up the subject. She no longer wanted her mother's opinion. Wanting to forget she'd ever seen the ghastly footprints, she deleted the picture.

This should have been one of the happiest days of Holland's life. She'd finally gotten Jarrett's attention. The hottest boy at school was actually interested in her. He said she was pretty, and wanted to teach her to bowl.

Ordinarily, she'd be calling Naomi and giving her every juicy detail about her encounter with Jarrett, but tonight her heart wasn't in it.

Phoebe was right. Something strange was going on, and whatever it was, Holland didn't like it. She'd never entertained the silly idea that she could possibly be a witch, and she didn't want to start.

The doorbell rang and Holland jumped at the sound. The Ouija board and microwave incidents had her spooked. She checked the time. Ten o'clock on the dot. Her mother's client had arrived.

"Mom!" she yelled out into the hall. "Your client is here!"

Phoebe poked her head out of her bedroom door. She was in the midst of dressing and had on a black caftan with silver threads stitched along the V-cut collar.

"Can you let my client in, Holland? Her name's Rebecca Pullman."

"Aw, Mom! I don't wanna be involved in this."

The bell rang again.

"Get the door, please," her mother said, sounding a bit aggravated. "Offer Ms. Pullman a seat, and tell I'll be with her in a few moments."

Holland opened the door and was surprised that her mother's client didn't look spaced out and crazy. Standing on the other side of the screen door was an African-American woman with flawless, mahogany colored skin. The attractive black woman looked completely normal. Holland stared at her and decided that attractive wasn't the right word. *Beautiful* was a more accurate description.

"Hi, come on in," Holland invited, feeling guilty that this unsuspecting person was going to be duped by her mother. Her mother meant well, but she really had no business charging people for her services.

The woman looked at Holland skeptically. "Are you Phoebe Manning?"

Holland giggled. "No, I'm her daughter. My mom will be with you in a few minutes." Holland directed her to the living room and gestured toward the couch. "Have a seat."

Ms. Pullman gave Holland a long look. "You smell divine."

"I do? I'm not wearing perfume." Holland gave a puzzled shrug.

Ms. Pullman closed her eyes and inhaled deeply. "Must be your natural pheromones."

Holland laughed uneasily. Looks were obviously deceptive. Ms. Pullman was a kook, after all. Beautiful, but still a little screwy.

"Good evening, Ms. Pullman." Phoebe Manning glided into the living room. Dressed for the occasion, she was wearing the black and silver caftan and a turban. In the center of the turban was a big rhinestone, clip-on pin. A zillion bangles clinked and clanked on her wrists. Every one of her fingers, including both thumbs, was adorned with chunky rings purchased from thrift shops.

Holland was mortified. Her mother was trying too hard. She should have left on the casual jeans and the shell top that she had on earlier this evening.

"Come into my consultation room. We'll work some magic on your financial affairs." Phoebe motioned for Ms. Pullman to follow her into the family's former dining room.

Oddly, Ms. Pullman kept her eyes fixated on Holland. "Your daughter has a lovely scent," she said as if enthralled.

"Her aura is beautiful, too," Holland's mother added with a trace of pride.

Two kooks! Holland awkwardly eased out of the living room and returned to the privacy of her bedroom.

It wasn't easy having a mother like hers. She needed to talk to someone. Though she wouldn't dream of discussing her weird-mother issues with anyone other than Naomi, she wished Jarrett would call her. Simply hearing his voice would make her feel so much better.

She could hear the vibration of a drum. *Oh, God!* Her mother was beating a drum—something she called drum healing. Holland groaned and covered her head with a pillow. The pillow was ineffective when the sound of a second drum filled the air. Ms. Pullman was fully cooperating with her mother's wacko methods and was beating a drum along with Holland's mother in an unorthodox pursuit of money.

The annoying drumming went on for at least thirty minutes or longer. And just when Holland thought she'd finally have some peace and quiet, there were two soft knocks on her bedroom door.

"Yes!" she said sharply, trying to deter her mother from coming in her room and telling her all about her kooky witchcraft session. But it wasn't her mother who opened her door. It was Ms. Pullman.

"I wanted to tell you how wonderful it was to meet you."

"Okaaay?" Holland said with a perplexed look on her face. She wondered why her mother had allowed her client to roam through the house and come to her bedroom.

"We'll meet again," Ms. Pullman said. She gave Holland a lingering look, her dark eyes blazed with a sort of longing that Holland was unable to make sense of.

After Ms. Pullman closed the door, Holland sat stunned for a few moments. *What was that about?* She waited until she heard the front door close and then raced out of her bedroom.

"Mom!" Holland yelled. Phoebe was sitting on the floor, her back rigid, her eyes closed, caught up in a trance.

"Snap out of it, Mom!" She shook her mother's shoulder.

Phoebe blinked and finally opened her eyes. "Oh, my goodness. I lost consciousness. I was in a really deep state." She turned her head right and left. "Where's Ms. Pullman?"

"She left."

Holland and her mother simultaneously spotted the two fifties that Ms. Pullman had placed on top of the tom-tom that she'd used during the session.

"What a nice lady," Phoebe said. "I hope I was able to help her."

⊕ ⊕ ⊕

Sleep eluded Holland. From the footprints, the Ouija board, and the microwave malfunction to Ms. Pullman knocking on her bedroom door, there'd been far too many bizarre occurrences today.

Ms. Pullman was one creepy lady, and Holland could only hope that she never sought her mother's services again. If she did, Holland would make sure she wasn't around. She'd hang at Naomi's house or go for a long walk...she didn't want to see the strange woman ever again.

She plumped her pillow and tried to drift to sleep, but she couldn't shake the icky feeling or the troubling sensation that someone was watching her. Her eyes roamed around her darkened bedroom. Ms. Pullman's presence was thick in the air. Holland got out of bed and turned on the light. After checking the closet and under her bed, Holland made a mental note to give her bedroom a cleansing with sage first thing in the morning.

CHAPTER 9

Jonas pulled his hand away from the intricate patterns on the bottom of his foot, and stroked the bullet hole in the center of his chest. It was a tragic reminder that he was no longer human.

He heard something approaching. Fast-paced, determined footsteps treaded through leaves and crunched twigs. Jonas sniffed the air but couldn't detect man or beast. Then suddenly, out of the darkness, a figure appeared. A young man, slightly older than Jonas, but no more than eighteen or nineteen.

He was dressed in a nineteenth-century costume that was more ragged and filthier than Jonas's clothing. The necktie that was formed in a fanciful bow sagged to his chest and was matted with dirt. The cuffs of his sleeves were hanging by threads. Soil clung to his face and his head, disguising the true color of his hair. His eyes, however, a vivid blue, sparkled with confidence and gleamed like jewels.

Jonas stood upright, his fingers closed into fists. He was surprised by the low, rumbling growl that emanated from his throat.

"Friend or foe?" the oddly dressed young man asked in a challenging tone.

"Neither," Jonas answered, his voice gruff. "Go away; I don't want to hurt you." Jonas found it strange that he didn't detect a whiff of human scent emanating from the strange-looking person.

The hunger continued to gnaw at him, but he had no desire to sink his teeth into the stranger's flesh.

"I'd like to make your acquaintance," the young man said in a Southern drawl and extended his. "My name's Zacharias Hamilton. It's a mouthful, so you can just call me Zac."

"I'm not looking for a friend," Jonas muttered in a surly tone.

"We have a lot in common. Like you, I was also called from my resting place."

Shocked, Jonas flinched. "How do you know that I was pulled from the ground?"

"I saw you crawl out of a hole. I watched as you wandered about, foraging for food." He chuckled mockingly. "I watched you kill a half-dozen rodents—a couple raccoons. Personally, I don't know how you do it—you know, substituting forest critters for a delicious meal."

"That's none of your business," Jonas said angrily. It was embarrassing that he'd been secretly observed while he'd scavenged through the woods. "Why were you spying on me?"

"For pure entertainment," said the bedraggled young man in his Southern twang.

"There's nothing amusing about my predicament."

"I didn't expect you to be so touchy. Accept my apology." Once again, Zacharias Hamilton extended a dirt-encrusted hand. And again, Jonas refused to accept it.

He gazed curiously at Jonas, trying to figure him out. "What are you? Vampire…werewolf?" Zac asked. His eyes glinted, and amusement stretched his mouth into a mocking smile.

Jonas scowled in disgust. "I'm neither. I'm a human being." He gave a bewildered shrug. "At least, I used to be human. I don't understand what's happened to me, but I'm not a vampire or any of those creatures from horror movies. Someone used a poisonous powder to put a hex on me. The powder is what changed me."

"Changed you into what?"

"I don't know. I'm bewitched. I don't think there's a name for what I've become." Jonas glanced surreptitiously at Zacharias. "You said that you were called out of the earth also. What happened to you?"

"Long story," Zacharias muttered. "What's your name, fella?" he asked, flashing a bright smile as he abruptly changed the subject.

Zacharias seemed a little dodgy—somewhat devious—and Jonas was hesitant to give him any personal information.

"Like I said, my friends call me Zac. What name do you go by?"

"Jonas," he finally answered.

"You don't talk like a Southerner, Jonas. And judging from the clothes you're wearing, I'm gonna assume that you're not from these parts."

Jonas instantly thought of Haiti and felt a tug in his heart.

Zac peered at him closely. "The West Indies, huh?

It was if Zac had read his mind, and Jonas felt a chill go through him. "Yes, I'm from the Caribbean," he acknowledged softly.

"You're a long way from home."

"I have relatives here in Florida, but I can't let them see me in this condition."

"Well, you're not in Florida." Zac stamped a scuffed boot on the ground. "This here is Georgia soil you're standing on— Frombleton, Georgia. It'll probably take a week or so to get to Florida by buggy. Much faster by railroad."

"Buggy? What are you talking about?" Jonas asked, bewildered.

A look of confusion crossed Zac's face. "You know…Horse and buggy."

Jonas gazed at him curiously. "You can't be serious."

"Never mind the horse and buggy. We can travel on foot. I

have to get out of these woods and find shelter before sunrise."

Jonas backed up slightly. "What are you...a vampire?"

Zac nodded with pride. "That's exactly what I am."

"You're a killer," Jonas snapped, grimacing in disgust. He looked at Zac with revulsion. Despite what Jonas had become, he didn't want anything to do with a vampire.

"I do what I have to for survival," Zac said in an unapologetic tone.

Jonas forced the gruesome memory of his own attack on the farmer out of his mind. "I'm not like you," Jonas insisted. "I can live off animals forever if I have to."

"Stop pretending to be so innocent. You've had a taste of human flesh," Zac said knowingly.

"Shut your mouth! You don't know anything about me. I've never taken a human life." Jonas whirled around and stormed away from the vampire.

In a flash, Zac stood directly in front of Jonas, staring him down. Jonas flinched in surprise. "How'd you do that?"

"I have my ways. Nice trick, huh?" Zac fixed his mouth in a smug expression. "I think we have more in common than you realize. Let's be friends, Jonas. We can help each other." His voice was low and seductive.

Zac's face was hideously caked with dirt and mud, yet his handsome features were evident. His lips stretched into a forced smile—a smile that held a hint of malevolence.

"I don't associate with vampires." Jonas folded his arms, adamant.

"In a world where people want to destroy our kind, we should band together and help each other." He spoke in a gentle, persuasive manner.

"I'm not *your* kind!"

"We're more alike than you want to admit. Come with me, my friend; it's not safe to lurk in the woods. We need shelter. We'll figure out your problem together."

Exasperated, Jonas sighed. Zac was deliberately engaging him, ignoring the fact that he'd clearly stated that he wanted nothing to do with him.

"What island are you from...Jamaica?"

"No, I'm Haitian. Well...I *was* Haitian when I was normal; I don't know what I've become."

"You're reborn," Zac said.

Jonas snorted. "A rebirth is something to celebrate and rejoice over. Hiding out in the woods like a scared animal is not a rebirth; it's a living hell."

"Then let's get out of here. Let's begin the new life we've both been given."

"How can I begin again?" Jonas yelled. Then, in a lowered voice, he admitted, "I miss my family. It's agonizing to know that even if I found my way back home, my mother and my sisters would never accept me. Not like this."

"I've never traveled to any island, but I've heard tales about Haiti and voodoo curses. Perhaps we can find a way to reverse the spell that was cast on you."

"That's impossible. The woman that hexed me is dead. This spell is irreversible."

"Don't be so sure of that."

Refusing to get his hopes up, Jonas shook his head. "My only desire is to return to my resting place. I'd take my own life if I could. But I'm already dead...I guess."

"If we find out who pulled us from sleep, we can get them to return you to your eternal slumber. Is that what you want?"

Jonas nodded.

"Not me. I have a different desire. I don't want to lurk in the shadows forever. I want to exist among the living."

Jonas looked at Zac with interest. "Is that possible?"

"I did it before. I had a wonderful time, living among mortals." Zac gave a wistful smile.

Jonas didn't completely trust Zac, but he was stirred by the possibility of living as close to a normal life as possible. Perhaps he could make a home here…send for his family.

Then Jonas pictured the face of the girl that had walked along the trail. Hoping that a hint of her remarkable scent still lingered, he sniffed the air. There was nothing but the smell of trees and forest animals, but in his mind, he remembered her glorious smell.

Zac interrupted Jonas's reverie. "After we've cleaned up, we'll both look like mortals. No one will be able to tell that we're different."

"Are you sure?"

"Positive. You'd be able to be a part of your family again. You'd like that, wouldn't you?"

"More than anything," Jonas whispered.

"Then let's get moving."

With an image in his mind of being reunited with his mother and his sisters, Jonas fell into step beside Zac.

CHAPTER 10

Taking purposeful strides along a trail that twisted and turned, Zac seemed to know exactly where he was going. After a few hundred yards, they found themselves in a meadow. Through the meadow and around a couple of bends, they passed an old horse farm.

Jonas slowed his steps when a sudden and powerful yearning twisted his insides.

Zac put a hand on Jonas's shoulder, nudging him along. "Killing horses is not a smart idea, fella."

"Why not?" Jonas was practically salivating. An animal as large as a horse could keep his hunger at bay for many hours. Maybe days.

"You gotta be discreet. Eating wildlife is one thing, but slaughtering horses won't go unnoticed."

"Who cares? What more can anyone do to me? I'm already dead," he said in an agonized voice.

"Around these parts, there's nothing worse than a horse thief."

"How do you know? Are you a horse thief? Is that why you were put in the ground?" Jonas's surly attitude was the result of raging hunger.

"I ain't no horse thief, but I know human nature. Folks around here don't take kindly to horse thieves, so be careful. You've already gone through the torture of being buried alive. Would you like to suffer that fate again?"

Jonas shuddered at the thought, and then he eyed Zac warily. "How do you know so much about me?"

Zac flashed a cocky smile. "Intuition."

"What about you? How'd you end up buried in the woods?" Jonas was only striking up a conversation to keep his mind off of his growing hunger.

Zac ignored the question, and once again, he changed the subject. "I know you're hungry, and I'll make sure that you feed when it's safe."

Feed! It was a terrible expression with hideous connotations. Jonas had no intention of *ever feeding!* Feeling petulant, he tagged along quietly. For a few miles, they traveled along an old gravel road that came to a fork. Zac yielded to the right, and after another mile, they came upon a creek.

"We're close," Zac informed.

"Close to what?"

"Shelter. Come on, we have to cross the water."

The cool water felt good on Jonas's bare feet. Heeding the desires of his former life, he bent over, cupped his palms and scooped up water from the creek.

Zac watched with great interest as Jonas sipped water from his hands.

Jonas grimaced when the water touched his tongue. It had such an acrid and disgusting taste, it was unpalatable. He expelled a blast of creek water, misting the air and nearly splashing Zac in the face. But with his supernaturally quick reflexes, Zac dodged the spray of water.

Muttering a few choice curse words in Creole, Jonas wiped his mouth with the back of his hand.

"We have more in common than you'd like to admit," Zac said with laughter. "Our thirst can only be quenched with blood."

Jonas recalled that the farmer had given him water. He also

remembered that the water had never entered his mouth. The farmer's presence…the sound and smell of blood pulsing in his veins had stirred a dark desire that Jonas was unable to control.

That one bite from the farmer's shoulder had tasted amazing. There was nothing to compare to the flavor. Jonas groaned inwardly. The very thought caused him unbearable hunger.

Jonas and Zac continued their trek. Another desolate gravel road and they finally came upon an old deserted sugar mill. It was a huge structure with several adjacent buildings. The battered sign at the chained gate cautioned, NO TRESPASSING, but there was no presence of security.

"How'd you know about this place?" Jonas asked.

Astonished, Zac's muddied fingers gripped the rusted metal gate. "What happened to the sugar mill? Seems like only yesterday that construction began. Folks from around here were delighted to have steady work."

Jonas gave Zac a baffled look. "You were around when this place was built?"

Zac nodded.

"How old are you?"

"Twenty-two. I was changed a few days after my twenty-second birthday."

"When was that…what year?"

"Seventeen-ninety-two."

"And when were you put in the ground?"

Zac winced at the memory. "Late eighteen hundreds."

"Welcome to the twenty-first century. Lots of things have changed in these modern times." Jonas cracked a smile. It felt good to have an advantage over Zac.

Zac scratched his head and regarded Jonas. "What year is it exactly?"

"Twenty-twelve."

Zac let out a long whistle. "A lot of years have passed by... more than a century." He shook his head, dumbfounded.

"I thought your clothes...well, I actually thought you were wearing a costume."

Zac ran his hands over his filthy garments. "This here is gentlemen's attire, suitable for Sunday service and a moonlight stroll with a lady friend."

Zac tried the door handles, but every door was locked tight. "Let's take a walk around the back. I know this building like the back of my hand. Hid out and slept in the bowels of this factory more times than I care to count."

At the rear of the main building, Zac tore away boards from an entryway. Inside, the vacant building was dark and decayed. It was pitch black inside, but Zac and Jonas had no difficulty seeing in the dark. Like laser beams, their eyes probed the old, rundown factory.

The walls and floors were corroded, and the dilapidated structure was filled with exposed pipes and rusted industrial equipment.

They came upon a huge boiler with two heavy metal doors. On the outside, the boiler looked like a humongous pot-bellied stove with circular piping at the top that spiraled high into the rafters.

Zac poked his head inside to inspect the deterioration inside. "Roomy! Exactly the way I remember it. With a little dusting, it'll be like old times," he exclaimed.

Jonas was appalled. Though he didn't require a soft mattress for comfort, he doubted if he'd be able to get a wink of sleep if he were closed up inside that claustrophobic-looking boiler. He and Zac were obviously two different breeds of undead. Zac was comfortable in his skin while Jonas was sickened by his monstrous transition.

With his mouth turned down, Jonas's unhappiness was apparent on his face.

"Why so glum?" Zac inquired.

"I'm not overjoyed at the idea of living inside a bleak, old factory."

"It's only temporary. We have to hide out until we learn the customs of today's society."

"I'm not from another era; I understand today's customs," Jonas stated tersely.

"But you won't be able to fit in until you get used to your transformation." Zac paused and gave Jonas a curious look. "Can you walk in the daylight?"

"Yes," Jonas said emphatically. "How many times do I have to tell you...I'm not a vampire!"

"You live off blood, exactly as I do, so if you're not a vampire... then what are you?"

"I don't know!" Jonas yelled. He was furious with Zac for probing, and even more upset with himself. Zac seemed to revel in being a vampire, but Jonas was sickened over his monstrous transition. Yes, blood was the elixir that he needed to survive, but living flesh was also a necessary component of his revolting diet.

"There's nothing supernatural about me," Jonas declared. "I'm under a spell, and once it's broken, I'll be my old self. I'm sure of it," Jonas muttered as he glanced around the unrelenting gloom of his new living quarters.

Zac gave Jonas a sympathetic pat on the shoulder. "That bad mood of yours will improve after you feed. I reckon it's time for us to go hunt up a nice, hearty meal for ourselves."

CHAPTER 11

Quite the spectacle in their dirt-encrusted and ragged clothing, Jonas and Zac traveled undetected on back roads. Zac sauntered onward, seemingly unfazed by hunger, but Jonas was so famished he was beginning to feel half-crazed with the need to eat. With his senses on high alert, he sniffed the night air; his eyes swept the bushes and tall grass alongside the road, searching for sizeable living creatures.

A pair of halogen headlights suddenly lit the dirt road.

Zac stood in a confrontational pose with his hands fisted at his sides, as if ready to do battle with the pickup truck that was barreling toward them.

"We have to hide!" Jonas grabbed Zac by the wrist and pulled him down into a crouch in the tall grass beside the road.

The truck screeched to a halt. Waxed to a high gloss, the Chevy glistened in the moonlight. Loud music that pumped from the speakers rocked and vibrated the vehicle.

"What the hell was that?" said the driver, stretching his neck out of the window, scanning the darkness.

A shaky voice from the passenger's seat said, "I don't know… deer?"

"That wasn't any deer," the driver said suspiciously, looking around and squinting at the weeds.

"What was it then?" the passenger asked shakily.

"Looked like two hobos wandering around—and probably up to no good."

"You're hallucinating, man. Those were deer."

"I know what I saw—bums! Drunken migrant workers."

"So what? We're pissy drunk our damn selves. We took this back road to avoid the cops, so keep driving, man. Let's get out of here."

"Nah, I wanna have some fun. Let's interrogate those guys."

"Interrogate 'em for what?"

"To shake 'em up and find out what they've been up to. Those migrant workers are all illegals; they don't have any business roaming around at night," the driver said in a slurred voice. "Grab the flashlight out of the glove box."

"For what?"

"So we can find those thieving nomads."

"Now they're thieves? You're weird, man. And your imagination is over the top."

From their positions on the ground, Jonas and Zac could clearly see and hear the occupants of the truck. Two teenage boys. The driver was freckle-faced with a youthful, athletic build. The passenger was broad shouldered and had thick russet-colored hair that was styled in a layered cut, presenting a controlled tousled look that had been accomplished with styling gel and a number of hair products.

The night breeze stirred the tall grass, revealing a pair of glowing blue eyes.

"Shit! Did you see those eyes, man? Must be a couple of big cats."

"I didn't see shit. You're freaking me out, though. Let's get out of here."

"Not until I investigate. I need my gun." The driver reached over his friend and jerked the glove compartment open.

"What do you need a gun for?" the passenger asked in an incredulous voice.

With uncanny speed, Zac leapt from his hiding place and stood beside the driver's door. He reached inside the truck, grabbing the stunned teenager by the throat.

Looking stricken, the passenger screamed for help and jiggled the door handle.

In awe of Zac's audacity, Jonas watched in fascination, but when the passenger tumbled out of the truck, taking off in a stumbling run, Jonas instinctively gave chase.

Though not nearly as fast as Zac, Jonas surprised himself with his panther-like speed and agility. His feet barely touched the ground as he ran. In airborne pursuit, he launched himself at his prey, catching him by the back of his collar.

Held in Jonas's tight grasp, the boy jerked and twisted. "Lemme go! What the hell is wrong with you?" the boy demanded in a terror-filled voice.

The smell of the boy's fear was tantalizing. Out of his mind with hunger, Jonas did not battle with his conscience. At that moment, he felt no remorse. Surrendering to bestial impulses, he bared his teeth and drew the boy closer.

The back of the boy's neck was greasy from a combination of sweat and hair pomade that had trickled down from his trendy hairstyle. Mouth wide open, Jonas had no qualms about biting into the uncommonly seasoned meat.

The boy's ear-splitting scream mixed in with the loud music that blasted from the truck. Wanting privacy, Jonas dragged the kicking and screaming boy into nearby bushes. He cut a glance at Zac and noticed that he was still standing outside the truck.

Zac had pulled the driver's upper body out of the open window. Clutching the driver by the shoulders, Zac seemed to be whispering in his ear. Then his mouth swept over the driver's neck in a somewhat teasing and seductive manner. Oddly, the boy didn't put up a struggle as Zac slowly and almost sensually began to drain him.

Turning his attention away from Zac, Jonas shoved the passenger. The boy swayed dizzily and then fell to the ground.

Injured from the bite and losing blood, the helpless boy's face was pale with fear. Moaning pitifully, he made a futile attempt to scoot away from Jonas. He held up a defensive hand. "Please. You don't have to do this. I have money—sixty bucks. It's in my pocket. You can have it," he pleaded in a croaking voice.

His desperate offering sounded like nothing more than white noise to Jonas. Growling and gritting his teeth, Jonas advanced. The boy screamed. Ignoring the boy's plaintive wail, Jonas savagely ripped off his shirt, chomping through chest muscles and tendons, biting wherever flesh was visible. He chewed on a mouthful of flesh, muscle, and tendons, and then noisily slurped the boy's blood.

Long after the boy's agonized cries became silent, Jonas continued the bloody carnage, grunting as he feasted on the soft internal organs.

⊕ ⊕ ⊕

Covered in blood and a splattering of human tissue, Jonas gnawed at the skeletal remains, picking off miniscule bits of skin like a vulture.

Footsteps brought Jonas to awareness. "There's not much left of him," Zac said, frowning at the clumps of russet hair that clung to Jonas's blood-caked shirt.

Jonas looked down at the remains of his victim. A deep and

nauseating shame overcame him. "Oh, God. What have I done?"

"Looks like you filled up your belly," Zac said in a matter-of-fact tone.

Jonas's dirty clothes were splattered with his victim's blood and innards, but there wasn't a drop of blood on Zac's mouth or the clothing that he'd been wearing since the 1800s.

Zac's eyes had become a more brilliant shade of blue, but aside from his enhanced eye color, there were no blood spatters on his clothing, and no outward signs that he had depleted the driver of every ounce of blood.

"Can you operate that…uh…" Zac paused and eyed the pickup, trying to come up with a word to describe it. "Do you know how that machine functions?"

"It's a truck," Jonas clarified. "Sure, I can drive."

"Good. We have to get rid of the bodies."

The driver's corpse lay in a pile on the dirt road. Using unnervingly swift movements, Zac hefted the passenger's carcass out of the bushes and dropped it in the back of the truck.

Guilt-ridden and filled with self-loathing, Jonas watched as Zac loaded the blood-drained boy next to his mangled victim.

Jonas got in the driver's seat and gripped the steering wheel. With a grim expression, he looked over his shoulder at the dead boys lying side by side.

Jonas was an atrocity; he deserved to burn in hell for what he'd done. Tormented and filled with revulsion, he put the truck in gear. He stepped heavily on the gas pedal, sending the truck lurching forward.

He hadn't been totally honest when he'd said he could drive. He'd taken a few lessons, but had never had an official license. By no means was he an experienced driver.

"Turn right at the end of the road. And try not to collide with any trees." Zac sighed and propped his feet on a canvas bag on the floor mat of the passenger side. Curious, he picked it up and rummaged through it, slipping into his own pocket, a plastic bag filled with crudely shaped, white rocks.

"We're in luck," he told Jonas, holding up shirts, a pair of khakis, and a pair of jeans. "After we get cleaned up, we can get out the filthy rags we're wearing and strut around in these snazzy garments."

Jonas had no interest in the dead boys' clothes. Wearing a haunted expression, he kept his eyes straight ahead as he bumbled at the wheel, swerving like a drunkard.

CHAPTER 12

Holding each boy by the scruff of his shirt collar, Zac dragged both teens to the edge of the river.

In the depths of despair, Jonas sat in the pickup contemplating suicide. According to legend, sunlight was like kryptonite to vampires. He wasn't a vampire and he didn't know which despicable and unnatural species he belonged to, but Jonas supposed that if he could get his hands on a gun and put a bullet in his head, he'd be able to once and for all put a permanent end to his miserable, so-called life.

After disposing of the bodies, Zac whistled merrily as he returned to the truck.

"Your belly's full, so why so glum, fella?" he asked, noticing Jonas's brooding disposition.

"You wouldn't understand. You have no conscience. No soul."

"And you do?"

"Yes, I still have a conscience! I feel horrible for what I did to that boy."

"Then why'd you do it?"

"I'm possessed! Cursed! Forever damned!" Jonas ranted. "I can't go on like this—this detestable spell has got to be broken."

Zac's eyes turned icy cold. "Face the facts—you're no longer human. You kill for self-preservation."

"But I feel human."

Zac clapped Jonas on the back of his shoulder. "Cheer up, fella. Let's get cleaned up and changed, so we can mingle with the mortals."

"I'm too dangerous to mingle with people," Jonas lamented.

"Sure, you can. You've already fed tonight; you should be satisfied for awhile."

"How long is awhile?"

Zac shrugged. "If you're anything like me, you should be able to go without feeding again until tomorrow night."

"I'm nothing like you," Jonas hissed. "I'm not a monster. I don't take pleasure in killing. I...I'm sickened by what I did."

"So you've said, and I'm getting sick of listening to you whimpering and whining. You have to accept what you are."

"I don't know what I am, so how can I accept it?" Jonas spat.

"You like the taste of living things," Zac pointed out. "It seems disgusting now, but over time, you'll feel different. Biting into a human will become as ordinary as biting into a tasty piece of chicken."

Jonas grunted in disagreement.

"Meanwhile, if we plan to survive another night, we have to get out of these bloody shirts and britches. Come on, fella. Let's clean ourselves up in the river and change into this modern wear," Zac said with uncharacteristic warmth.

⊕ ⊕ ⊕

"How do I look?" Zac smiled confidently.

Jonas looked him over. With the dirt and blood washed away, Zac looked like a normal person. Dressed in faded jeans and a powder blue button-down shirt, he was the perfect image of a contemporary young man. His hair was long and wheat-colored.

His skin was extremely pale, but his lack of pigmentation didn't detract from his good looks.

"These dungaree britches are more comfortable than I thought they'd be, and I prefer my leather boots to these shoes made out of fabric and rubber." Zac frowned down at the Nikes he'd retrieved from the canvas bag.

Jonas had changed into khakis, a striped pullover shirt, and black Puma running shoes. Bathed and dressed in clean clothes, Jonas felt refreshed. He wondered if he looked human.

"You look thoroughly modernized and completely human," Zac responded.

Jonas gazed at him curiously. "Did you read my mind?"

"Sure did," Zac said, grinning.

As if to guard his thoughts, Jonas covered his head with his hand. "Cut it out, man; that's intrusive."

"It's one of the many benefits of being a vampire. I don't read humans as clearly as I can an immortal's mind, but I get the gist of their thoughts." Zac glanced at Jonas. "What are your special traits?"

"I'm a lot stronger than I used to be. I can see in the dark, hear the faintest whisper, and track scents like a bloodhound. But aside from this sickening desire to slaughter innocent people, there's nothing remarkable about me."

"You can walk in the sunlight," Zac reminded him with a wink.

"Thrilling," Jonas muttered sarcastically and slouched against the truck.

Grinning, Zac stuck a hand in his back pocket and pulled out a wad of cash and waved it in Jonas's face. "No sugar mill for us tonight. We can afford upper-class lodging for a few days."

Jonas raised an eyebrow. He was so taken off-guard by the thick pile of currency, he stammered, "Wh— where'd you get all that money?"

"I rifled through the traveling bags and the pockets of those two boys before I ditched them in the river."

Jonas pushed away from the truck and moved closer to Zac. "How much?" he asked, mentally counting along with the vampire as he sorted through the bills.

"I used to enjoy stacking twenty-dollar gold pieces, but this paper money will do just fine," Zac said and began the count again. "We got ourselves two thousand and fifty dollars!" Letting out a cheerful whistle, he portioned off a slim section of the bills and handed it to Jonas. "This is your share."

Too guilty to accept the blood money, Jonas inched away. "No thanks." Imagining his family suffering and hungry at home, he felt doubly guilty for declining.

"Your family could use some financial help," Zac said slyly.

Jonas sighed loudly. "You're doing it again. Stay out of my head, man."

"Imagine how much you can help your family with a portion of this money."

"I don't want it," Jonas said stubbornly.

"Suit yourself." Zac returned the money to his back pocket. He walked around to the driver's side of the truck. "I'm driving," he announced, and boldly pulled open the door.

"But you don't know how to drive."

"I catch on quick. I watched you and figured out how to operate this contraption." Zac fired up the engine and put the truck in gear.

Not wanting to be left behind, Jonas hopped in the passenger seat. He didn't trust Zac and hated having to depend on him. But having nowhere to go, he was pretty much at the vampire's mercy until the spell was broken.

Jonas wondered if Madame Collette, the woman that Captain

Henri did business with, had any knowledge of removing hexes. From what he'd overheard, she didn't seem like the type of person who'd reverse a spell from the kindness of her heart. She'd want American dollars.

"Nothing in life is free," Zac quipped as if Jonas had spoken out loud and had asked his opinion.

Exasperated by the mental invasion, Jonas rolled his eyes skyward and then leaned his head against the seat rest. Attempting to protect his privacy, he tried to clear his mind of all thoughts.

As if he'd been driving for years, Zac expertly steered the truck down a back road. "Do you think she's a witch?" he asked.

"Who?"

"The woman in Florida. The woman you believe can change you back to your mortal self." Zac chuckled at the idea.

"It's possible," Jonas said with quiet hope.

"We could drive there in a few hours."

"No, not in this truck."

"Why not?"

"The authorities will be looking for those boys. They'll have a description and the license plate number for this truck."

"We'll be out of town long before the sheriff can find us."

Jonas shook his head. With a long sigh, he explained the high-tech modern world and how vehicles could be tracked by innumerable methods.

"Well, I guess if we don't wanna get caught, we'd better get rid of this buggy," Zac suggested and slammed on the brakes.

"Let's walk, my friend." He put a hand on Jonas's shoulder. "We'll get to Florida one way or another, but first we must find lodging," he said, his voice deceptively soft and compassionate.

CHAPTER 13

After a few miles of gravelly roads, they came upon a back-woods tavern. Neon letters over the door read, "Tully's Place."

Zac slowed his steps as they approached the parking lot that was filled with cars, trucks, and minivans.

"What's up, man? You're gonna try to steal one of these vehicles, aren't you?" Jonas asked anxiously.

"No. I want to go inside and see how well we fit in."

"I can't go in there."

"Why not?"

"I'm underage, and I don't have any documentation." Jonas pointed a finger at Zac. "You need ID, too. Something that proves that you're at least twenty-one," Jonas explained.

"Relax, Jonas. You worry too much." Zac boldly pushed the door open and Jonas timidly followed him.

A small band was on the makeshift stage, blasting instruments and singing loudly. The place was packed with people. In the air were the unusual mixtures of tobacco, alcohol, and the over-powering scent of human sweat. It was maddening to be around so many humans at the same time. Jonas involuntarily began grinding his teeth.

"We got live entertainment tonight; you boys gotta pay the cover charge," the big muscled bouncer announced as Zac attempted to brush past him.

Zac halted and frowned in annoyance at the bouncer. "Pay what?"

"How much is the cover charge?" Jonas interjected quickly, relieved that the bouncer wasn't hassling them about ID.

"Ten bucks a piece," the bouncer replied gruffly.

"Pay the man," Jonas whispered.

Zac peeled a twenty off of the thick wad of cash, and the bouncer's stern expression changed to a look of surprise. "You boys make yourselves at home," he said, grinning.

"We plan to," Zac replied with a firm head nod.

As they pushed their way through the crowd of people, Jonas grabbed Zac by the elbow. "You have to be careful. Showing off all that money could get us in a world of trouble."

"I can handle a little bit of trouble," Zac boasted.

There were no empty seats, but that didn't seem to bother Zac. He shepherded Jonas to a dim corner where they leaned against a wall, shrinking into the darkness.

"This isn't a hotel…it's a bar. Why did we stop here?" Jonas asked.

"Plenty of time before sunrise, so let's enjoy ourselves."

"Doing what? I don't think I can bear the taste of liquor."

"We don't need alcohol to have a good time. We're gonna mingle—make new friends," Zac said with a malicious chuckle. "The man at the entrance is gonna send a girl back here to keep us company."

"How do you know?"

"I took a peek inside his mind. Couldn't read him word for word, but I got the general idea."

Jonas looked around warily. In the crowd, he noticed a young lady heading in their direction. Zac spotted her, too. "Ah, she here comes. Now let's see if I can convince her that I'm one of her kind."

The girl looked to be in her early twenties. Her eyes were made up with heavy, dark eyeliner and her Cupid's bow lips shimmered with a fresh coating of lip gloss. She was wearing a black, low-cut top that revealed deep cleavage. Her light brown hair was fixed in a ponytail that was pulled to the side.

Jonas couldn't take his eyes off of her. But it wasn't her breasts or her luscious lips that he found enthralling. He was attracted to her satiny skin. Without the benefit of an alcoholic beverage, he was quickly becoming intoxicated by the delicious aroma that emanated from her pores. Unconsciously, he began grinding his teeth again.

"How are you boys feeling tonight?" The girl flashed a sparkling smile at Zac, correctly pegging him as the man with the money.

"I can't speak for this here fella…" Zac nodded to Jonas, "but I'm feeling mighty nice now that I've met your acquaintance, Rosie," Zac said, his voice silky smooth and oozing with Southern charm.

"I didn't get a chance to introduce myself…how'd you know my name?" Apparently impressed by Zac's vampire trick, the girl giggled and blushed.

"I got a gift for guessing names," Zac said with a seductive smile. "But only pretty girls," he added. "My mind goes as blank as a clean sheet of paper when an ugly girl crosses my path."

Rosie laughed harder. "You're a hoot. What's your name, cutie?"

"Zacharias Hamilton. Friends call me Zac."

"Hi, Zac," Rosie said, eyeing him seductively while provocatively running a finger down her cleavage.

Zac nodded toward Jonas. "And this here is my buddy, Jonas. He's visiting from the West Indies."

"Welcome to the States, Jonas," Rosie muttered, avoiding eye contact with Jonas.

Jonas realized that the way his teeth were grinding together was making the girl uncomfortable.

"You schoolboys seem a little young to be in here drinking," Rosie said.

"I'm a lot older than I look," Zac piped in. "But I'm laying off the booze tonight. Just looking to have us some fun."

"Oh, yeah? What's your pleasure? You wanna get high? I have grass...Ecstasy? I can get you whatever you're looking for." She cut her eyes in the direction of the bouncer at the front door.

"Don't know what that stuff is and I don't need it. I wanna get high on you," Zac told her.

Zac patted his pocket. "I can pay you for your trouble. How much you asking, pretty lady?"

"For both of you?" Her eyes became narrowed and calculating.

"Count me out," Jonas said, shaking his head.

Zac laughed. "He doesn't like participating, but he likes to watch. Is that okay with you?"

"I guess," Rosie replied. "But I gotta charge him full price for watching. All total, you boys are gonna have to cough up two hundred bucks." She paused for a beat. "Oh, yeah. My manager expects me to get the money up front."

"Not a problem." Zac discreetly extracted the money and produced a friendly smile.

Rosie twirled her ponytail. "I have a van parked in the rear of the lot. That's where I do my business. The windows are tinted... you know, for privacy."

Before exiting the tavern, Rosie slipped the money to the bouncer. Jonas felt sorry for her. She seemed like a sweet girl. The bouncer was clearly taking advantage of her, and there was no telling what Zac was going to do to her once he got her out of the bar.

Rosie led Zac and Jonas to the van, and hit the keypad, unlocking the doors.

"How'd you work that magic?" Zac inquired, impressed that pressing a button could open doors.

"How'd I do what?" Rosie asked, frowning at the nonsensical question.

Rosie climbed into the back and gestured for Zac and Jonas to join her. "What do you want—a BJ or the regular? If you want both, you'll have to pay extra."

For an instant, Zac looked perplexed by Rosie's terminology. Then as he roamed inside her mind, his face brightened with enlightenment. "I only want to kiss and cuddle."

"You're kidding!" Rosie's eyes lit with astonishment.

"I'm just an old-fashioned country boy, and I've got a sweetheart that I'm saving myself for."

"Okay. It's your money, and you can spend it any way you want." She leaned close to Zac. "You're real handsome," she said and then offered her lips.

Zac encircled her in an embrace and gently placed his lips against hers.

"Mmm. You're a good kisser...and such a gentleman," Rosie murmured.

"And you smell delicious, darlin'," Zac whispered, his mouth finding its way to her neck.

"My neck is real sensitive...it's my hot spot," Rosie uttered, tossing her head back and inviting Zac to cover her neck with smoldering kisses.

Rosie's human scent intermingled with the smell of lust was an agonizing combination. Jonas feared that he'd grind his teeth down to nubs if he didn't get far away from the girl. He yearned to get out of the van; clear his head by inhaling the cool night air.

But a young Haitian refugee roaming a parking lot would draw suspicions. A suspected car thief might be punished with a gunshot to the chest and dumped into a hole in the ground. Being murdered again was not an option.

Suffering in silence, Jonas shivered and grinded his teeth miserably as he fought off mounting desire.

Rosie's excited moans suddenly quieted down. Jonas glanced at the passionate couple and what he saw caused his mouth to gape. Zac's fangs glittered in the darkness. Jonas had never seen his fangs. They looked both deadly and magnificent at the same time.

Zac lifted Rosie's chin with a finger and stared into her eyes, holding her in a mesmerizing gaze. Rosie's eyes were wide open—glassy and unblinking, as if hypnotized. Zac began to stroke her neck, and in a trance state, Rosie began purring like a kitten.

Zac alternated kissing and stroking her neck and then after a long moment, he whispered as sensuously as a lover, "Do you want me to bite you?"

"Yes," she agreed. "Bite me good and deep," she added and then gave a lustful sigh.

Zac cut a triumphant eye at Jonas before sinking his teeth into the girl's neck. With her legs spread wide, Rosie writhed in passion as Zac extracted her blood. He sipped for only a few moments and then licked at the two tiny puncture wounds that oozed residual droplets of blood.

"Would you like to taste her?" Zac asked Jonas.

Jonas nodded briskly. He was so enthralled, he couldn't find his voice.

"Can I trust you to merely sip? I don't want her to end up ripped to shreds."

Jonas shrugged and edged away. He couldn't say for sure how he'd behave after getting a taste of blood.

"Suck my neck, Zac," Rosie urged impatiently. "You got me so hot and bothered, I don't care if your buddy does a little more than watch. He can take a turn with me while you suck on my neck."

Licking droplets of blood from his lips, Zac gave Jonas a wink. "She's nice and ripe for you, fella. But you have to promise you won't hurt her."

As if she were under anesthesia, Rosie began talking out of her head, speaking in a voice that sounded faraway and dreamy. "I want him to hurt me," she said, hitching up her skirt. "Let's get this ménage started—no extra charge."

Zac's hand wandered beneath Rosie's skirt. "Get over here, fella, and get yourself a couple of sips of blood."

Jonas hesitantly swiped his tongue against the twin punctures on Rosie's neck. At the rich taste of her blood, Jonas groaned and nearly swooned. Determined to control himself, he sucked gently, coaxing out a steady stream. A warm current of blood flowed into him, flooding his veins. Euphoria! He was close to howling with ecstasy.

"You're doing an A-okay job at pacing yourself," Zac encouraged as if speaking to a vampire pupil.

"Ooo, you boys are really kinky," Rosie said lazily. Her closed eyelids fluttered blissfully as Jonas sucked and Zac worked his fingers between her parted thighs.

"That's enough, Jonas," Zac said sternly when Rosie's hips ceased rotating.

Jonas didn't want to stop. He couldn't. She tasted so good, his puckered lips sucked more deeply.

Zac grabbed him by the shoulder. "You're gonna drain her," Zac warned and then gave Jonas a hard shove, knocking him against the back window.

Growling and panting, it took a few moments for Jonas to collect himself. The taste of blood clung to his palate, and as he slowly calmed down, he licked his lips and ran his tongue along the insides of his mouth.

Zac gave Jonas a smoldering look as he administered to Rosie who was sprawled like a rag doll. A few light smacks to her cheeks brought her around.

"What happened?" she asked, her eyes blinking in confusion.

"I got a little frisky while I was working on your hot spot. Gave you a couple love bites," Zac said with a wink.

Rosie touched the affected area of her neck and smiled. "That's all right. It just stings a little."

"Well, we got to be on our way. It was nice making your acquaintance," Zac said, throwing in a charming smile.

"I like your old-timey way of talking," Rosie said as she readjusted her skirt. "Sounds real sexy."

"Thank you, ma'am," Zac said with a head nod, overdoing the old-fashioned, Southern charm routine.

"Where are you boys headed?" Rosie took a compact out of her purse and began fussing with her hair.

"We're looking for a hotel. Any nice ones around these parts?"

"The Atwell Hotel is a couple miles from here. Swanky and expensive."

"Money's not a problem." Zac patted his bulging pocket.

Rosie's eyes became narrowed and cunning. "How'd you come by all that cash you're carrying? You a rich boy or something?"

"Naw, we're just farm hands. We save our earnings and every now and again, we like to get out and have a good time."

"What are you driving?" she asked.

Zac gave a helpless shrug "We're on foot."

"I can give you a lift to the hotel."

"Much obliged. I'll pay you for your trouble."

"Give me your phone number; that's all the payment I need," she said breathily.

"My phone number?" With a puzzled expression, Zac looked from Rosie to Jonas.

"He doesn't have a cell phone," Jonas piped in, interpreting for Zac.

"Well, I'll give you mine." She jotted her number on a slip of paper. "Call me the next time you wanna have some fun. We can cut out the middle man, and I'll do you for half-price next time."

While Rosie drove the van, Jonas explained to Zac in a whispered voice that they needed identification to rent a hotel room. They reached the hotel and Zac gave Rosie a goodnight kiss that had her swooning.

Once Zac finished the kiss, Rosie got out of the van with her driver's license in hand. She went to the front desk and booked a suite in her name.

⊕ ⊕ ⊕

Zac and Jonas appraised the lavish rooms with admiring eyes. There was a sitting room, a dining area, two bedrooms and a large bath. Zac was awestruck by the modern features.

After living in a hut in the crumbling ruins of Haiti, and then surviving in the woods for a while, Jonas was impressed by the spacious luxuriousness also.

Zac claimed the larger bedroom with a king-size bed, and relegated Jonas to the smaller room. Jonas didn't mind. He grabbed the remote and clicked on the wall-mounted TV. High definition images sparked to life. Zac let out a surprised hoot. "How the hell did those people get in there?"

"Technology, my man. That's called a television. Those people on the screen aren't real; those are digital images. You know… like film," Jonas explained as if speaking to a dull-witted child.

"A talking and moving photograph?" Zac asked, fascinated.

"Yeah, I guess you could say that. I've been playing the role of pupil, but there are many things that you can learn from me. When it comes to explaining this modern world, I'm the teacher," Jonas boasted, deliberately trying to get under Zac's skin.

"If you say so," Zac muttered snidely, and then crossed the room and closed the drapes. "The sun will be coming up shortly. Where are you going to rest?"

Jonas patted the mattress. "Right here in this comfortable bed."

Zac frowned. "So close to the window?"

Jonas's full lips spread into a cocky smile. "Remember, I'm not like you. I don't have to hide from sunlight."

Zac rolled his eyes and tugged on the drapes, pulling them even tighter. "Luckily I don't have to depend on you entirely. Rosie's eager for me to share my wealth with her. We're going to a place called a shopping mall tomorrow at dusk. You're welcome to tag along if you'd like."

"All right, but I don't want to stick around here in Frombleton too long. If I don't get to Florida, a lot of innocent people may get hurt."

Zac gave Jonas a reassuring pat on the back. "Don't worry, we'll get to Florida in due time. I'll dazzle Rosie with more of my Southern charm, and she'll happily drive us to Florida. After you visit that voodoo lady, you'll be good as new. You can start making an honest living; get that education you've been pining for. I bet you're smart enough to go to college."

Jonas smiled at the compliment. Furthering his education was the main reason his mother had sacrificed so much to get him to America.

With the drapes closed securely, the suite was as dark as a tomb. Jonas put the "Do Not Disturb" sign outside the door and then removed his clothes and curled beneath the covers, enjoying the feeling of crisp sheets against his skin.

Zac, on the other hand, ignored the king-size bed in his room. He selected the tight space inside the closet as his sleeping area.

CHAPTER 14

The days leading up to her date with Jarrett had gone by in slow motion. Holland had spent half a day sprucing up the yard—pruning, trimming hedges, and mowing the grass. She'd studied several how-to videos, but taking on a painting job was out of her comfort zone, and so the front door remained an eyesore.

On Friday night, Jarrett was right on time for their bowling date, and Holland was waiting for him at the door. As soon as he pulled up, she darted out of the house.

"I hope I don't embarrass myself with too many gutter balls," Holland said as she climbed into the Durango. "Are you sure you wanna do this bowling thing? It might be safer to take in a movie."

Jarrett could have said that he preferred going to the moon and it wouldn't have mattered. Holland was excited being in his company.

"Let's stick to our plans. We'll catch a movie next time."

Next time? Yay! He wants to see me again!

"I have to stop home for a second. My phone died, and I need to grab my charger."

"All right," Holland said affably.

Jarrett lived on the other side of town—about six miles away—in an upscale housing development. Though within a short distance, their neighborhoods were separated by Burke's highway. On one side of the thoroughfare were the haves and the have-nots such as Holland lived on the other side.

Jarrett eased out of his parking space and steered toward the highway.

Feeling relaxed, Holland reclined her seat a little and enjoyed the ride.

They didn't talk much, but every so often she'd catch Jarrett looking her over with a faint, approving smile. When they reached Meadowbrook Drive, Jarrett made a left and then parked in the driveway of an impressive, colonial-style home. He invited her in.

"That's okay; I'll wait in the car."

"Come on in. I want to introduce you to my parents."

Honored and scared at the same time, Holland unlocked her seatbelt and took a deep breath. She hadn't planned on trying to make a good impression on Jarrett's parents, but refusing to meet them would be extremely rude.

Jarrett's house was very neat and furnished expensively. His football trophies were on display all over the living room.

"Be right back; I have to run upstairs and grab my charger." After Jarrett went upstairs, Holland admired his sports awards, team pictures, and trophies.

She gazed at the portraits of the Sloan family through the years. They were a good-looking family, and their picture-perfect image gave her a twinge of envy. She missed her dad—missed being part of a regular, nuclear family.

Carrying his charger, Jarrett trotted back down the stairs.

"Where are your parents?" Holland asked.

"I thought they were here, but I guess they went to pick up my little brother from his friend's house. They're on the same football team and tonight their team had a scrimmage and a pizza party."

"Your little brother plays football, too?"

"Yeah, we're an athletic family. We call my little brother the triple threat," Jarrett said proudly. "He's only twelve and he's the star player of his middle school's football, baseball, and basketball teams."

"Wow!" Holland couldn't think of anything else to say.

"My mom is a tennis instructor, my dad played football in college, and I've been playing football since second grade. I shoot a mean game of hoops, too!"

"I've never seen so many trophies! How many do you have—like a hundred?"

Jarrett laughed and shrugged. "Too many to keep track of. There are more in the recreation room, downstairs." He grabbed her hand and led her toward the stairway. She followed him down the stairs to the basement.

The Sloans' recreation room was impressive. There was a ping pong table, a pool table, electronic games, and the largest flat-screen TV that Holland had ever seen. There was a showcase in the family room that displayed the entire family's sports trophies and plaques.

As Holland gazed at the dazzling exhibit of sports proficiency, Jarrett plugged the charger in a nearby outlet and set it on the pool table.

How did I get so lucky? Holland wondered as she stole a glance at Jarrett.

Wearing what looked like a bashful smile, he paced toward her. Her heart skipped several beats when he stood close to her—so close, she could feel the heat of his body. She had a sort of electrical reaction when he draped his arm around her shoulder—her skin seemed to sizzle.

"You're really pretty, Holland." Jarrett's voice was low-toned and amorous.

Blushing, she mumbled a thank you. A new haircut, a revamped wardrobe, and now the boy of her dreams was doling out compliments. Life was incredibly good!

Jarrett pressed against her and kissed her neck. "That tickles," Holland said, smiling and inching away. He enveloped her in his arms and a mild shock went through Holland's body. She inhaled slowly to calm her thumping heart.

"Why do you keep running from me, Holland? I really like you." His voice felt like a soft kiss, and when he placed his thumb beneath her chin, and turned her face toward his, Holland didn't resist.

Jarrett's kiss was tender and sweet. She melted inside his arms, loving the feeling of his hands caressing her back. His hands glided downward and moved to the front of her jeans. His fingers groped at the button in front. He unsnapped her pants and began sliding them down over her hips.

Holland was so lost in the kiss, so entranced by the intimacy of his touch, she wasn't aware of what was happening until she felt Jarrett's insistent hands tugging on the elastic band of her panties.

"No. Stop." She pulled away and slid her jeans up and snapped them closed.

"Okay, I'll behave myself," Jarrett promised. He gave her a faint smile and kissed her again. This time his warm tongue parted her lips and his tongue intertwined with hers. When he slipped his hand under her shirt, Holland broke the kiss.

"It's way too soon for this, Jarrett."

"I'm sorry. I keep getting carried away."

"If we're going bowling, shouldn't we be on our way? I can meet your parents another time."

"What's wrong, Holland?" he asked, reaching out, attempting to pull her close again.

Holland stepped out of his reach. "Nothing's wrong. It's just... well, it's just that we're still getting to know each other."

"You like me, and I like you. So, what's the big deal?"

She scrunched up her face. "Aren't you sort of seeing Chaela Vasquez?" She hadn't meant to bring up Chaela, but the words tumbled out before Holland could stop them. Now that she had spoken, she was relieved. She wanted to hear it straight from the horse's mouth whether or not he was still going out with Chaela.

"Chaela and I are over. We broke up a few weeks ago. You don't have to worry about her. I'm trying to get to know you better, Holland. Are you going to let me?"

"Wh-what about your parents? Aren't they on their way home?"

"No." He looked at his phone. "My mom sent me a text. My lil' bro' is staying the night at his friend's house and she and my dad are going out with a few of their friends."

Jarrett sounded sincere, and the way he was looking at Holland was causing her resolve to weaken—making her melt.

"You're so pretty," he said, giving her a kind of smoldering look that made her feel like the most desirable girl in the world. He enfolded her in his arms; his lips brushed against her hair... her forehead and her cheeks.

Jarrett cupped her face and kissed her, his tongue driving deeply inside her mouth. He moved his hands to her breasts and she didn't fight him off. She shuddered in excitement as his thumbs massaged her nipples. Jarrett's hands moved downward, nearing her thighs.

Then his hands got busy, working on the front of her jeans, again. She didn't try to stop him. She'd never imagined losing her virginity like this, but why not? She was one of the last virgins at her school. She told herself that losing her virginity to a hunk like Jarrett Sloan was something to be proud of. This time when her pants glided over her hips, she didn't yank them back up. She didn't utter a word of complaint. Filled with anticipation, she trembled as Jarrett guided her down to the fluffy rug on the floor.

Jarrett came out of his shirt swiftly. Holland timidly removed her top and placed it on the seat of a chair. She kicked her jeans from around her feet, and Jarrett had already shoved his pants down to his ankles when the doorbell began ringing persistently.

Holland grabbed her jeans. "Is that your parents?" she whispered, quickly sticking a leg into her pants.

"No, they'd use their key." Jarrett's voice sounded shaky. His cell phone that was charging on the pool table began chiming. Wearing only a pair of briefs, he got up and retrieved his phone. Worry lines creased his forehead as he stared down at a text message.

"Holland, you have to get out of here. Chaela's at the door," Jarrett said with panic in his voice.

"But you guys broke up. Can't you just ignore her?" In Holland's mind, Jarrett was now her boyfriend and she was feeling territorial.

"No, I can't ignore her. And you have to go. Seriously! Chaela will explode if she catches us together."

"B-but you said… You said you two broke up."

"Yeah, we did. But now she's saying that she wants to work it out." His phone rang. He cut an eye at the phone and then glared at Holland. "I'm not kidding; you have to get out of here, Holland." Jarrett's eyes were cold and hard.

Holland gawked at him. "You really want me to go home? You can't seriously expect me to walk across Burke's Highway at this time of the night!"

"Look, I'm sorry, but you have to understand." Jarrett held up a palm.

"One minute you're acting like you're into me, and the next

minute, you're treating me like trash. I don't get it." Holland's voice cracked with emotion. With a little whimper, she grabbed her top and pulled it over her head. The lump that had formed in her throat felt as large as an apple. Humiliated, she wriggled back into her jeans; all the while the doorbell kept chiming, and Jarrett's ring tone kept going off.

Impatiently, he grabbed Holland by the arm and physically dragged her toward the basement door.

"Jarrett!" Holland whimpered his name in disbelief as he opened the door and shoved her out.

"See you around." Jarrett's facial expression was hard and un-apologetic.

Before Holland could utter a response, Jarrett closed the door. Right in her face!

The backyard was brightly illuminated, showing off wind chimes, a tree house, colorful flower beds, rose bushes, and a cobblestone walkway that was lit with fancy, garden lights.

Shocked and mortified, tears shimmered in Holland's eyes. She prepared herself for the trek from his backyard to the front of his house, which would lead to Burke's Highway. Suddenly, all the lights in the back went out.

Why, Jarrett? Why? Holland wondered as she stood alone in the pitch darkness. She usually enjoyed the peace and tranquility of the night, but not now—not under these circumstances.

Horribly humiliated and shrouded in unrelenting gloom, Holland felt like she was in the midst of an outer body experience. *This can't be happening!*

A neighbor's dog began barking vigorously, startling Holland, causing her heart to lurch. Expecting to be attacked by a vicious dog, she pressed her back against Jarrett's back door, shuddering in fear.

Only a few feet away, inside the recreation room, she could hear Chaela's voice as she grilled Jarrett about his whereabouts.

"Why didn't you answer your phone?" Chaela hissed.

"I fell asleep."

"That's a lame excuse, Jarrett, and I don't believe you. What the hell were you doing that was more important than me?" Chaela screamed.

"I wasn't expecting you, Chaela. I'm sorry, baby," Jarrett replied in a soothing tone.

Holland couldn't bear to hear any more. Risking being mauled by a dog, she crept into the deep shadows. With trembling legs, she crossed the lawn and made her way to the main street.

What just happened? Holland asked herself after getting her bearings. *I almost lost my virginity to a jerk!* Jarrett and Chaela were the most self-absorbed, awful people on the planet. They deserved each other. And when she saw Jarrett at school, she wouldn't give him the satisfaction of even looking his way!

Holland was indignant. But she was also hurt and ashamed. Bitter tears stung her eyes, and she couldn't hold them back any longer. Crying softly, she walked along Meadowbrook Drive.

Unfamiliar with Jarrett's neighborhood, she wandered in circles for a while. The upscale neighborhood was hushed and serene; there was no one around to ask directions.

Holland kept ending up on dead-end streets as she tried to find her way to Burke's Highway. Sniffling and crying, she wondered how she could have been so foolish to think that Jarrett was interested in a D-lister like her.

After circling the luxury development for what seemed like an eternity, she found herself back on Meadowbrook Drive.

She heard an engine, and out the corner of her eye, she spotted Jarrett's Durango. Chaela had taken over Holland's spot in the passenger seat. Fervently wishing that she were invisible, Holland lowered her head in mortification as she moved along the tree-lined street.

She cringed when she heard Chaela's taunting voice. "You're on the wrong side of the tracks, loser!"

The Durango accelerated, and the sound of Chaela's malicious laughter echoed in the wind. Humiliated twice in the same night, Holland wondered if her life could get any worse.

⊕ ⊕ ⊕

Following the same route that Jarrett and Chaela had taken in the Durango, Holland was relieved when Burke's Highway came within view. The loud roar of traffic reminded her how difficult maneuvering across the busy highway would be.

Picking up her pace, she walked hurriedly, wanting desperately to get home where she could cry her heart out in the privacy of her bedroom.

A horn honked. Reflexively, Holland looked in the direction of the sound. She squinted at the dark-colored Buick and was surprised to see her mother's client, Rebecca Pullman, sitting behind the wheel.

"Get in, Holland. I'll give you a ride home," Ms. Pullman said in an anxious voice.

Relieved that she didn't have to cross the busy and dangerous highway, Holland hurried over to the car. Her hand was on the handle, ready to pull open the door, when she noticed an odd look in Ms. Pullman's eyes. There was something that Holland could only describe as hunger radiating in the woman's eyes. Filled with sudden dread, Holland instinctively let go of the handle and backed away.

"Uh...no thanks, Ms. Pullman. I prefer to walk."

"Don't be silly; get in. It's not safe for you to walk alone at night." Rebecca Pullman fixed an intense gaze on Holland. She attempted a smile, but her mouth twitched, betraying what Holland interpreted as creepy behavior.

Recalling how the woman had come into her bedroom, Holland wondered if the stunningly gorgeous woman was gay.

"I'm trying to help you, Holland. Now get in the car," Rebecca Pullman said in a disturbingly gruff tone.

Frightened and distrusting everyone at this point, Holland took off running.

Holland dashed through traffic, causing a commotion as horns beeped and tires screeched.

For the remainder of the walk home, Holland was uneasy, casting suspicious glances at everyone she passed. In her own neighborhood, Holland still didn't relax. She kept looking over her shoulder, hoping that Rebecca Pullman hadn't followed her.

Trotting up the steps to the front door, Holland's shabby little home had never looked so good. "Hey, Mom, I'm home," she yelled and rushed to her room. Thank goodness she'd had the foresight not to tell her mother about her date with Jarrett. Had she divulged that information, she'd be getting grilled by her mother right now. She could hear her mother, now: 'How'd it go, hon? Did you have a good time? Are you going out again?'

Tomorrow, she'd tell Naomi every dreadful detail of her degrading experience with Jarrett, but she couldn't tell her mother. There were some things that a girl simply didn't share with her mother.

I'm so stupid. I almost had sex with that lying, no good Jarrett. Ugh! I hate him; he's such a pig! And I hate Chaela, too!

Inside the confines of her bedroom, Holland pressed her face into her pillow and surrendered to terrible, gut-wrenching, body-wracking sobs.

CHAPTER 15

Flavors drifting from the kitchen awakened him as usual. But the aromas smelled more like pig guts than his normal morning meal. Downstairs the odor was stronger, reminding him of sewage.

"What's that smell? Don't tell me another critter done crawled up in the walls and died," the farmer said grouchily as he entered the kitchen, sniffing at the air.

"I don't smell anything, Walter." His wife rolled her eyes toward the ceiling and then placed his big, country breakfast before him: a cup of steaming coffee, a glass of orange juice, four sunny-sides up eggs, six strips of bacon, a slice of ham, grits and cheese, and fried potatoes with Vidalia onions—handpicked from their fields.

Having the appearance of an award-winning country breakfast, the food was attractively arranged on the plate and cooked to perfection.

Walter sniffed his plate. "Are these eggs rotten?"

His wife reared back in indignation. "Walter! What's gotten into you? You know I wouldn't serve you spoiled food."

He stabbed the slice of ham with his fork. "Maybe the meat went bad."

"The meat is fresh," his wife snapped, clearly irritated.

"Something's wrong, Angie. I'm not crazy. This food is reeking; I can't eat it." He shoved the plate away from him and picked up the glass of orange juice. He took a sip. Frowning, he spat the juice back into the glass.

"Walter!" his wife shrieked.

"You're trying to poison me, aren't you? What'd you do...put arsenic in my food?"

"I don't have to listen to your crazy ranting. You've been acting like a crazy man ever since you got back from that convention in Miami. You should see a doctor about that bite on your shoulder. The dog that nipped you might have been carrying rabies."

Walter's cheeks were flushed with anger. "I don't have any goddamn rabies. Don't try to wiggle your way out of this, Angie! Are you trying to kill me?"

Angie looked aghast. "No, of course not. I'm merely suggesting that you go see a doctor and check out that dog bite. Why would you try to pick up a stray animal in the first place?"

Walter pounded his fist on the table. "I told you why...the dog was on the side of the road, limping and hurt."

"That dog has infected you, Walter. Something's not right."

"I'll tell you what's not right...the way you're trying to collect on my insurance policy ain't right."

"That's it; I'm not listening to another vicious word out of your mouth. It'll be a snowy day in hell before I slave over the stove for you again. You can starve for all I care!" Angie yanked Walter's plate off of the table and slammed it on the kitchen counter. She tore off her apron and flung it on the floor. Indignant, she fled the kitchen.

Walter started to go after her. He wanted to apologize for losing his temper. Accusing his wife of trying to poison him was insane. Angie was right; he needed to see a doctor. But how would he explain what had really happened without implicating himself in the murder of an insane Haitian refugee?

It was always something! If it wasn't one problem, it was another. He had the bank breathing down his neck over his heavily mortgaged farm. He had a pack of illegal aliens working on his farm. He didn't need to bring any unnecessary attention to himself.

He had no idea why everything stank to high heavens. His sense of smell was acting up like crazy. Hopefully, it was only a temporary thing. An allergic reaction.

He'd apologize to Angie later. Call and have some flowers delivered. A beautiful bouquet would sugar her up real good.

Imagining Angie rewarding his loving gesture with a steamy night in the sack, Walter smiled as he idly picked up the mug of coffee and took a swig.

He spewed out a mouthful of coffee, splattering the brown liquid over the white tablecloth. "Ugh! That shit tastes like goddamn turpentine. That whoring wife of mine is blatantly trying to knock me off."

The farmer's growing fury sent him barreling up the stairs. "Angie! Where are you, bitch!" he shouted.

He burst into the bedroom and found his wife folding laundry.

Holding the ends of a fitted sheet, Angie looked at her husband with surprise in her eyes.

In the bedroom, the air was thick with a heady scent that was enthralling. The farmer stopped in his tracks. He inhaled deeply, filling his lungs and his chest with the delicious, musky odor. "What's that smell?"

Angie shook her head in exasperation. "Oh, for goodness sake, Walter. Now what? Don't tell me you smell a dead animal in our bedroom, too."

Turning his head from side to side, he sniffed the air. Determining that the intoxicating aroma was emanating from his wife, the farmer stared at his wife leeringly.

Angie gave a nervous laugh and then self-consciously finger-combed her salt-and-pepper-colored hair. "Wh-what is it, Walter?"

Drawn to his wife like a shark to blood-spilled water, he edged toward her. His movements were sluggish, but determined. Motivated by hunger alone, his gray eyes were vacant, seeing nothing.

Dropping the rounded corners of the sheet, Angie called her husband's name and snapped her fingers, trying to snap him out of what appeared to be a sleepwalking stupor.

"Walter! Honey, you're scaring me," Angie said in a shrill, panicked tone. Neither her frightened voice nor her frantic finger snapping had deterred her husband; he kept on advancing. She took a few steps backwards, hugging herself as if the air in the bedroom had taken on a frosty chill.

Walter reached for her.

In pure amazement, Angie gawked at her husband's outstretched arms. At first, she regarded him with furrowed brows, but the yearning in his eyes and the sight of his arms stretched out insistently, made her feel a little sorry for him.

Angie dutifully moved within Walter's reach, giving him the hug of affection that he seemed to desperately need. A quick hug and a few pats on the back was all she was willing to give. Walter's sex drive was dreadfully annoying at times, and if he thought that she was going to lie down and spread her legs for him right in the midst of her morning chores, he had another thing coming!

Holding his wife in a bear hug that she couldn't squirm out of, Walter sank his teeth into her forearm. Being that there wasn't another home for several miles, Angie's painful shriek went unheard.

Blood moistened Walter's lips as he chewed greedily. The farmer lifted his wife and callously tossed her on the bed. In a breathless state of terror, Angie landed atop a pile of folded laundry. Pleading words formed on her lips but she was too dumbfounded to speak. Her mouth moved wordlessly as her husband yanked up her dress.

Angie gasped and shuddered. Was Walter actually going to rape her? Finally finding her voice, she breathlessly protested.

But it wasn't sex that her husband was after.

Walter buried his face between her thighs and then ripped into the soft skin, savagely tearing out a chunk of flesh.

Angie howled like a wounded animal as she tried to fight him off of her. Walter pinned her down with a firm palm pressed against her chest; he chewed contentedly and then lowered his head again, lapping at the blood that oozed out of the open wound, drizzling onto his freshly washed undershirts and boxers.

With his wife screaming and thrashing beneath him, Walter feasted on her ample thigh. He alternated between chewing living flesh and slurping the rivulets of blood that streamed out in multiple directions on top of the white flower-appliquéd bedspread.

After ravaging the flesh of both thighs, he worked his way up to the swell of his wife's hip.

In shock, Angie's body twitched occasionally, but weakened from blood loss, she no longer put up a struggle. Holding her down was no longer necessary; and Walter was able to feed with ease.

Using his free hands like claws, he shredded flesh from her hip, her buttocks, and her belly, and greedily shoved fistfuls of the bloody meat into his mouth and chewed vigorously.

Closing his eyes blissfully, the farmer stuffed himself. His peculiar appetite finally satisfied, he carried the carcass of his wife downstairs and hid it inside the walk-in refrigerator. Robotically, he went about the tasks of cleaning up the murder scene. He burned the red-stained bed linen and his blood-soaked clothes, and then scrubbed the bedroom clean.

From his closet, he retrieved a pair of green uniform pants and a tee shirt that bore the name, "Sutton Farms" emblazoned across the front.

Whistling a tuneless melody, Walter Sutton contentedly drove to his onion fields.

CHAPTER 16

Jonas awoke at noon. Acutely aware of a hunger that rose like a fever and threatened to overtake all sense of reasoning, he yanked open the drapes and gazed at the bustling life on the street below him. People were out in droves, and their human scent was so potent it was maddening.

He watched them intently, and growled with yearning as people strolled along the pavement. He could hear their murmurings. Some laughed and talked without a care. Others were discontented, arguing and vocalizing petty complaints. No one realized that they were being watched. They didn't have an inkling that four stories above them, a predator lurked.

As if a million knives were slicing at his insides, Jonas groaned and clutched his stomach. The hunger was agony, far worse than before. The feeding last night seemed to increase his appetite; making him more ravenous than ever.

Obeying the demands of his voracious craving, he left the room. Shunning the elevator, he took the stairs and exited the hotel at a back entrance that spilled out to an isolated area that was filled with a variety of Dumpsters.

Sniffing, Jonas detected the scent of rotting food blended with the smell of rodents. He rushed to the nearest garbage can, and then stopped. Small creatures couldn't satisfy him today.

Suddenly, he heard a woman's voice calling, "Sparky. Come back, boy. Sparky!" Barking, a Great Dane frolicked to the back lot.

Jonas silently beckoned the dog with a soft whistle. Too friendly for his own good, the poor creature trotted over to Jonas, tongue lolling and primed to lick Jonas's hand in affection.

Jonas grabbed the dog by the throat. Holding it an iron grasp, he cut off the animal's bark of alarm, and then dragged the pooch out of sight, behind the Dumpster.

The pet owner rushed to the open area. Holding a leash, she called her dog in a voice that had risen to hysteria. As a last resort, she banged on the hotel's kitchen door. Weeping and wailing, she babbled that her dog had gone missing on the hotel grounds. A befuddled kitchen worker attempted to calm her down, insisting that he had not seen a dog or any other animal on the premises.

Obscured from view, Jonas satisfied his craving, leaving behind the ravaged carcass of the friendly dog.

⊕ ⊕ ⊕

As if an alarm had gone off, Zac pulled open the sliding closet doors the moment that the sun went down. He emerged looking frightful with his hair disheveled and his complexion ghastly and pale from hunger.

Rubbing his eyes, Zac stumbled into Jonas's room. "I'm starving; what about you?"

Relaxed in a chair, Jonas was watching a movie. He shook his head. "I'm not hungry."

Zac pointed to the telephone. "How do you work that device?" he asked impatiently. Clasped between his fingers was the slip of paper with Rosie's number.

Jonas put the movie on pause and walked over to the phone on the desk.

Zac gasped softly. "That's amazing!" he exclaimed as he gawked at the frozen TV screen. While Jonas dialed Rosie's number, Zac tinkered with the remote, examining the menu and exploring the features.

"Hello, Rosie? This is Jonas. Zac would like to speak to you." He laid the receiver down and returned to his seat, taking the remote from Zac's hand.

Zac eyeballed both ends of the handset, quizzically.

Sighing, Jonas rose from his seat again. He took the handset and demonstrated how to hold it properly.

After finishing the conversation with Rosie, Zac said, "She's on her way. Be here in fifteen minutes." Zac studied his reflection in a wall mirror. "I look rather gaunt; what do you think?"

"You look all right," Jonas replied disinterestedly.

"I'm gonna need a couple sips of Rosie until I can get my hands on a full meal." He gave Jonas a sidelong glance. "You seem pretty calm, fella. Not as jumpy as usual. Let me guess…you gorged on vermin while I was asleep?" Zac said with a derisive snort.

"I had a light lunch to hold me over," Jonas commented.

"Well, it's suppertime now, and I'm starving. Are you coming with us to the shopping mall, or are you gonna sit around watching that picture box?"

Jonas clicked off the TV. He didn't relish the idea of hanging with Zac and Rosie, but Zac was his ticket back to Florida and he couldn't let the vampire get too far from sight.

Rosie arrived and was all smiles when Zac and Jonas got into her van. Zac sat next to Rosie in the front and Jonas climbed into the back. Rosie was sporting a wide Band-Aid on the side of her neck.

"You got real frisky last night, Zac. My roommate thinks I'm covering up a hickey. But I've got four teeny lil' holes in my neck."

Rosie rolled her eyes upward. "I don't remember much of last night, but you sure got carried away. If I didn't know any better, I'd think you had some vampire in you." Rosie and Zack shared a laugh at the outrageous idea of him being a vampire.

Zac's laughter trailed off, and he jerked his head toward Jonas. The smile no longer visible on his lips, he fixed his gaze on Jonas, revealing to him the raw hunger that blazed in his eyes.

Jonas wondered if Zac intended to hunt while at the mall. The idea of Zac killing in a public place was a fearful thought. However, hunting in the mall was preferable to draining Rosie. Losing Rosie meant losing his ride to Florida. Jonas felt guilty for thinking of Rosie as nothing more than a source of transportation, but under the circumstances that was her only purpose in his eyes.

The gleaming shopping mall was spectacular. It was as bright as daylight inside the mall, but he noticed that Zac didn't flinch. Apparently, only natural sunlight affected the vampire.

Jonas thought he and Zac would stand out from the crowd, but no one gave them a second look. Jonas stared at his surroundings—amazed by the opulence. No one was ragged or hungry. These privileged people—these consumers—were spending money with a dizzying urgency. They were all too busy ogling their next purchase to take notice of Zac and Jonas.

A chaos of scents filled the shopping mall. Jonas forced himself to ignore the alluring smell of the shoppers as he took in the incredible sights. For a moment, he almost smiled as he stood and gawked. The mall was magnificent—the kind of place that accurately represented his idea of the American dream. There were no sad faces. Everyone seemed in high spirits, enjoying their prosperity as they dangled shopping bags with impressive logos.

In a fleeting burst of cheerfulness, Jonas felt like a normal teenager. He wanted to capture the moment and take pictures to send home. Of course, he didn't have a camera or a cell phone, and that was probably for the best. With a sinking heart, he thought about his family's plight. They desperately needed money for survival, not photographic images of excess and abundance.

Feeling guilty, Jonas reconsidered accepting the money that Zac had offered. He decided to speak to Zac about it later—in private. An envelope stuffed with money and a short note to his mother, assuring her that he was okay, would ease her troubled mind.

"I'm thirsty. I could go for some lemonade. Let's go downstairs to the food court," Rosie suggested and stepped on the escalator.

Grasping Zac's elbow, Jonas helpfully guided him onto the moving stairs. "It's called an escalator," Jonas whispered discreetly.

Zac frowned and pulled away from Jonas, seeming more annoyed than grateful for his assistance.

On the lower level, Jonas was hit with the nauseating scent of cooking food. "I'll wait here," he said, taking a seat on a nearby bench.

"I'll wait with Jonas," Zac agreed, holding a finger under his nose to block out the unpleasant odors from the food court. Turning his head back and forth, he took in the sights, his blue eyes gleaming at the hoards of humans, all conveniently under one roof.

"What's that place?" Zac asked Rosie, pointing to a dimly lit store with flashing colored lights. Young people drifted in and out of this noisy hub of activity.

"That's an arcade. Don't they have arcades where you're from?" Rosie inquired, her face scrunched in confusion.

"Been so busy doing farm work, I guess I never noticed any arcades," Zac said.

"That's weird. Haven't you ever played videogames?"

Losing his patience, Zac glared at her. "No!"

"What about you?" she asked Jonas.

"Now and then," Jonas said sheepishly.

"Wow, it's like you boys just fell off the turnip truck." Rosie giggled.

Zac clamped a hand around her wrist. "Don't mock me," he said to her in a warning tone.

"Jesus, you sure are touchy." Rosie twisted her hand free.

"He's sensitive...you know, about growing up poor," Jonas said, trying to salvage the situation. He didn't want Rosie storming out of the mall and ending her friendship with Zac before he made it to Florida.

"Let's go take a look at the arcade," Zac suggested, giving Rosie an apologetic smile.

"I don't like arcades," she said, pouting. "After the way you manhandled me, I need my lemonade and a little retail therapy."

Not understanding the expression, "retail therapy," Zac had a blank expression. Then picking up on Rosie's thoughts, he lifted his brows his understanding. "Oh! Yeah, sure...go get yourself something fancy." He pressed a few hundred dollars in Rosie's palm and she rewarded him with a kiss on the lips, and then dashed away.

With Jonas on his heels, Zac hurried toward the teen hangout. There were aisles and aisles of videogames. Kids stood hunched over the high-tech machinery, battling with aliens and other digital images. Smaller children were being trailed by their parents.

The mingled human scents were pleasant, their thick aromas extremely seductive. Despite being in a state of distress, Zac walked slowly...silently as he scanned the gamers, pretending to be a spectator as he intently considering his options.

He spotted a smaller and more secluded room in the rear of the arcade, and gestured for Jonas to follow him there. In the back room, there was only one person standing in front of a steel cage playing electronic basketball.

Zooming in on his prey, Zac silently crept up behind the tall, broad-shouldered boy as he shot a series of three-pointers. With each toss of the ball, the muscles in his forearms popped up enticingly. His body appeared as fit and athletic as the boys they'd killed the previous night.

Leering and grinning, Zac flicked out his tongue, moistening his lips as he observed the appetizing specimen.

The boy's strong odor floated to Jonas's nostrils, tantalizing him. If Jonas hadn't fed earlier, he would not have been able to stop himself from publicly devouring the delicious-smelling teen.

When the boy raised his arms to shoot another basket, his shirt lifted, revealing a tapered waist and a fleeting glimpse of a strong lower back.

While Jonas fantasized about the sweetness of the boy's blood, the tanginess of his flesh and how delectably chewy his tendons might be, Zac went into action. Zac tapped the teen on the shoulder. Startled, the boy jerked around, revealing a handsome face with large, curious eyes.

"Excuse me. Are you going to be using this apparatus much longer?" Zac asked politely.

"Yeah, man. I'm trying to beat my score," he said breathily and with an edge of irritation. Perplexed, the boy looked at the vacant steel cage next to his. "Why don't you get on that one?" He returned his attention to his game.

"I don't want that one; I want yours!"

The boy frowned and tilted his head in confusion, but before he could get out a single word out, Zac had seized him, clenching him by his V-shaped waist.

"What's your problem?" the boy managed to blurt, his voice

lilting in indignation. Any further protestations were abruptly cut off as Zac cruelly jabbed his claw-like fingernails into the young man's sides and then swiftly pushed him between the two electronic basketball games, shoving his back into the wall.

An observer might have thought that Zac and the boy were romantically involved, using the isolated gap between the basketball cages as a secret love nest.

Covering the teen's mouth with his hand, Zac muffled his cries and pressed his lips against the boy's neck.

Aroused by the scent of blood, Jonas squeezed into the tight confines behind Zac and the desperately struggling athlete. He loathed himself for giving in to his unnatural craving.

While Zac fed from the ball player's neck, Jonas crouched down and lapped at the bloodied waistline, which had been pierced by Zac's sharp fingernail.

Jonas fed from the jagged wound. The blood was so immensely flavorful that Jonas soon dispensed with feelings of guilt and fed his hunger.

Though he yearned to take a huge bite of the smooth, fragrant flesh, he fought the urge. *No killing tonight!* He contented himself with nibbling on the ragged skin surrounding the wounds and gently sucking the boy's thick, syrupy blood.

CHAPTER 17

Zac showed Rosie the plastic bag filled with the white, little pebbles that he'd found in the two football players' gym bags. "Do you know what this is?"

Grinning, Rosie's opened the bag and fondled the drug. "It's crystal meth."

"Is it worth anything?"

Rosie's eyes widened in an "are you crazy" kind of way. "Uh… yeah. That's a lot of product." Through narrowed eyes, she scrutinized him. "You're no farmer, are you? I get it," she said, nodding. "You're operating a meth lab, aren't you?"

Zac smiled mysteriously, but didn't comment.

"I know plenty of buyers. I can help you move it…uh, for a cut, of course."

"Of course," Zac said.

Rosie reached for the plastic bag.

"Hold on, little lady. I can't give you all of it."

"Don't you trust me?"

"I don't trust anyone. Let's see what you can do with a small portion and then I'll give you more."

"Fair enough." Rosie emptied out the contents of her small makeup bag and Zac filled it with the white substance.

Surrounded by Rosie's shopping bags, Jonas sat miserably in the back. He and Zac had left the basketball player slumped and unconscious, but his heart was still beating when they'd hurried out of the arcade.

Jonas wondered if the boy would report the attack to the police. Probably not, he decided. His wounds were miniscule and he'd sound like a crazy person if he spoke of being bitten and sucked by two young men in an arcade.

The basketball player had only been an appetizer for Zac. The next person that Zac encountered tonight wouldn't be so lucky. Jonas didn't intend to tag along on Zac's next fresh kill. Nor did he want to be a part of drug dealing. His mother would be horror-stricken to learn that her son had traded a promising future as a physician to deal illegal drugs.

"Pull over, Rosie. I'm going to walk back," Jonas said.

"Why?" Zac asked suspiciously. "Thinking of going hunting without me?"

"Hunting at night?" Rosie asked, perplexed.

"I'm giving you and Rosie some privacy."

"You're such a sweetheart...and so thoughtful," Rosie said, smiling at Jonas.

"We don't need any privacy," Zac interjected bitterly. "Rosie was going to drop us off at the hotel and then go take care of some business for me."

"I thought we were going to hang together at the hotel for a while," Rosie said, sounding hopeful.

"No, I'll see you after you're finished doing business."

"All right," Rosie said with obvious disappointment. "What time do you want me to come back?" Her tone was so pathetic. Jonas lowered his eyes, unable to bear witness to her shameless plea.

"Call me at the hotel...around midnight," Zac instructed.

"Cool. I'll see you around midnight," she said.

"I said, *call* me!" Zac shook his head in exasperation.

Eventually, Zac would suck Rosie dry, but the poor girl was so head over heels, she couldn't comprehend the danger she was in. Needing to survive to take care of his family, Jonas couldn't allow himself the distraction of feeling sorry for her. Couldn't risk trying to defend her.

He didn't trust Zac and had already grown weary of his company. Jonas promptly decided that he and Zac should part ways as soon as possible. The repugnant existence he'd been leading had to come to an end. Realizing that he was able to fit in easily with humans, Jonas determined that he didn't have to depend on Rosie for a ride to Miami.

Undoubtedly, Zac would go out and kill tonight while Rosie was selling his drugs. With his affable manner, Zac would befriend some poor soul and then turn on him, leaving the body limp and depleted. Then Zac would return to the hotel satiated and in good spirits as if returning from dining in a fine restaurant.

While Zac was in a good mood, Jonas would ask him for the money to purchase a bus ticket to Miami—to salvation. The journey would be lengthy and the hunger would be as torturous as a long prison stint, but Jonas would endure it. As long as he filled himself with the flesh and blood of small creatures, he wouldn't have to worry about attacking his fellow passengers.

⊕ ⊕ ⊕

Zac returned to the suite, and roughly shook Jonas's arm, waking him from a pleasant dream. Though hazy eyes, Jonas stared at Zac. "What is it? What's wrong?"

"Did Rosie call?"

"I don't know; I was asleep. Did you call the front desk to check for messages?"

Zac glared at Jonas, his wordless response informed Jonas that he hadn't mastered using a telephone.

"Using a phone is easier than driving, man," Jonas said. "You just pick up the receiver and push zero, and you'll get the front desk."

"Do it for me," Zac said in an authoritative tone of voice.

Jonas noticed that Zac's cheeks were flushed from recently feeding, yet his mood was as sour as when he hungered. The vampire had many mood swings and was a complete mystery at times.

Jonas sat up and reached for the bedside phone, content in knowing that soon he'd be free of Zac's erratic temperament.

"Any messages?" Jonas asked the person on the other end of the phone. "No? Okay, thanks." He hung up and glanced at Zac. "You have Rosie's number. Do you want to call her?"

"I told her to call me at midnight. She's going to regret stealing my money."

"Rosie's crazy about you; she wouldn't steal from you?"

"Come, we have to find her." Zac snatched impatiently at the bedspread that Jonas was cocooned inside. "Get dressed."

"You disturbed my sleep, Zac," Jonas said crossly. "I'm not a nocturnal creature like you, and I don't enjoy running around in the middle of the night."

"You expect me to give you bus fare to Miami, yet you deny assisting me," Zac said sneeringly, letting Jonas know that he was well aware of his plans.

Jonas shrank back from Zac. "My thoughts are supposed to be private!"

"Well, they're not! You should guard your thoughts as carefully as you avoid feeding on humans."

"You read my mind, so you realize that I've reconsidered your offer. I really need to see Madame Collette as soon as possible."

"I don't have any traveling money for you. It's all gone—I spent it."

Jonas looked aghast.

"Tracking humans on foot is time-consuming. I bought myself a driving machine. Nothing snazzy, but it'll get us around."

"You bought a car!"

"I sure did. I've got the title."

Jonas sighed. "I don't want to depend on you to drive me to Miami. Listen, I'm not like you, Zac. I don't want to survive on living flesh." He pressed his palm against his heart. "Don't you understand; I want to salvage the last bit of humanity that's left in me."

"You should be in the theater. You deserve applause for that fine performance." Zac clapped his hands sarcastically.

"I'm being sincere. From the time you saw me, you knew that I despised being under this hideous spell."

"You're not under any spell. You've been changed into a..." Zac shook his head. "Well, I can't say for certain what you've been changed into. But I do know that you thrive on living things, just as I do. The only difference between you and me is that you're much more brutal...more savage in the way you go about killing."

Jonas dropped his head in shame.

"The truth hurts, doesn't it?"

Memories of his victim's screams and anguished pleas flooded Jonas's mind.

Zac narrowed his eyes. "You know, I've seen some gruesome sights in my time, but the way you mutilated the boy that you yanked out of that driving machine was like nothing I've ever seen."

"I couldn't help myself," Jonas whispered in a tortured voice.

"And neither can I; so what makes you better than me?"

The ringing telephone interrupted their argument. Zac shot Jonas a look that commanded him to answer the phone.

Jonas willfully crossed his arms in front of his chest. "I'm not your servant. If you can drive a car, you can surely pick up a phone."

Zac yanked up the entire headset and console. When the headset toppled to the floor, Rosie's voice could be heard saying, "Hello? Zac? Are you there?"

"Yes, I'm here." Zac spoke in an unnaturally loud voice directed at the receiver that rested on the floor.

Giving Zac a look of disgust, Jonas picked up the receiver. "Hi, Rosie. Are you on your way? A few minutes? Okay, I'll let him know." Jonas looked at Zac. "She'll be here shortly. I'm assuming she's bringing you cash, so I'm repeating my request…can I have the money you offered a few days ago?"

Zac stared at Jonas stonily. "Yes, but you have to earn it."

"I won't do anything that involves killing."

A quick, elusive smile played at the corners of Zac's mouth. "I'm not asking you to kill."

"What do you want me to do?"

There was a soft tap on the door.

"Ah, Rosie's here! I have important business to take care of."

"But… What about—"

"We'll talk later." Moving with a slow and graceful confidence, Zac went to the door.

CHAPTER 18

Rosie entered the hotel room in a cloud of perfume. Though she was thoroughly doused in the floral fragrance, she had hardly masked her alluring human scent. She took a stack of worn bills from her purse. "Count it," she said to Zac.

Zac methodically sorted through the pile, straightening and organizing the currency by denomination, and then he gave Rosie her cut.

"Good job." Zac patted Rosie on the shoulder.

"A pat on the shoulder—is that all I get?" she asked, her face upturned, her lips puckered.

Zac's eyes slid away from her glossy lips and fixed on her neck. He bent close to her, and lightly stroked the bandage. Brushing his mouth against her throat, he murmured, "Take it off."

As if stripping away a layer of clothing, Rosie slowly, seductively peeled away the adhesive. Not yet healed, the punctures were a fiery red.

Zac caressed the bite marks. Rosie trembled in response.

"Does it hurt?" Zac asked.

"Not much," she whispered, her eyes closed and her neck outstretched in offering.

Though he was sitting on the other side of the room, the soft beating of Rosie's heart was enticingly audible to Jonas, thrilling him with waves of excitement. He wanted her as badly as Zac did. Maybe more.

Zac had fed sufficiently and was only toying with Rosie, using her as a nightcap. Jonas, on the other hand, was famished.

Zac licked the twin wounds. A sigh of arousal escaped Rosie's painted lips.

The sight of her exposed wounds; the sound of blood pulsing through her veins was so tantalizing, Jonas felt his heart constrict.

Standing on her tiptoes, Rosie's short black skirt hitched up higher, exposing her thighs and giving a glimpse of her plump buttocks. The urge to reach for her was overwhelming. Sweetly tormented by the thought of filling his mouth with chunks of Rosie's juicy buttocks, Jonas shuddered.

Near delirium, Jonas snatched the key card from the bedside table, stuffed it in his pocket, and made fast strides toward the door.

"Where are you going? Don't you want to join Rosie and me?" Zac inquired, holding a swooning Rosie in his arms.

"No, I need some fresh air. I'm going for a walk."

"You don't have to walk. Do you want the keys to the driving machine?"

"No!" The roar of the blood that coursed through Rosie's veins grew louder, beckoning Jonas—beseeching him to draw her in his own arms and drink from her. But he was ravenous, aching for more than trickles of blood.

Absorbed by the pressing desire for a more substantial meal, Jonas left Zac and Rosie and went out into the night.

Denying himself the speed of the elevator, he once again selected the darkness and obscurity of the exit stairs.

In the crowded commercial strip where the Atwell Hotel was situated, streetlights blazed abundantly. But in an effort to save money, the ones on the less populated side streets of the city had all been extinguished.

His silhouette barely visible, Jonas paced down a narrow back street with his hands in the pockets, his head hung low. En route to the city park, the rough rustle of his denim pants legs broke the eerie, late-night quiet.

Rabbit, squirrel, pigeon, and opossum were hardly filling, but that was all the city park, with its meager dining options, had to offer. White-tailed deer were elusive creatures, but hopefully one would make an appearance on tonight's menu. Grinding his teeth in anticipation, Jonas hastened his steps.

The park was particularly bleak. Pitch black in most areas. The trunks of a few trees were decorated with white, decorative lights. Aside from providing much needed illumination, the effect of the white lights was peaceful and soothing.

Shying away from the lighted areas, Jonas sought the shadows. As he walked deeper into the darkness, his footfalls alerted the small, furry creatures that inhabited the park. He ignored them as they scurried out of his path.

Startled by an unexpected smell, Jonas stopped suddenly. There was a familiar sweet aroma—a human scent that was uniquely fragrant. Tracking the source of this titillating scent, he noticed a slender female figure sitting on a park bench. She was bent forward, her hands cradling her cheeks, her head bowed in contemplation.

She removed her hands and looked toward the sky as if searching for a heavenly answer. Her face, hallowed in moonlight, was a breathtakingly familiar sight.

His heart leapt in his chest. *It's her!* The lovely girl that he'd secretly watched walking the path near his burial site.

Standing behind a large tree, Jonas merged deeper into the shadows. And through the darkness, he stared at the girl with undisguised longing as he inhaled her unusual, heated fragrance.

He searched her face, and was surprised to see gleaming tears beginning to trickle from her eyes. Her despair seemed palpable; the air seemed to thicken with her sorrow, and Jonas longed to come out of hiding and comfort her.

But he didn't dare reveal himself. He was a predator, after all. Absolutely unable to trust himself. Nights like this, he wasn't sure if he could control his monstrous nature.

The girl's sweet scent was potent as it drifted on the night breeze. His senses were thoroughly aroused, and a vicious hunger rose in Jonas, twisting and knotting his insides. He had to get away from her.

Intending to slip to a more remote area of the immense park, Jonas stealthily stepped away from the tree. The sole of his right sneaker inadvertently crunched into a discarded cellophane bag. The sound reverberated as loud as an explosion.

The girl gasped. Her misted eyes, wide with fright, shot in his direction. Her nervous fingers groped for the clasp of her purse. "Don't come near me. I have a gun!"

Amazed that he was only a few feet away from this beautiful angel—this dream girl—his throat felt as if it were closed tight, choking off his words. For a moment, he couldn't speak. Pushing past his nerves, he found his voice. "I'm sorry; I didn't mean to scare you." Jonas spoke as calmly as he could.

"What do you want?" she shrieked, jabbing her hand inside the opening of her purse.

"I don't want anything. I was taking a stroll through the park—"

"At this time of the night?" The girl's voice was shrill with suspicion. Jonas saw that her hand was wrapped around a cylinder object. Most likely mace…not a gun. Taking another bullet to the chest was unendurable; he gave a sigh of relief.

"I won't hurt you," he assured her, backing away, his hands held up in surrender.

It took a tremendous amount of inner strength not to attack her, but he continued moving away from the girl. He desperately needed to feed, and with the glorious scent the girl emitted, he was certain she'd make a delectable meal.

The girl wiped the tears that streaked her face. "I'm sorry for the way I reacted. I mean…the way I yelled at you, you'd think that you tried to accost me." She gave a little laugh that had a tinkly, musical sound.

"It's okay. I'll leave you in peace. Good night," Jonas said, unable to take his eyes off of her face.

"Wait. Where are you from? Your accent…"

"I'm from Haiti. I'm here doing farm work to pay for my education."

"Are you enrolled in school?"

"Not yet. But soon, I hope."

"What's your name?"

"Jonas."

"My name's Holland. Maybe I'll see you when school starts."

"Yes, maybe." Jonas rushed past her, walking fast. And when he was out of her range of vision, he broke into a run. Fleeing as if the Devil himself was on his heels, Jonas didn't stop running until his legs nearly gave out.

Miles from where he'd left the girl sitting, Jonas found himself on an unpaved, deserted part of the immense park. A hiking trail. Surrounded by boulders, wild foliage and trees, he bent at the waist, panting as he tried to catch his breath. From the corner of his eye, he saw a pair of wide, expressive eyes watching him with curiosity.

Caught off-guard, a white-tailed deer stood momentarily frozen in fear.

Jonas captured the animal, grabbing it by a hind leg as it made an attempt to leap from harm's way. Breathing raggedly and growling unnaturally, Jonas dragged the struggling animal behind a boulder. With both forearms holding the deer in place, he bit into its side, viciously tearing out large hunks of meat with his strong teeth. Oblivious to the mournful cries of the wounded animal, Jonas stuffed himself, eating its flesh and slurping from a cavity that was pooled with blood. Motivated by a blinding hunger, he ferociously consumed the animal in minutes.

The night's kill was not at all what he craved. But the meal had been substantial. His hunger satisfied, Jonas covered the ravaged carcass under twigs and brush.

Deep in thought, he took the long route out of the park.

⊕ ⊕ ⊕

Back in the hotel suite, Jonas was surprised to find Rosie sprawled across the bed. One arm rested at her side, and the other was flung over the edge of the bed. There was no rise and fall of her chest, and her feeble heartbeat was barely perceptible.

"She's dying!" Jonas gawked at Rosie in astonishment.

"No, she's resting. Gathering her strength. In another hour or so, she'll awaken and she'll be fine," Zac said.

"How do you know?"

Zac shrugged.

"This is lunacy, Zac. How could you do this to her…right here in the hotel? She's not an anonymous stranger. The room is in her name, for God's sake. Are you trying to get us both arrested?"

"Get a hold of yourself; she's going to be fine," Zac's said, his voice quivering with anxiety. The cheeks of his pale face were tinted scarlet, and Jonas wasn't sure if the burst of color was from embarrassment or Zac's overindulgence in drinking Rosie's blood.

Jonas gazed at Rosie and listened intently. "Her heartbeat is faint. Look at her! She's not taking a nap; she's unconscious, and she's not going to make it if her blood isn't replenished."

"What should we do? I don't know the ways of this modern world." Zac sounded helpless, like a frightened child.

"We could drop her off at a hospital. The doctors will know in an instant that she needs a transfusion."

Zac rubbed a blood-tinted cheek. "But the police… The police will question her when she comes around. And they'll come after us—with guns!" Zac said anxiously, deliberately playing on Jonas's fear of guns.

The idea of being brought down by a hail of bullets caused Jonas to shudder. He couldn't endure another untimely burial. He had to get to Miami to reclaim his humanity, and he wouldn't allow Rosie or anyone else to stand in his way.

"Perhaps there's another method we could use to revive her." Jonas recalled the vampire myths and said, "Why don't you feed her your blood?" It seemed like a ridiculous suggestion, but was worth a try.

Zac stiffened and frowned in revulsion. He was slow and hesitant in his answer. "I… I don't… Giving her my blood will turn her into a vampire. And vampires are completely untrustworthy. I can't read their minds," he said, shaking his head regretfully.

"You don't have a choice; we have to save her."

"I don't want a vampire mate. I want Rosie to remain human, at my command to continue doing my bidding."

As if called from the grave, Rosie's eyes suddenly popped opened. In near-delirium, she moaned and clumsily tried to sit upright.

"Lie down. You need to rest," Zac said, feigning compassion for the mortal woman as he brushed away errant strands of hair that had fallen in her face.

"I can't rest; I have to take care of you," Rosie uttered. Though weak and feverish, she propped herself up on a shaky elbow.

Rosie lifted her chin, and in her weakened state, her head lolled awkwardly to one side.

Jonas gasped at the sight of the multiple punctures and the red and bluish bruises on Rosie's neck.

"Come on, Zac; bite me again, baby," she whispered in a raspy voice, the words sounding both vulgar and sensual at the same time.

Zac spoke to Rosie in a gentle, lover's tone. "Not tonight, Rosie. I'll bite you tomorrow."

"Promise?" Rosie asked dreamily, her glassy eyes slowly fluttering closed.

"I promise," Zac vowed. Glancing at Jonas, Zac's eyes flashed in triumph.

CHAPTER 19

Keeping Angie on ice had worked for a short while, but soon her rotting flesh had become indigestible.

At first, he replaced her with live pigs that he bought from the slaughterhouse that was down the road a piece from his onion fields. Those squealing pigs kept the hunger at bay somewhat but didn't satisfy his craving the way human meat did.

Walter had always been a prominent member of the community, but this live meat-eating habit of his was causing him to lose his high standing. Tongues had started to wag with regard to the way he kept turning up at local slaughterhouses, buying live pigs one day, and baby calves the next. Rumor had it that his onion business was in deep trouble and that Walter was hacking up slabs of meat and selling them as a side job.

Though annoying, he could live with the rumors and withstand his decline in popularity. It was the gossip that he'd personally created about Angie that was starting to get to him, making him feel less than a man.

Angie's church friends had come calling, inquiring about her whereabouts. Their combined scents gave him a powerful craving, causing his eyes to well from the unbearable yearning. Keeping a safe distance from the Bible-toting parishioners, Walter wiped the tears from his eyes and insinuated that Angie had ran off with one of his strapping, young migrant workers.

"I'm a forgiving man, and I'm praying that she'll come back to me," he had told the church members in an overly emotional voice.

Rumors about Angie leaving Walter for a younger man—an exotic type—spread like wildfire.

Angie's sister, Gladys, who lived up north, had been ringing the house phone off the hook and leaving desperate messages, pleading for Angie to get in touch with her and let her know that she was all right.

Weary of Gladys's unceasing phone calls, Walter yanked up the receiver and bellowed into the mouthpiece, "After all I've done for her, your whoring sister upped and left me for a worthless field hand!"

Gladys drew in a deep intake of breath. There was a ring of truth in Walter's claim. After all, he'd met Angie at a farm convention that he'd attended fifteen years ago in Cincinnati. At the time, she was working as a hooker.

"But she's been deeply religious for years; I thought she'd gotten those heathen ways out of her system," Gladys said regretfully.

"Leopards don't change their spots," Walter said vehemently. "I should have never walked that hooker down the aisle."

"I'm so sorry, Walter," Gladys said. "When I hear from Angie, I'm going to give her a stern talking to. She's probably going through some sort of phase. She'll be back."

"I don't want her back! Your sister is dead to me!" he shouted, sounding infuriated. Feigning indignation, he hung up on Gladys.

It wasn't that Walter was completely heartless. He missed Angie and regretted what he'd done to her, but the hunger was stronger than his concern for the dead. Life goes on.

His biggest regret was letting that Haitian con man, Alain, talk him into getting on that refugee boat in the first place. He should have followed his gut and left the comatose boy exactly where he'd found him. He should have never fooled with someone under the influence of a botched spell. Walter's wife would still be alive today if he'd never gone after that free zombie labor.

Some zombie! From what Walter had heard, the typical Haitian under the influence of zombie poison merely walked around in a daze and did whatever they were told. They worked free until the poison wore off, and then they came back to their senses. Never had he heard of a Haitian zombie biting and attacking folks.

Worse than a case of rabies, that refugee's bite had poisoned Walter's system and had changed him into a ravenous animal. That shiftless, lazy Alain was to blame for Walter's troubles. Instead of devouring his poor wife, Walter should have fed on Alain.

The Haitian hadn't gotten along with the other workers; he was always complaining and stirring up trouble. Alain was a boat man and working in the fields eight hours or more a day, clipping, bending and lifting in the oppressive Georgia heat made him a surly, mean-ass, son of gun. On top of being antagonistic, Alain was lazy…the slowest worker Walter had ever set eyes on. That worthless Alain had brought a horrible curse upon Walter. And now Walter couldn't get revenge. The beady eyed con man had fled the onion fields immediately after getting his first week's wages.

At the end of the workday, Walter sat in his cool, air-conditioned truck observing the sweaty migrant workers. He took notice of one of the new men, a curly-headed Latino named Raul. Raul was an illegal with no family ties that Walter was aware of. Like many of the workers, Raul spoke limited English.

Eating animals simply wasn't doing it for Walter anymore, and so he appraised Raul through calculating eyes. He needed one more taste of a live human being. *Just one more*, he promised himself.

Raul was short in stature, but was thick and burly. Taking him down might not be easy; the man looked as strong as a bull.

As the workers piled into the back of an old, dull-gray truck that would take them back to the rooms they rented in town, Walter sneakily wagged a finger at Raul.

Raul walked briskly over to the truck

"Hey, Raul. How's it going, buddy?"

"Si, senor?"

"Uh…I wondered if you were interested in doing some overtime."

"Eh?" Raul inclined his head, uncomprehending.

"More work-o?" Walter said, struggling to communicate. Damn, he needed the foreman to interpret for him, but that wouldn't be a wise idea. He looked up in thought. "Okay, look…you do mucho work-o, and I'll pay you mucho dinero." *Hell, after all these years of hiring Hispanics, I should be able to speak a little Spanish.*

Frustrated, Walter looked around for another victim, but all the workers had already piled into the beat-up truck.

The driver fired up the loud, rumbling engine and Raul looked over his shoulder in alarm.

"No worries," Walter stated. "I'll drive you home." Realizing that Raul didn't understand a word he was speaking, Walter cut to the chase. He pulled out a stack of money that was fastened together by a sparkling silver money clip. "Mucho dinero for work-o."

This time Raul gave a radiant smile of understanding. Nodding eagerly, he said, "Si, senor!"

Walter nudged his head toward the passenger side. Raul climbed in; a happy smile was plastered on his face.

Headed for a main road, the truck bumped along over the field. Walter handed Raul a flask filled with bourbon.

"Gracias," Raul said and took a swig. He drank deeply and then passed the flask back to Walter.

Walter shook his head and gestured with a wave of his hand. "Drink up. Enjoy!" He patted Raul on the shoulder, encouragingly.

Raul tossed his head back and took another long swig.

"I used to drink a pint a day, but my taste buds done changed on me and the thought of drinking it makes me sick," Walter said, turning down the corners of his mouth. A whiff of Raul's rich, human scent put a faint, sinister smile on Walter's lips.

By the time they reached his home, Walter could tell by Raul's goofy smile and the way he slightly staggered, that the Latino was already hammered.

"Have a seat, Raul." Walter pointed to his favorite chair, a large, custom-made leather recliner with Walter's monogram on each side.

Raul sank into the oversized chair. Looking proud, he placed his hairy arms on the armrests. Walter's eyes roved from Raul's beard down to his arms.

With slowly accumulating disgust, Walter wondered if Raul's back and chest were as hairy as his face and his arms. That would be intolerable. Angie's skin had been hairless. Smooth and tender. He'd be bitterly disappointed if his next human eating experience reminded him in any way of a fur-covered animal. Walter wondered if he should try and talk Raul into shaving off his body hair before he feasted on him.

Impressed by the size and the attractiveness of the house, Raul sat swallowed in the huge chair, rambling in Spanish, his eyes gleaming at his boss's fine possessions.

"Be right back," Walter told Raul and raced to the kitchen, taking a six-pack of beer out of the fridge. Hopefully, mixing beer and bourbon would slow down the Hispanic's reflexes—rendering him putty in Walter's hands.

Raul was guzzling beer almost as fast as he was snapping open each can. After the fourth can of beer, Raul indicated that he needed to use the restroom.

Walter regarded Raul thoughtfully before responding. After the mess he'd made with Angie in his bedroom, he decided that any room with carpeting was off limits. The kitchen, with its ceramic tile flooring, would be easy to clean. Satisfied with his decision, he beckoned Raul, leading him to the bathroom that was right off the kitchen.

Walter ran upstairs and grabbed his shaving equipment. When Raul came out of the bathroom, Walter gestured for him to take a seat at the kitchen table. He sincerely hoped that he'd get over the desire to eat people if he fully and completely indulged himself one last time.

Walter plied the drunken worker with more liquor. He used gentle tones and gestures to get Raul to remove his shirt. As suspected, hair covered Raul's torso like a thick rug.

Walter gestured that he wanted to shave Raul and the worker didn't protest. He was too intoxicated to care. Tickled at being personally groomed and pampered by his boss, Raul giggled as Walter used an electric razor to remove his body hair.

Nearly crazed by Raul's musky scent, Walter broke into a sweat. His hunger was agony. Still, he fought the ever-growing desire to drop the razor and devour Raul…body hair and all.

Finished with Raul's chest, Walter grasped the man's thick arms. His anxious fingers tingled as he urged Raul to turn around. Raul's rapid pulse seemed to welcome him. Delirious with desire, Walter groaned with such fervor, the buzzing razor slipped from his hand.

Raul jumped at the sound of the electric razor hitting the floor.

Overcome by the scent of bare skin and warm blood, Walter drooled as he lunged for Raul.

Wild-eyed and swinging in self-defense, Raul fought to keep Walter away from him. His senses dulled by alcohol, he threw clumsy, ineffective blows.

Hands clawed, Walter gouged Raul's chest.

Raul cried out in pain and shock; his own hand flew to his chest, covering the horrendous wound. Walter swatted Raul's hand away. And with his mouth wide, he bit into the center of Raul's chest, crunching through the writhing man's ribcage. Teeth that were unreasonably strong tore a ragged path to Raul's thudding heart. Biting soft tissue and guzzling blood, Walter fed so greedily, he nearly choked on the migrant worker's blood.

CHAPTER 20

Having transportation, Zac had already gone out to feed before Rosie was scheduled to arrive. Zac fed on Rosie so frequently, Jonas was surprised that she hadn't succumbed to an illness due to blood loss. Jonas noticed that Rosie's complexion had changed from its original healthy pallor to a sickly shade of gray. And she was losing weight.

Being utilized as Zac's late-night snack was taking an awful toll on Rosie. And she wasn't Zac's only regular source of nourishment. There were others that Zac kept alive for his personal pleasure.

Jonas wasn't exactly sure how Zac lured humans, but he thought it might have something to do with his mesmerizing gaze. On more than one occasion, he'd witnessed Zac staring intently into his victim's eyes, holding them spellbound.

Zac was a gluttonous vampire. Some nights he went out two or three times. It wasn't hunger that drove him out into the darkness repeatedly. The blood of the first victim of the night was enough to satisfy his appetite. Zac enjoyed the sport of killing. After every kill, he returned to the hotel wearing his victim's clothes, and his wardrobe was becoming quite impressive.

He gifted the clothing and costume jewelry of his female victims to Rosie. Diamonds, gold, silver and other ornaments of value went into the hotel safe.

Zac had finally given Jonas the money he'd promised—six hundred dollars—more money than Jonas had ever held in the palm of his hand. A portion of the money had been placed in a stamped envelope, addressed to his mother. He'd spent some of his small fortune on badly needed new clothes and a small nylon backpack. The remaining funds would pay for transportation to Miami and also for Madam Collette's services.

Rosie entered the hotel suite wearing a new accessory. Hiding bites and bruises, a fashionably knotted scarf was draped around her neck. By now Rosie should have known that Zac was a vampire, yet Jonas got the impression that Rosie considered him overly passionate and a bit kinky. She didn't seem to have any conscious memory of the bloodsucking sessions.

Having had small meals throughout the day, Jonas could easily tolerate Rosie's presence. They chatted politely until Zac came in a few moments later.

"I ended it with Hugo," she announced as she passed Zac a bundle of money.

"Who's Hugo?" Zac asked.

"The bouncer at the bar."

"Oh, that guy," Zac said absently as he counted the money.

"He's pissed. Says he's not going to help me move the packages anymore."

"Doesn't matter. I don't have anything left."

"Are you serious? What are you gonna do for money? This place isn't cheap…" Her eyes wandered around the plush rooms.

"I'm pretty handy; I should be able to find some night work," Zac said with a teasing smile.

"Night work, huh?" She squinted in thought. "There's a bartending gig at Tulley's. Six at night 'til two in the morning."

"Six?" Zac shook his head emphatically. "Can't do it. Too early for me."

"I'm cool with the owner; maybe I can talk him into letting you start later. Would seven or eight work for you?"

"Yeah, sure," Zac murmured, more focused on counting money than having a conversation with Rosie.

"You don't need any real bartending experience. The clientele at Tulley's doesn't drink those fancy umbrella drinks. All you'd have to do is crack open bottles of beer and pour shots."

"Sounds easy."

"We can go talk to the manager tonight, if you'd like." A worried expression came over Rosie's face. "Hmm, maybe that's not a good idea…Hugo's working tonight and seeing you and me together might set him off."

Finished counting, Zac gave Rosie her payment. "Do you think I'm afraid of Hugo?" he asked Rosie, excitement glinting in his eyes.

"I'm just saying…he's a big guy," Rosie said nervously. "And mean," she added, her face tightly drawn with concern.

"Why don't you introduce me to that bar owner tonight?"

"That's not a good idea. You don't know Hugo."

"And you don't know me." Zac's voice rang with superiority. Chuckling, Zac left the room to put the money away in the hotel safe that was secreted away in a cubby near the closet where he slept.

"Are you coming with us, Jonas? You know…for backup in case Hugo flies into a jealous rage?" Rosie asked in a whisper, unaware that Zac could clearly hear her.

"I have other plans," Jonas told her.

"Can't you put your plans on hold for Zac? Hugo's a big guy, and he's extremely violent. He'll beat the crap out of Zac."

Recalling Zac's lightning fast motions—the way he moved with such swiftness was baffling—Jonas couldn't suppress an amused smile. "Zac can handle himself. But if you're so worried about his safety, why did you invite him to work at the same place as Hugo?"

"After he gets hired, he'll be safe. The owner won't allow employees fighting and carrying on."

"I'll let you in on a little secret," Jonas said in an equally low tone, though fully aware that Zac could hear him. "Zac knows martial arts. He's good. So don't worry about him."

Zac rejoined Jonas and Rosie. "You're looking mighty spiffy, Jonas. Where're you off to?" He gazed at Jonas. "Let me guess… you're going out to rendezvous with your sweetheart again tonight?"

"I don't have a sweetheart. You don't know what you're talking about," Jonas snapped, but he knew that Zac was in his head again. After tonight, he'd be far away from Zac and his constant prying.

⊕ ⊕ ⊕

The clothes he'd stolen from the boy in the pickup truck were a constant reminder of the ghastly crime. Dressed in dandy new clothes: crisp jeans, a sleeveless hoodie, and black Nikes, Jonas looked thoroughly Americanized. And more importantly, he felt more like his former human self and less like the monster he'd become.

He hadn't done a lot of sightseeing, and he thought about wandering around the city on his last night in Georgia, but there was a tug on his heart that led him back to the park. And it wasn't merely for prey.

He wanted to see Holland again. Hoped there was a chance that she'd returned to the park. As soon as he'd crossed the main entrance, he smelled her unmistakable personal scent. Her sweet fragrance led him straight to her.

His breath caught. There she was, seated on the same bench as the night before. Only this time she wasn't crying. She was wearing ear pods, listening to music. Her face, serene. He studied her flawless features in secret, and had to admit that it was more than her beauty that attracted him. She seemed wise and kind. An old soul that he could talk to about the mysteries of life.

What bothered him was that she was so vibrantly alive and warm, he could practically feel heat radiating off of her skin. His attraction to Holland was confusing. He suffered conflicting emotions, wanting to protect and devour her at the same time.

He wasn't exactly hungry, but there was a low growl in his throat, a primal instinct that compelled him to attack. It occurred to him that he should vacate the park at once. How could he ever forgive himself if he hurt Holland?

She raised her head and saw him. The lights from the sparkling trees illuminated Jonas's face. A welcoming smile blossomed on her face. "Hey, Jonas." She pulled the ear pods out and waved him over. "I was hoping I'd see you again."

He cautiously approached her. The closer he got, the more heady her scent. He willed himself to keep control over his impulses.

"Glad to see you smiling tonight," Jonas said in a voice that was much calmer than he felt.

"Yeah. Teenage stuff. I'm over it," she said. "Hey, I heard that enrollment for new students' starts tomorrow."

Jonas's face clouded. "I won't be able to enroll—not yet."

"Are you planning to get homeschooled?"

"I'm not sure. I have to go visit family members in Miami tomorrow. I'll probably work for a few months. I won't have the luxury of being a student until my finances have improved."

"Was your family, uh, back in Haiti…were they affected by the earthquake?"

His eyes dropped in sorrow. "Everyone was affected by that disaster. Terrible times in my country."

Holland lowered her head, nodding in understanding. Jonas got a better look at her on the sly. Her tough girl image: the edgy haircut and the bold, two-toned color screamed that she was a rebellious, troubled child. Yet her conversation told a different story. Holland seemed good-natured and completely centered.

"Where have you been staying?" she asked.

"I'm staying in a hotel. Provided by the Red Cross." He hated lying, but the truth was a horror story.

"I'm glad you've had stable lodging."

A silence stretched out for a few uncomfortable moments as Jonas recalled his former unstable dwelling place in the woods. Holland would have fled screaming if she'd seen him in his filthy burial clothes.

It bothered him not knowing the meaning of why he'd been uprooted from the grave. Perhaps that was something else that Madam Collette could explain.

Sensing his solemn mood, Holland patted the top of his hand. "Things always work out in the end. That's what my mom always says." She stood. "It's getting late. Time for me to call it a night and get home. Nice seeing you again, Jonas."

"Yes, very nice," he said, standing up also. Though he barely knew her, having to say goodbye to Holland was distressing.

"We can exchange numbers if you'd like," Holland suggested.

"I'm not your typical American boy; I don't have a cell phone yet."

Embarrassed, Holland averted her eyes briefly. "Sorry. I guess I can't fully grasp what you've been through...what you're still enduring."

"I'll be all right," Jonas said with a brave smile. His stomach was beginning to rumble. Soon, his entire system would be in turmoil, yet he didn't want to say goodbye quite yet.

"It's pretty late for you to walk the streets alone," Jonas said.

"Oh, I'm fine. I'm a night creature," Holland joked. "I love the solitude of darkness. Besides, it's safe around here. Small town. Everyone knows each other."

There were forces that Holland didn't know about and Jonas would hate for her to cross paths with Zac. The thought of Holland being pulled into the vampire's fatal embrace caused Jonas's heart to quicken.

"I'd feel better if you allowed me to walk you home."

"Okay," she said with an easy smile.

They chatted about their favorite subjects, and then the topic changed to fave movies. Back in Haiti, viewing films was a rare luxury, but since being in the hotel, Jonas has watched his share and was able to contribute to the conversation.

When they reached the front of her house, a small, one-story bungalow, Holland opened her handbag and scrawled her number on a piece of paper. "Call me and let me know how you're doing in Miami." As if committing his features to memory, she scrutinized his face.

Taking Jonas off-guard, Holland lifted up on her toes and brushed her lips across his cheekbone. "I hope we'll be friends, Jonas. And don't forget to call me."

"I will," he promised and then, unable to control his attraction to Holland, Jonas bent and softly kissed her on the lips.

Increasing the intimacy of the kiss, Holland encircled his neck with her arms, pulling him closer, and parting her lips.

He felt a tingling within. The sweet taste of her tongue, the rush of warm breath that was transferred from her mouth to his, was intense. His arms slid around her back, pressing her chest against his. His mind was spinning out of control. Agony practically oozed from his pores. Feeling the familiar low, primal growl building inside, Jonas abruptly pulled away.

Sweat broke out on his forehead. He mopped it away with the back of his hand. "Good…goodnight, Holland," he stammered.

There was a look of bafflement on Holland's face.

"I'll talk to you soon," he said with a hint of an apology in his voice.

He turned around and rushed away. He could feel Holland's curious eyes on his back, and somehow he made it to the end of the block.

Walking with the brisk stride, he reached the corner and turned around. He waved at Holland; she fluttered fingers and he could see the sad look in her eyes. Reluctantly, he tore his eyes away from her face and made a sharp turn.

Out of Holland's view, Jonas's posture changed, his shoulders slumped as his blazing eyes swept the ground, alleyways, and up into the branches of trees. His hands formed into a clawed position, ready for an attack. And his breathing became loud, panting…animalistic.

All traces of humanity had vanished. Once again, Jonas was a monster, prowling the quiet streets in search of prey.

CHAPTER 21

"**M**om!" Holland called as she placed her keys on the hook near the door. Her mother was a night owl like her, and rarely went to bed before midnight. She wanted to tell her all about Jonas.

"I'm in my bedroom," Phoebe called back in an unusual drowsy tone. Holland glanced at the time. Eleven-fifteen. Early for her mother.

Holland tossed her purse on the couch, and then hurried through the small living room to her mother's bedroom.

Phoebe was propped up by pillows, her laptop in front of her.

"What happened to your neck?" Holland asked, stunned to see a piece of gauze taped to the side of her mother's neck.

Phoebe gave a dismissive hand wave. "A couple of mosquito bites."

"Oh!" Holland furrowed her brow, giving the bandage another quizzical look. "You look a little pale. Are you okay, Mom?"

"I'm fine. Guess who stopped by?"

Holland lifted a brow.

"That polite young man that bought the car from me—Zacharias. He said that he felt guilty over the low price he paid and he insisted that I accept an additional three hundred dollars." Wearing a smile tinged with pride, her mother shook her head as if in disbelief. "A real Southern gentleman. Only a few years older than you."

"That's great, Mom. But I hope you aren't trying to set me up with an older man," Holland said, laughing.

"He's twenty-two and very handsome. I hated having to sell my car, but we needed something to tide us over until my business picks up."

"Maybe you should hook up with the guy that bought your car. At thirty-seven, it's time for you to embrace your cougar tendencies," Holland teased.

"I'm not a cougar! I'm still in love with your father—my true soul mate. We'll meet again one day on the other side." Her mother's eyes drifted off wistfully. "Zacharias and I had a lengthy discussion about reincarnation, soul mates, witchcraft...all the topics that interest me."

"Zacharias! That's a weird name," Holland said with her mouth turned down.

"I like the name. It has a certain Southern elegance. Anyway, Zac set up a session...tomorrow night."

Holland groaned. "Oh, Mom, you are absolutely shameless. What did you promise him...a love casting spell?"

"No. He's interested in becoming an entrepreneur. I'm going to help him with his finances."

"Sounds great," Holland muttered sarcastically. "We can barely make ends meet around here, but yet you think you're qualified to help people with their finances. Seems a little unethical."

"You know I wouldn't do anything unethical, hon. I'm not even charging him for his session. It's my way of thanking him for the extra bonus he gave me."

"Okay, that's cool," Holland said in earnest. She felt a little guilty for suggesting that her mother was dishonest. "I'm sorry to see the old Saab go. I've only had my driver's license for a month...would have been nice to have a set of wheels."

"We'll get another car—a newer model. I've yet to reach the full potential of my powers. But as I continue to learn and my spells improve, I'm sure I'll be raking in money," her mother said, her eyes filled with hope.

Her mother's money troubles had become serious once the money she'd been granted from a medical malpractice suit a few years ago had run out. Holland and her mother had been living off the settlement after her mother sued the hospital where her father died. It had been a large sum of money, but nothing lasts forever—especially when the beneficiary is a little loopy and a terrible money manager.

Often times, Holland felt like the parent in the mother/daughter relationship. Something had changed in her mother after her father's untimely death. After all these years, her mother was still grieving, but masked her pain with all her New Age hobbies.

Feeling like she'd been overly harsh and critical toward her mother, Holland said, "You know what, Mom, your spells have been improving. You helped me get Jarrett's attention."

"Really?"

"Yeah, but I'm not so sure that he's the right guy for me." She kept it brief, fearing that if she went into detail, admitting that Jarrett was a coldhearted creep, she might burst into tears. And that would be embarrassing.

"You're probably too mature for him, honey. Those school boys aren't up to your level of maturity, hon. Now, a guy like Zac—"

"Not interested, Mom. Christ, I'm only sixteen—I'm jailbait!"

"I was only suggesting a friendship—an intellectual equal. Nothing more."

"He's *your* friend; not mine!" Holland couldn't imagine why on earth her mom was pushing for her to make a connection with an older man. It was crazy, even for her kooky mom.

Now, Jonas...he was Holland's kind of guy. Well-mannered, sensitive, and he'd suffered a horrendous tragedy that most people could never fathom...let alone survive. Too bad Jonas was leaving town. She would have loved to have gotten to know him better.

And that kiss. Oh, my God! Holland had felt her knees go weak when she'd felt his tongue hesitantly touch hers. Jonas had abruptly broken the kiss and backed away from her. His expression was hard to read. But he seemed nervous. He most likely thought her legs were about to buckle, and was anxiously preparing to catch her. How chivalrous of him. She smiled at the sweet memory, knowing that she was going to be waiting anxiously for his call.

Deciding against talking about her newest crush—Jonas, Holland bent and gave Phoebe a kiss on the forehead, and then regarded her with concern. "You look tired, Mom. I'm going to bed and you should get some rest, too."

"I am feeling a little sluggish." She shut the laptop and closed her eyes. "All right, hon, sleep tight." Phoebe closed her eyes and, in only a few moments, she was snoring softly.

Holland clicked the light switch near the door, darkening Phoebe's bedroom. Those mosquito bites on her mother's neck worried Holland. Some mosquitoes carried diseases, she'd heard. *I hope my mom didn't pick up some kind of rare infection.*

⊕ ⊕ ⊕

Jonas was surprised to find Zac and Rosie still hanging around in the suite. "I thought you were going on a job interview," he said to Zac with a smirk.

"George, the owner, said the place was packed; too busy for him to talk to Zac," Rosie chimed in. Her scarf was slung over the back of a chair, and her exposed neck had fresh puncture wounds added to the collection.

"We're leaving in about a half-hour. Wanna come along?" Rosie asked.

Zac waited for Jonas's response, looking at him with a cold, sterile gaze.

Wherever Zac went, trouble erupted. Jonas didn't want any part of trouble. "No, I'm going to hang back here and—"

"Fantasize about your sweetheart," Zac said in a way that was intended to sound playful, but Jonas detected an undertone of hostility.

After Zac and Rosie left, Jonas tried to watch TV for a while, but he couldn't concentrate on what was happening on the screen with his thoughts fixated on Holland.

He pictured her almond-shaped, honey brown eyes, and her soft pink lips. Those lips! He could still taste the sweetness of her kiss. A kiss that almost caused him to reveal the brutality of his nature.

He retrieved the slip of paper that she'd given him from his pocket. Stared at the numbers and the handwritten script of her full name: Holland Manning. It would be nice to hear her voice before he closed his eyes for the night. Glancing at the clock, he realized it was well past midnight. His eyes darted to the telephone. He shook his head. It would be rude and insensitive to call her at such a late hour.

But he couldn't sleep; couldn't stop thinking about her. Tonight might possibly be the last time he'd have an opportunity to talk to her. Though he hated to think negatively, there was the possibility that Madame Collette would not be able to break the spell. He could be doomed to continue his monstrous existence forever.

Having a justifiable excuse, he picked up the phone and called Holland.

She answered on the second ring.

"Hi. It's Jonas. I apologize for calling at such a late hour. Did I wake you?"

"No, I'm glad you called. I was thinking about you."

Her warm words soothed him instantly. Merely hearing Holland's voice was like a ray of sunshine bursting through his bleak existence. His unspeakable burdens felt momentarily lifted, and he smiled broadly.

"I wanted to hear your voice before I leave tomorrow," he said. "I don't know what to expect in Florida. I may not have access to a phone once I get there."

"Where are you gonna be working?"

Jonas went silent for a moment. "I'm not sure. My uncle is going to help me find work. Like I told you, my family is in a pretty desperate situation back in Haiti, and I'll take any job that's offered."

"I can't even imagine what you and your family went through in Haiti, and I hear that despite all the charitable organizations involved in rebuilding the area, there hasn't been much improvement."

"That's true. Our home wasn't completely destroyed, but it's barely habitable. Many of my friends weren't as lucky, though. They're still living in tent cities."

"That's so sad. Our school collected donations, but obviously we don't have control over what's done with the money." Holland sighed quietly before continuing. "Having to live in tents after all this time is hard to fathom."

"Yes, our plight is unimaginable unless you've lived it."

"I'd like to go back to Haiti with you one day and…you know… to volunteer."

"I'll keep your words in my heart. Something to look forward to."

"Jonas," she said softly. "I barely know you, but I like you a lot. Is it crazy of me to want to stay in touch?"

"No, I don't think it's crazy. I feel the same way." He wanted to tell her that he'd felt a strong connection to her the first time he'd set eyes on her, right after he'd clawed his way out of the moist earth. But how could he confide the forbidden truth about himself? How could he reveal his detestable nature without scaring her out of her wits?

"I'm glad you called me, Jonas," Holland said, her voice lilting like musical notes. "Make sure you call as soon as you can. I want to know that you made it to Miami safe and sound."

"I will. Goodnight, Holland," Jonas murmured, wishing he could taste her sweet lips once more before he set off on his journey.

CHAPTER 22

While asleep, Holland was aware of a presence. Someone stood over her, observing her as she lay in bed. It had to be her mother—checking on her. Who else could it be? She wanted to open her eyes to make sure, but it seemed too much of an effort to awaken fully. And she was reluctant to come out of her sweet dream. She could only manage a soft, wistful sigh as she was pulled deeper into sleep.

The footfalls that retreated were not the soft padding of her mother's slippers. The steps were confident and decidedly masculine. In her sleeping state, she imagined that she was hearing her father's footsteps. But wait! How could that be? Her dad had died six years ago.

Jolting awake, Holland's heart quickened as she caught a fleeting glimpse of a man's silhouette moving toward her open bedroom door. Had she been thinking rationally, she would have grabbed the phone and dialed 9-1-1.

But feeling inexplicably heroic, she rushed out into the hallway, clicking on the light switch as she chased after the intruder.

She pursued the shadowy figure into the kitchen, and immediately switched on the light. The room was empty with everything in its place. She grabbed a knife out of a kitchen drawer, and crept to the living room. The window near the bookcase was pushed halfway open. The curtains blew in the night breeze. Holland slammed it closed and then twisted the lock in place.

Fearing that her mother had been attacked—or killed—she raced to her mother's bedroom, screeching in terror, "Mom!"

Holland burst into Phoebe's room. She pressed a palm against her thudding heart, gasping in relief when she saw that her mother had not been hacked up by a sadistic killer and left in a pool of blood. She was alive and in one piece.

"What's wrong, hon? What are you doing with that knife?" her mother implored, her drowsy eyes blinking in curiosity.

"Someone was in the house—a man. He came in my room, and then escaped through the living room window."

"Holland, sweetie," Phoebe said indulgently. "I had a male visitor, but he didn't leave through a window."

Holland's eyes flitted to the clock at her mother's bedside. "It's four-twenty. Why did you invite that man over in the wee hours of the morning?" Holland questioned, her voice raised in disbelief.

"It was my friend, Zac."

"The transaction is complete. Why does he keep coming back?"

Phoebe shrugged. "Lonely, maybe? He grew up here, but he left town years ago. I don't think he has any friends."

"But...what do you have in common? He's like half your age. Are you actually being a cougar, Mom?"

"Don't be silly. We're just friends. He got a new job, tending bar at a little place on the outskirts of town. That spell I cast has been bringing a lot of good luck his way. I really think my spells are improving."

Holland noticed that the gauze on her mother's neck was dotted with two specks of blood. "Those bites are starting to bleed, Mom," Holland said, frowning as she stared at her mother's neck.

Phoebe brushed her fingers across the white bandage. "Those mosquito bites were itching something terrible. I must have scratched too hard." She gave Holland a tired smile. "Stop worrying so much. Listen, I personally walked Zac to the front door and saw him out. Everything's okay, hon. It really is."

"But Mom, the window was wide open. How do you account for that?"

"I started getting this woozy feeling while Zac was here. I must have cracked it…you know, trying to keep my eyes open with a bit of fresh air."

"I think it's very inconsiderate of that guy to come over here bothering you at any hour of the night. He's taking advantage of your kindness. What a selfish prick!"

"He's not taking advantage of me," Phoebe protested. "He called me and I invited him over."

Holland looked warily over her shoulder. There was something terribly disturbing about her mother inviting that Zac guy over for an after-midnight chat. It dawned on Holland that her mother was starved for male attention, and she hoped there wasn't anything sexual going on with Zac. And it wasn't the cougar factor that bothered her. Though she hadn't met him, she'd already decided that Zac was a creep and she didn't want him hanging out at her house.

As far as seeing a man leaving her bedroom… Holland sighed and reluctantly accepted that she'd been half-asleep and had merely imagined the shadowy figure.

⊕ ⊕ ⊕

A half-hour before dawn, Zac slipped into the suite.

Sensitive to the slightest sound, Jonas woke. Being that this would be the last time that he was in Zac's company, Jonas decided to have a friendly farewell conversation before Zac sequestered himself in the closet.

"Did you get the job?" Jonas asked, coming out of the bedroom into the outer area.

"Of course," Zac replied in a pompous tone.

"That's cool, man. Congratulations." Jonas flopped down into a chair, unperturbed by Zac's arrogant attitude.

"Where's Rosie?"

"With Hugo."

"They're back together?"

"I guess you could say that. They like getting high together. And that's why I'm completely out of my product," Zac said scornfully.

Jonas raised a brow.

"I found out they've been sampling my product. A lot of it." Zac's face was tense with hostility. "I punished Hugo. Put a couple of deep gashes in his neck. I would have drained him, but I don't like the ways he tastes. His blood has a bitter aftertaste—from the drugs, I reckon."

"What about Rosie? Does she taste like Hugo?" Jonas was curious since Zac drank from Rosie regularly.

"Not as bad, but I won't be feeding on her anymore. You can have her if you want…Hugo, too. They're both worthless."

"No, that's okay," Jonas said, shaking his head.

"Are you sure? I can get them over here just like that!" He snapped his fingers.

Jonas gave Zac a doubtful look.

"I've tasted their blood, and now they're bound to me for life." Zac had a sudden faraway look in his eyes, and then fixed his gaze on Jonas. "I won't be tapping into their tainted bloodstream again, but I'll figure out a way for those two addicts to be useful." Zac laughed and the sound was filled with malice.

Zac whisked past Jonas and walked over to the safe. As Zac stocked the safe with cash and a gleaming array of stolen trinkets,

Jonas caught a familiar whiff as he inhaled the thick scent that hung in the air and that clung to Zac's most recently procured clothes.

"What's that smell?" Jonas's brows knitted together in fear and suspicion.

"It's wonderfully unique, isn't it?" Zac smiled but his eyes were cold. He turned his back to Jonas and began his nightly ritual of arranging the stacks of bills inside the safe. "That girl is something special, but I can't figure her out."

"What girl?"

"That lil' sweetheart of yours," Zac said, tauntingly.

Jonas leapt from the chair and stalked over to Zac and grabbed him by the arm. "What did you do to her?"

Zac wrenched himself free. "Calm down. I didn't do anything. I just peeked in on her. There's no harm in looking, is there?"

"You shouldn't have gone near her. You have the whole town to prey upon. Why her? What's your problem, man?"

"You're leaving, so why do you care?" Zac glared at Jonas; each word dripping with disdain. "That lil' lady has a fascinating aroma. Sweet and pungent. It lingers in the air—so thick you can practically taste it."

A smoldering rage overtook Jonas. His nostrils flared. Resisting the urge to growl and snarl like a wild beast, he hissed through his teeth. Fists clenched, he imagined strangling the life out of Zac.

"Get that thought out of your head…I'm immortal, remember? You can't kill me," Zac reminded after telepathically seeing the angry flashes in Jonas's mind. "Listen, I was only kidding. I'm not interested in your sweetheart; I'm involved with her mother."

Jonas scowled confusedly.

"Phoebe's a generous donor," Zac explained with a smirk. "She extends invitations to her home and I eagerly accept. All I have to do is stare at her with these pretty blue eyes, and the next thing you know, she's tilting her head back, offering me a taste of blood."

"You deliberately chose her mother because you know how important Holland is to me."

"Merely a coincidence," Zac said with a shrug. "I bought her mother's car and we clicked."

"There's more to it than that. You're a devious son of a bitch," Jonas said sharply. Using profanity was usually out of character for Jonas, but he was so enraged, he couldn't control his tongue. Two seconds from pouncing on the vampire and eating him alive, Jonas gave Zac a dark, threatening look.

Grinning in amusement, Zac gave Jonas a long, knowing look. "You should get a grip on yourself. You can't destroy me. And furthermore, until you learn how to shut off your thoughts, I'll always know what's on your mind."

"Why are you doing this?" Jonas asked, his voice lowered in defeat.

"I need you to stay here and look after me—keep those cleaning women out of here while I sleep."

"You don't need me for that! You can get Rosie, Hugo… anyone you've drawn blood from will obey your command."

"I don't trust anyone the way I trust you. A silent call woke us from an eternal sleep—pulled us from the ground. We have a united mission…a common bond."

"We have nothing in common!" Jonas spat.

"You actually have a point," Zac said sneeringly. "In comparison to your kind, we vampires are virtuous beings. Vampires give mortals a dignified and humane demise while you savagely rip them to shreds, leaving nothing behind—nothing for their families to identify except ravaged bones." Zac wore an expression of revulsion. "I don't think your sweet-smelling little darling would fancy you so much if she caught a gander of your barbaric nature. She wouldn't be so moony eyed for you if she met that angry beast that lives inside you."

"I'm warning you, Zac. Stay away from Holland."

Zac held his hands up in surrender. "Okay…okay. For you, my friend, I won't touch her. But that doesn't mean that she'll be safe from other vampires."

"Others? There're more vampires around here?"

"I've noticed a few. They mostly lurk in the shadows, hunting in secrecy. They're not out and about…they don't mingle with mortals as I do."

Worried and confounded, Jonas dragged his fingers down the side of his face, and rubbed his jaw.

"The girl's captivating scent will draw them out of hiding."

Jonas walked back to the chair and slumped into it. Holland was in danger and he was responsible. His friendship with her had piqued Zac's interest, prompting the devious vampire to finagle an open invitation inside her residence. If that weren't bad enough, there was a nest of underground vampires that would be chomping at the bit once they caught a whiff of Holland's distinctive fragrance.

Zac eyed the window warily. The deadly sun would soon peak over the horizon. He took strides toward his bedroom. Jonas followed.

"May I have some privacy, please!" Zac snapped.

"We have to talk."

"We'll talk when I wake up."

"But I'm leaving for Miami."

"That's a pity," Zac said sarcastically and tugged on the handle of the closet, pulling it open only partially. Jealously guarding the interior of his resting place, Zac carefully edged inside and closed the door.

Jonas returned to his bedroom and made a point of keeping Holland out of his thoughts. He was only able to have mental privacy when the sun was blazing in the sky and Zac was deep in slumber. Waiting for daybreak, Jonas focused on the mundane thoughts: TV shows, music, car models. He even recited the names of states in alphabetical order.

At six-fifteen, certain that Zac was asleep and unable to penetrate his mind, he finally allowed thoughts of Holland to absorb his thoughts.

Zac was using Phoebe to be close to Holland's enchanting scent. Jonas realized that Zac's loyalty to him was tenuous at best. Before long, he'd go after Holland. And how much longer before those underground vampires sniffed her out?

Holland's life was at stake, and Jonas couldn't abandon her. As desperately as he wanted a normal life, Miami would have to wait. Perhaps there was a Haitian priestess in Georgia—someone as knowledgeable as Madame Collette—someone who could reverse the spell.

CHAPTER 23

Walter's company was taking a hit. He couldn't concentrate on farm business. He could barely communicate with his jowly, plump foreman without having to resist the urge to take a couple of bites out of the man's fat, juicy cheeks.

Agricultural conventions had always been a source of big fun. Walter enjoyed the camaraderie among his peers, the wheeling and dealing, and he especially loved the nightlife, which consisted of heavy drinking and carousing around with hookers.

But the fun times were over. He had to steer clear of conventions. Too many tempting aromas mingled together under one roof. God forbid if he lost all self-control and went berserk—attacking, biting, and mauling—as he became caught up in an unstoppable public feeding frenzy.

Since feasting on the illegal named Raul, Walter's desire for human meat had been gnawing at him something terrible—the craving simply wouldn't let up. But Walter had been exerting a great deal of will power. Keeping his dangerous passion under control, he survived off livestock: cattle, goats, horses, and pigs.

Getting an early start, at six-fifteen in the morning, Walter began the twenty-five mile drive to Morgan County, where he'd recently purchased an old slaughterhouse. The place was tucked away in a heavily wooded area. At the slaughterhouse, Walter was granted the privacy he needed to eat his meals in peace. He could get as bloodied as he wanted without worrying about prying eyes. He didn't have to concern himself about the level of noise, either. Ever since that Haitian refugee had turned him into a loathsome and vile, flesh-eating ogre, Walter's dining experience always produced a cacophony of gruesome sounds, with animals balking and protesting loudly as he hungrily tore into their flesh.

Hooked onto the back of his truck was a small aluminum trailer that contained three succulent pigs. Walter frowned, thinking that he was more in the mood for raw beef.

Passing miles of cornfields, he suddenly caught sight of a flash of yellow a few yards ahead. The yellow turned out to be a windbreaker worn by a young woman, running on the side of the road, getting in her morning workout. A pair of black shorts revealed that the girl had a nice pair of legs on her—long and muscular.

His salivary glands working overtime, Walter wiped drool from his mouth with the back of his hand. He opened the window and allowed the girl's scent to fill his nostrils. He groaned and grit down on his teeth. Overcome with yearning that had nothing to do with a sexual attraction, his truck veered slightly out of control.

Acting on predatory impulse, he pressed down on the gas pedal, quickly accelerating from forty miles per hour to seventy. Driving up on the jogger fast and furiously, Walter slammed into the back of those sturdy legs, throwing the girl face down in the dirt and gravel.

His face lined with false concern, Walter got out of his truck and rushed to the girl's aid. Kneeling, he asked, "Are you okay? It's so foggy out here, I didn't see you?"

The jogger moaned. "My head hurts. And my right leg...I can't move it."

"Yeah, looks like you're in pretty bad shape," he said grimly as he noticed that her leg was turned at an impossible angle and her hair was matted with blood. "No telling how long it's gonna take for an ambulance to get here."

On the ground, the girl moaned and grimaced in pain.

"Guess I'd better drive you to the hospital myself," Walter decided.

"Thank you," the girl murmured. Overtaken by pain, she bit down on her lip as Walter lifted her off the ground.

Carrying her in his strong arms, Walter headed for his truck. The sight of the blood that oozed from the gash in her head whetted his appetite.

"You're bleeding like a stuck pig. I'm really sorry, miss, but I can't put you in my nice, clean truck. You understand, don't you?"

The girl opened her eyes questioningly. "Where're you gonna put me?"

Walter swiped his thick tongue across her forehead, lapping up a good amount of thick, bright red blood.

"Stop! What's wrong with you? Are you crazy?" the girl shrieked.

"Mmm-umph! That's the taste I've been hankering for," he said, nodding and licking his lips.

"Let me go, you lunatic!" With terror and rage in her eyes, she squirmed inside Walter's brawny arms, but Walter held her close, his grasp as firm as iron.

The girl screamed and writhed, but Walter seemed to not hear her. He kept on lapping up blood, running his tongue along her cheek and across the bridge of her nose. Not wanting to miss a drop, he went so far as to dip the tip of his tongue into the corner of her eye where a small amount of blood had pooled. "You got a sweet taste to yourself; and I can tell that you're gonna make for some real good eating!"

"Help!" The girl kicked out her good leg, and flailed her arms, trying to propel herself out of Walter's grasp. He loosened one arm and opened the back of the aluminum trailer. The two pigs were squealing like crazy, upset from all the commotion.

"In you go," Walter said in cheerful tone as he tossed the maimed girl into the trailer with the pigs.

Back behind the wheel, the taste of the girl's blood still on his tongue, Walter trembled in anticipation. The slaughterhouse was only ten miles away, but he was of a mind to pull over, crawl into the trailer, rip off the girl's clothes, and commence to eating.

CHAPTER 24

Jonas had his hand on the doorknob to the closet, and was tempted to open it. Exposing Zac to the deadly rays of the sun would put an end to the threat he posed to Holland.

But Zac was only part of the problem. Jonas needed backup to protect Holland from the swarm of vampires that prowled in the murky shadows.

It was odd that they had never posed a threat to Holland before. What had prevented the other vampires from attacking her long before Jonas and Zac had risen from the ground? Puzzled, Jonas turned away from the closet and paced the floor. He was too wound up and anxious to sleep. There was no time to waste. He had approximately ten hours to put together a plan before Zac awakened and began probing his mind again.

⊕ ⊕ ⊕

The first thing Holland did when she opened her eyes was reach for her phone to check her messages. There were two texts from Naomi, but nothing from Jonas. She didn't actually expect to hear from him so soon, but it would be a nice surprise.

Jonas had said that getting to a phone wouldn't be easy. Not wanting to risk missing his call, she stuck her phone in the pocket of her PJs and took it into the bathroom.

After her morning ritual of brushing her teeth for three minutes and then splashing her face with cold water, she trotted down the hallway.

The house was awfully quiet, which was weird. Normally, Phoebe was in the kitchen clattering pots and pans as she concocted a love potion or other spells.

"Mom!" she called, tapping on her mother's bedroom door.

"Come in, honey." Phoebe's voice was faint; she hardly sounded like herself.

When Holland opened the door, she was surprised to find her mother buried under the covers. Her laptop, which was the lifeline to her witchcraft business, was on the bed next to Phoebe, but the lid was closed.

"What's wrong, Mom. Are you sick?"

"A little under the weather. I'll live; it's nothing major."

"What are your symptoms?" Holland asked. Acting like the parent, she touched her mother's forehead with the back of her hand. "You don't seem to have a fever."

"I'm feeling a little lightheaded. The room actually started spinning when I tried to get out of bed."

"Really? You're scaring me, Mom. You never get sick."

"I'm not sick. Just a little woozy."

"You said you felt woozy last night while that Zac dude was here. What's going on with you? Have you been blacking out... having fainting spells?"

"No. All I need is a little bed rest and I'll be fine."

"You may have picked up an infection from those mosquito bites."

"I don't think so."

"Let me have a look." Holland gently peeled back the adhesive and let out a little yelp when she saw the discolored, swollen skin surrounding three sets of punctures on her mother's neck.

"Oh, my God, Mom! Those wounds look serious...not like

mosquito bites at all. It looks like you've been bitten by something with fangs. Like a rat or something. Maybe a bat! I really think you should see a doctor."

"Don't be silly, Holland. I don't trust doctors. I'm going to mix up a balm that will heal those bites and I'll be good as new."

Holland knew it was pointless to try and talk her mother into seeing a doctor. Her mother hated doctors; she blamed them for misdiagnosing Holland's dad—treating him for appendicitis when he actually had pancreatic cancer.

"Are you hungry? Want some breakfast?" Holland asked, wanting to do something for her mother.

"No, my stomach's a little queasy. Just a cup of tea."

"Okay. I'll fix you lunch this afternoon. Hopefully, you'll have an appetite by then."

In the kitchen cabinet, Holland sorted through Phoebe's vast assortment of tea and selected a lemon and orange spice mixture. Her mind was completely off of Jonas and totally focused on the weird wounds on her mother's neck. Something had certainly bit her mother, but it sure wasn't any mosquito.

Do we have rats? Holland wondered, grimacing at the terrible thought. Some of the money that her mother had gotten from selling her car would have to go toward pest control. Holland planned to call around and get some estimates.

Their money situation was getting critical. It was obvious that Phoebe's witchcraft wasn't going to pay the bills, and the money from selling the car was only a temporary fix to their financial woes. Holland babysat from time to time, but the money she earned was only chump change—enough for personal items. If she planned to help with the bills, she'd need a real job and a dependable income.

⊕ ⊕ ⊕

Naomi and Holland walked to the mall together. Naomi chatted endlessly about her new obsession, fashion and makeup, while Holland was quiet and pensive.

"What's your preference—working in retail or fast food?" Naomi inquired.

"Doesn't matter; I'm not picky."

"You'll have fewer encounters with Chaela if you work in a fast food joint. She's too worried about her figure to munch on burgers and fries."

"Chaela is the least of my worries."

"Chaela and the rest of the bitch squad are retail junkies, and there's no way to avoid her unless you get a job selling appliances or cleaning products. I mean…anything that has to do with housework would be taboo to a girl like Chaela. She might break a nail or something, you know what I mean?" Naomi giggled.

"I don't care if I bump into Chaela. She has what she wanted— she got Jarrett back. There's nothing I can do except move on. And by the way, I have moved on."

Naomi grinned with excitement. "Moved on with whom? You should consider starting a romance with one of Jarrett's football buddies. That would be the perfect way to get even with him!"

"I don't want anything to do with Jarrett's crowd. My new friend isn't from around here. He's Haitian."

"Whaaat? How come I'm just hearing about your new man?"

"He's not exactly my man. Not officially. There's definitely an attraction, but we're just friends." Holland pushed her hair out of her eyes. "Look, it's complicated. We're trying the long distance thing. Phone calls and emails…you know," she said with a sheepish smile.

"No, I don't know. I've never had a long distance relationship or any other kind. You can't spring this kind of news on me without providing details, Holland. When, where, and how did you meet this boy? And as your best friend, I'm insulted that you're just getting around to telling me."

"His family sent him here from Haiti to go to school, but he's having some sort of difficulty with finances…maybe his citizenship. I don't know all the particulars. I've only known him for a short while. But I do know that whatever's going on between us is really intense."

"You hooked up with a Haitian guy after Jarrett Sloan? Hmmm. Kinda strange, even for you."

"What do you mean?"

"You went from a blond-haired Nordic type to a guy from Haiti. I'm surprised. I've never known you to go for black guys. I'm just saying…"

"You're trying to psychoanalyze me, but there's nothing going on in my head except I discovered that I prefer a decent human being over a self-absorbed prick."

"Okay, I get it. No reason to go off on a tangent." Naomi rolled her eyes in exasperation. "So does the new boyfriend have a name?"

Holland's expression brightened. "His name is Jonas, but he's not my boyfriend. Not yet."

"Well, thanks for finally putting me—your best friend—in the loop," Naomi said, pouting.

"He's going to Miami for awhile. I have to wait and see how things go before I start putting labels on our friendship."

"So, tell me about him. Does he have a heavy accent? Is he cute?" Naomi inquired, pasting on a big smile that expressed her forgiveness.

Holland's expression brightened. "Ohmigod, his accent is so sexy. His English is excellent, though. And he's gorgeous! His complexion is…it's like a red clay brown. He has this killer combination of sculpted, high cheekbones and a strong jawline. Thick eyebrows and dreamy, dark brown eyes. I could stare into his eyes forever. And his lips…" Holland's eyes rolled upward as she was close to swooning. "His lips are soft. Plump. Succulent."

"You kissed him?"

Smiling dreamily, Holland nodded. "His kiss tops Jarrett's. I mean…there's no comparison, really. The chemistry between us is crazy. I'm crazy about him, Naomi," Holland confessed, blushing.

"I'm still trying to get over the interracial aspect. I never knew you were into black guys—you know, besides a celebrity—someone like Drake."

"Jarrett has been my major crush, but I've had others. And I don't base my crushes on color!"

"Who else have you been crushing on? I mean, which black guys, specifically. I can't believe you're so secretive."

"It doesn't matter. My former love interests are all in the past now. But I don't choose anyone based on color. You're my best friend and you, of all people, should know that about me."

"I know. I shouldn't have made it a black or white thing. But I am a little concerned."

"About what?"

"A few weeks ago you were all broken up over Jarrett. You were devastated! Now you're head over heels for some guy you barely know. I don't want to see you hurt again, Holland. Whatever's going on between you and that Haitian dude is an end-of-summer fling. Summer romances are typically doomed from the start."

"I'll keep your advice in mind," Holland said in a tone that indicated the discussion was over. She realized that Naomi had her best interests at heart, but what did Naomi know about relationships? Nothing!

"I'm gonna hit Wal-Mart first. I heard they're hiring," Holland said, steering Naomi toward the entrance of the store.

"While you're filling out the application, I'll go browse the beauty products."

"You have a giant tub filled with makeup that you never wear. What else do you need?" Holland asked, shaking her head.

Naomi shrugged. "I'm a hopeless junkie. See you in twenty minutes."

Sitting in front of the computer, Holland began keying in her personal information. Having held only babysitting jobs, she skipped past the work history section, hoping her lack of experience wouldn't be held against her.

Her phone jangled, and she groped inside her purse. The number on the screen was a shock. It was the number of the hotel where Jonas had been staying.

"Hello?" she answered breathlessly.

"It's Jonas. How are you, Holland?"

"I'm fine. Are you still in town? I thought you were catching an early morning bus to Miami."

"There's been a change of plans. I'm not going to Miami—at least not for a while." He sounded down in the dumps.

"What happened? Why didn't you go?"

"A couple of problems that I have to work out." Jonas didn't seem to want to talk about what had detained him, and so Holland let it go.

"I need to talk to you. It's pretty serious. Can we meet some-where?"

"Sure. I'm at the mall filling out job applications. But you can stop by my house at, uh…around two?"

"Uh, I'm not sure about coming to your house."

"Why not?"

"I don't want to risk anyone overhearing what I have to tell you. Do you mind meeting me at the park?"

"Not a problem. See you at our favorite spot—at two." Holland disconnected, feeling a mixture of joy and dread. She was super happy that Jonas was still in town. But his tone was so gloomy, she felt like she needed to brace herself for some really bad news. Was he going back to Haiti? Did she need to worry about him being deported?

Clasping a blue and white plastic bag, Naomi was at Holland's side when she finished the application. Honoring Jonas's desire for secrecy, she didn't mention his phone call, but it took a lot of willpower not to blurt out that he'd called her.

"Guess who was in line in front of me at the register?" Naomi said.

"No clue."

"Jarrett and Chaela." Naomi gazed at Holland inquisitively as she waited for her response.

Holland merely shrugged. "So. What do I care? Those two egomaniacs deserve each other."

"Jarrett was sporting a huge bandage on the side of his neck. Chaela must have scratched him in a fit of jealous rage!" Naomi giggled.

Holland's brows furrowed. "What kind of bandage? Gauze and tape?"

"No, more like a giant Band-Aid. And his skin looked sickly—really pale. He was alarmingly thin. Looks like he's going to have to sit out the season. Jarrett looks way too fragile to be effective on the football field."

"That's weird," Holland mumbled, thinking about her mother's neck injury and her sickly pallor. "Have you heard anything about a mosquito plague?"

Naomi turned up a corner of her top lip. "Don't tell me you think he was attacked by killer mosquitoes? I'll stick to my theory that Chaela caught him looking at another girl and went for the jugular using a sharpened fingernail."

Holland had a bad feeling in the pit of her stomach. Was it a coincidence that Jarrett and her mother were both pale and sporting large bandages on their necks?

"That's it for the applications."

"You only filled out one!"

"I know, but I'm worried about my Mom. She wasn't feeling well when I left. Said she was dizzy. I should check on her."

Naomi gave Holland a doubtful look. "Is this about Jarrett and Chaela?"

"No. Not at all. I'm over him. I swear."

During the walk from the mall, Jarrett's shiny Durango cruised up to Holland and Naomi. Chaela was at the wheel, and Jarrett was sitting slumped in the passenger seat. As usual, Chaela was tanned and gorgeous as ever. In stark contrast, Jarrett's complexion was ghastly pale. He had on dark sunglasses, presumably to hide his sickly appearance, but the camouflage wasn't working. His lips were set in a grim line of misery, like he was suffering unbearably.

"Hey, losers!" Chaela called out of the window in a saccharin-sweet voice typically used when giving a compliment. "Looks like you two could use a ride."

"No, we're okay," Naomi responded meekly.

Holland glared at Chaela and held up her middle finger. "Fuck off, Chaela!"

Chaela looked briefly stunned. Then her pretty face twisted into an ugly mask of rage. "You tried to steal my boyfriend and now you're giving *me* the finger!"

Jarrett looked at Holland. His mouth twitched into something that resembled an apologetic smile. "Let's go, Chaela. I'm going to be late for practice," he said in a weak, irritated voice.

"It's your lucky day, Holland Manning. Jarrett's in a rush, so I don't have time to give you the beat down that you deserve," Chaela said, still smiling and tossing her hair around. "But I'll catch up with you when school starts." Chaela narrowed her eyes threateningly. She sped away, leaving behind the echo of her taunting laughter.

"Oh, no. This is bad," Naomi whispered. "We worked so hard to redefine your identity so that you could gain acceptance. And it's all for naught. Chaela and the bitch squad are going to make your life hell."

"I don't need acceptance from Chaela and her crowd. There're more important things in life than fitting in with a pack of mean, shallow girls."

"I know, but…" Naomi gave Holland a look of sympathy. "I'm really worried for you. Look, Holland, I know your mom can't afford private school, but maybe you should consider transferring to a different public school." Fear for Holland shone in Naomi's eyes. "I don't think Chaela's going to be satisfied pulling cruel pranks. Did you see that vicious look on her face? She's out for blood."

"No offense, Naomi, but I'm not letting Chaela or any other bullies chase me out of school. I'm standing my ground, and I'm not going anywhere." Something had changed in Holland—a new confidence that went beyond a beauty makeover. She wondered if the humiliation she'd suffered over Jarrett had hardened her. Or maybe she'd evolved beyond teenage angst after hearing from Jonas a firsthand account of the tragedies that still prevail in Haiti.

Warm and compassionate, Jonas had touched her on a deep

level. She now realized that there was much more to life than an updated wardrobe. Holland wanted to help people. Fight for the rights of people who didn't have a voice. But how could she help others if she didn't start sticking up for herself?

Squinting in the sun, Holland looked ahead. Jarrett's truck had stopped at a red light. Hoping that Chaela was watching from the rear view mirror, Holland raised her middle finger high in the air, and shouted. "Bring it, Chaela Vasquez! I'm not afraid of you.".

Naomi gave Holland concerned side glances as they continued their trek home.

CHAPTER 25

When Holland and Naomi reached the midway point between their respective homes, they gave each other quick hugs and went their separate ways. Alone with her thoughts, an image of Jarrett popped in Holland's head. He looked far worse than Naomi had described. How on earth was someone so scrawny able to manage the rigors of football practice? Oh, well, Jarrett was Chaela's problem—not hers!

She wrinkled her nose, remembering the adhesive bandage on his neck. His condition seemed eerily similar to her mother's. *Strange!*

Thinking about her mother's illness, she picked up her pace. Holland had a little over an hour to check on her mother and fix her lunch before meeting up with Jonas in the park. Butterflies fluttered in the pit of her stomach as she wondered what was on Jonas's mind.

"I'm home, Mom!" she yelled after entering the house. She hurried to the kitchen, pulled the fridge open and peered inside. "Do you want grilled cheese on whole wheat for lunch?"

No answer.

"Mom!" she called again and worriedly rushed to Phoebe's room.

Hung in front of the blinds, blocking the sunlight was a navy blue blanket at one window, and the other was covered with a forest-green sheet. The room was as dark and as quiet as a tomb.

"What's going on, Mom? Why are you lying here in the dark?"

"The sun's too bright today; it's giving me a headache and hurting my eyes," Phoebe said, covering her eyes with her forearm.

"Do you want to take something for your headache? I have Tylenol in my purse."

Phoebe grimaced as she shook her head. "You know I don't trust the pharmaceutical industry."

Holland sighed. "Well, you gotta eat something, Mom. How about some soup and a grilled cheese sandwich?" Holland clicked on the bedside lamp. She flinched when she got a close look at her mother in the light.

"Mom, your complexion is all pasty and white. I'm worried; you don't look good." Holland began nibbling on her index finger, chipping away at the fresh coat of electric blue polish.

"All this self-medicating isn't a good idea. I mean…suppose there's something seriously wrong with you?"

"If I don't feel any better tomorrow, I'll go see a doctor. I promise," Phoebe said in a hoarse whisper.

Holland noticed that the tea she'd brought to her mother hadn't been touched. Feeling helpless, Holland bit her bottom lip. "You need some nourishment. Will you please eat some lunch?"

"I'm really not hungry."

"We have to get some nourishment inside you. Do it for me. Please, Mom."

"Okay, hon," Phoebe conceded with a weak smile.

Spoon-feeding her mother was totally weird, but it was the only way to make sure that her mother got some nourishment. Holland glanced over at the set of windows, wondering how her mother had found the strength to hang the blanket and sheet.

After eating half a bowl, Phoebe shook her head, indicating that she didn't want anymore. Holland wished there was a kindly old auntie or a grandmother that she could call, but sadly, she and her mother were all alone in the world. It occurred to her to get in touch with her mother's coven sisters. But that would probably be a big waste of time; they were only cyber buddies—not physical friends that could come over and lend some support.

Maybe her Mom's new friend, Zac, would lend a hand. As much as she disliked the idea, she decided that she'd sneak Zac's number from her mom's phone, put in a call and ask him if he could persuade her mother to see a doctor. And since Zac was the owner of her mother's car, he could provide transportation to the ER.

She checked the time and sighed when she realized that she had only fifteen minutes to get to the park. With no time to freshen up and change clothes, she ran anxious fingers through the front of her hair and was out of the door. She swiped on lip gloss as she race-walked to the park.

Jonas was waiting for her at the main entrance. She hadn't expected to see him standing there. The sight of him was an unexpected pleasure that took her breath away. Without thinking, she rushed into his arms. As she squeezed him tightly, Jonas suddenly broke the embrace.

Feeling self-conscious, Holland could feel her face flushing. Instead of brushing her hair out of her face, she raked it forward, attempting to hide her embarrassment. She could have kicked herself for gripping Jonas in a bear hug. She must have appeared awfully needy.

"Let's go sit down," Jonas offered, guiding her down the cobbled path that led to their favorite bench. When his hand reached for hers, she no longer felt off kilter.

"What did you want to discuss?" she asked as she took a seat on the bench.

He clasped her hand and looked her in the eyes. "What I have to say is going to shock you, so I won't beat around the bush."

Her eyes, large and questioning, latched onto his.

"Your mother is involved in a dangerous friendship with someone I know."

"Are you talking about Zac?"

Jonas nodded.

"How do you know him?"

"We're acquaintances," he said.

Holland scowled, wondering what Zac and Jonas could possibly have in common.

"Dangerous? My mom thinks the world of him. How is he a danger to her?"

"He's involved in activities that could put her health at risk."

"Is he biting her?"

Jonas nodded solemnly.

Holland gasped. She'd heard about people that played vampire games. Those weirdoes wore fake fangs and even shaved their own teeth to sharpened points. How had her mother fallen for Zac's lines? That Zac individual was more contemptuous than Holland had imagined.

Her heart quickened. "My God! My mom hasn't been feeling well. Her neck is swollen. I think it's infected."

"She has to rescind his invitation... Or he'll eventually deplete her," Jonas warned.

Holland gawked at Jonas. "Are you serious? Rescind her invitation...like in a vampire film?"

"Yes." Jonas swallowed, and then nervously cleared his throat. "Zac is a vampire," he blurted.

Holland burst out laughing. "You mean, he *thinks* he's a vampire, right?"

"Zac *is* a vampire, and he's been feeding on your mother. I don't think she realizes what's been going on."

Holland looked at Jonas with horror in her eyes. "Vampires are mythological figures; they're not real. Zac sounds psychotic." She gazed at Jonas suspiciously. "How do you know this wanna-be vampire?"

"He's the real deal. Vampires exist," Jonas said in a tone so serious, Holland felt the hairs rising on the back of her neck. "I'm afraid that you're also in danger. There are others and they're attracted to your smell."

Holland hugged herself, her eyes darting around fearfully. "Wh-what do you mean?" she stammered.

"According to Zac, you have a particularly noticeable and attractive scent. He told me that there are other vampires here in Frombleton, and they'll eventually locate you."

"This is crazy! Why are you hanging with a freaking vampire?" she whispered, her voice quivering in terror.

"I...uh. I thought we could be friends."

"Why would you want to befriend a vampire?" Holland was appalled.

"He lied to me. Led me to believe that he was harmless...that he only fed on animals. I'm sorry, Holland."

Holland abruptly stood. "We have to contact the police."

"We can't."

"Why not?"

"They won't believe us. They'll call immigration and deport me and who knows...you could end up in a mental hospital."

"Well, what do you suggest?" she asked in a tiny, fearful voice.

"The best defense is to get your mother to rescind her invitation."

Holland's mouth twisted in indignation. "The best defense

would be to put a stake through that bloodsucker's heart!" Holland spat, erupting into rage.

"That won't be easy. Zac is a powerful vampire."

"Look, I can't sit on my hands while he feeds off my mother. I have to be proactive. I have to do something."

"The first step is to keep him out of your house."

Holland nodded. She felt a shiver of fear as she recalled Zac's presence in her room last night. "What's his Achilles Heel? Garlic...a crucifix? How can I protect my mother and me?"

"He's terrified of sunlight."

Holland could not suppress a gasp. "My mom is avoiding sunshine, too. She has blankets up to the windows in her bedroom. I'll freaking die if my mom starts turning into a vampire!"

"That won't happen." Jonas shook his head.

"How can you be sure?"

"I don't know all there is to know about the vampire lifestyle, but Zac's only interest is in feeding. He hasn't made any new vampires to my knowledge. He doesn't seem to know very much, and I doubt if he has any idea how to spawn a new vampire."

"How long has he been feeding on people?"

"A hundred years or more," Jonas muttered. "That's what he claims, but he lies all the time."

"A century-old vampire probably knows a lot more than he's letting on. You seem like a really sensible person, Jonas. I don't understand why you entered into a friendship with him in the first place. How'd you meet him?"

"He introduced himself. He's a very devious fellow." Jonas lowered his eyes. "Out of desperation, I entered this country illegally. I was scared and vulnerable. Zac led me to believe that he could help me maneuver in this strange, new land. I thought he could assist me in getting a green card." It was a lie, but Jonas couldn't tell Holland the truth about himself.

"Did you know that you were making a deal with a vampire?" The idea was so repulsive, Holland's mouth was twisted in a grimace.

"I thought Zac could help me."

"I can't even wrap my mind around half of what you've told me. It's all so...so mind-boggling. Feels like a nightmare. And it's too much to deal with right now. I'm worried about my mother. I have to get home and warn her," Holland said in a panicked tone.

Jonas stood up. "I postponed my trip to Miami so I could stay here and..." His voice faded. "I stayed behind so I could protect you."

"I appreciate it. But you're only a mortal like me...how can you protect me from a vampire?"

Jonas visibly flinched and then mumbled, "I'll think of something."

Holland took a few hesitant steps away from Jonas, and then stopped and turned around. "I have to go. I'll talk to you later."

"I can stop by later. To check on you." Jonas stared at Holland; his eyes were deeply troubled.

"Give me a call before the sun goes down. I'm safe until then... right?"

Jonas nodded.

CHAPTER 26

All sorts of crazy thoughts ran through Holland's mind as she raced the six blocks to her home. Was Jonas mentally stable? His story was rather farfetched. And he'd failed to specifically tell her the nature of his and the vampire's relationship. God, she hoped that Jonas didn't help lure victims to Zac.

Her thoughts turned to Jarrett and that bandage on his neck? How'd he fit into the scheme of things? Was Zac using Jarrett as a personal blood bank, too?

As cruel as Jarrett had been to her, she needed to put personal feelings aside and give him a call…find out how he was doing. Like her Mom, Jarrett may have also been mesmerized by Zac. Jarrett had a right to know that a charismatic vampire was living among them—and possibly feeding on him.

Holland burst through her front door, and was stunned to find Phoebe in the kitchen bent over her cauldron with a towel tenting her head as she inhaled the steam that rose from the big pot.

"I was so worried about you, Mom. Thank God, you're feeling better!" A mixture of scents filled the air. Holland sniffed, recognizing the smell of cloves, mint, and sassafras.

Phoebe lifted her head from the pot and announced cheerily, "I came up with a healing potion, and it's working. I feel revitalized."

"You look much better. Your face has a little color." Holland scrutinized her mother's neck. "And those bruises are actually starting to fade," Holland noted in amazement.

"You can't keep a good witch down," Phoebe said, laughing. "I couldn't lie in bed all day. It's not my nature to accept illness without putting up a fight."

"Mom, we need to talk," Holland said grimly.

"About what?"

"Your friend, Zac. There's something you should know about him."

Phoebe gazed at her.

"Those bruises and punctures on your neck weren't from mosquitoes. I know it sounds crazy, but I'm not kidding…Zac's a vampire, Mom. He's been biting you."

Holland's mother laughed. "That's hilarious. Zac will get a good laugh when I tell him that you think he's a vampire."

"Mom, I'm serious. He can't come over anymore. You've got to resend your invitation."

"Holland…honey…get a grip. I'm a broadminded person, and I believe that there are supernatural forces, you know…more than meets the eye. I believe in witchcraft and the spirit realm… but vampires?" She shook her head. "I promise you that Zac is a mere mortal. He doesn't bite." Phoebe gave a little chuckle.

"Then how do you explain those puncture wounds?" Holland asked frantically. "A few hours ago, you didn't want sunlight filtering into your bedroom. What do you have to say about that?"

"The light was giving me a headache. But I'm okay now."

Holland shook her head, pityingly. "Zac has you mesmerized. I'm scared for you, Mom. I'm terrified for both of us."

"Zac is a sweet person. He's really harmless. What's come over you?"

"Think about it. He never visits in the daylight. I've had an uneasy feeling about him from the moment you mentioned his name."

"Holland, you're practically hysterical. This isn't like you."

"Call him, Mom," Holland challenged. "I bet you can't get him on the phone until the sun goes down."

"I actually don't know how to reach him; I can't call him. I have to wait for him to contact me."

Holland sighed. "Do me a favor, just humor me. When he calls...or if he takes it upon himself to drop by, please tell him that you rescind your invitation. That's the only way to keep him out of here."

"I don't want to keep him out of here. I enjoy Zac's company. What you're saying is ludicrous."

"Okay, Mom, forget about him being a vampire. But he was in my room last night—watching me while I was asleep. How creepy is that?"

"You were dreaming."

"I know what I saw!" Holland yelled. "Okay, you don't have to believe me, but doesn't the fact that this guy is upsetting me...don't my feelings matter?"

"Of course. But you're not being rational. You're being a little paranoid."

Holland sighed loudly. "What do really know about him, Mom? Nothing! He could be a thief, a sex offender...or something far more sinister. I don't feel safe with him lurking around."

"I don't know why you feel so strongly when you've never actually met him."

"I don't want to meet him." Holland looked her mother in the eyes. "You've always told me to follow my instincts, and my gut tells me that Zac's bad news."

Phoebe made a dismissive gesture. "You're wrong about Zac. He's really nice—"

"Seriously, you need to rescind your invitation," Holland

demanded, her voice high-pitched and shaking. The tremor in her voice was a combination of fear and frustration. Feeling helpless, her eyes welled with tears.

"Oh, sweetie…" Phoebe rushed to Holland's side, wrapping her arms around her daughter. "You don't have to worry about Zac coming around anymore. I'll end the friendship."

Holland breathed an audible sigh of relief.

CHAPTER 27

Jonas had danced around the truth, and he felt guilty. He'd misled Holland, only telling her partial truths. He'd nearly choked when she referred to him as a mortal. If only it were true. Still, he hadn't been completely deceptive. His fate wasn't sealed like Zac's. Zac was a full-fledged vampire—immoral and corrupt.

There was still hope for Jonas. He fought against his base instincts. It tormented him that he'd taken a human life, but since that mishap, he'd refrained from killing. That had to count for something.

He fervently believed that the day would come when he'd be able to walk among the living—not as a creature that savagely feasted on living animals, but as a normal member of the human race.

His cravings were torturous. When Holland greeted him at the entrance of the park, and had thrown her arms around him, he had to pull away from her. Her scent was so strong, it was maddening.

Now as he walked back to the hotel, Jonas ached with need. Hunger was a misery that clawed at his very soul. There were humans in their cars, riding bikes, and walking past him—they were everywhere—and their smells filled his nostrils, tempting and arousing him.

Inhaling deeply, Jonas detected another fragrance that stimulated his hunger. The scent led to a live poultry market on the other side of the street. He instantly began salivating. Changing directions, he walked to the corner and stood waiting for the traffic light to change.

Inside the market, people were lined up at the counter picking out chickens from cages. The market echoed with the squawks of the terrified birds.

In full view of the patrons, the birds were slaughtered by a heavyset man with bushy eyebrows and graying stubble on his face and chin. He wore a black plastic apron and long plastic black gloves. Some chickens were decapitated swiftly, while the necks of others were sliced with a knife and the blood flowed freely into a sink. Jonas's mouth watered as he witnessed blood spurting from the carotid arteries of one bird after another. Trying to control his impulses, he clenched his fists as he impatiently waited his turn.

Unspent money for his trip to Florida lined his pocket. He could purchase several crates filled with chickens to satisfy his hunger, but self-restraint was essential. He'd look extremely odd carrying crates of live chickens back to the hotel.

At the front of the line, finally, Jonas wasn't picky. He chose four random chickens. "I'll take them live, please," Jonas added.

The man wearing the black apron didn't bat an eye. He was apparently accustomed to the occasional customer that preferred to do his own kill.

"Here you go," the man behind the counter said, handing Jonas his purchases.

"Bonjour," Jonas said, slipping into his native tongue.

Casting a furtive glance, he noticed that some of the remaining customers were giving him dirty looks. With his superior olfactory skills, he heard a woman suck her teeth in disgust and then whisper to the woman behind her, "I heard about his kind. That boy's gonna sacrifice those poor chickens in one of those ritual killings."

The chickens were stuffed into paper bags and doubled with plastic. Protesting their captivity, the birds squawked and squealed, making a terrible racket.

Holding the ends of the bags tightly, Jonas took swift steps out of the live poultry market.

⊕ ⊕ ⊕

Jonas had done his best to clean up the mess he'd made in the bathroom of the suite. Chicken feathers were bundled inside trash liners and all the bath towels were covered with the blood and gook he'd wiped off the granite counter.

But with stray feathers here and there, and tiny blood spatters on the walls, the mirror, and other surfaces, the place could use a little extra cleaning.

While Zac was still asleep, it was an opportune time to get the rooms spiffed up and vacuumed. Jonas would make sure that the maid didn't open the closet.

He called the front desk, asking for someone from the housekeeping department to clean the rooms.

"Sorry, housekeeping is gone for the day," said the crisp, professional voice on the other end of the phone.

"Is it possible to get a few cleaning supplies?"

"We certainly can accommodate you, sir. What items do you need?"

Jonas requested plastic liners, cleaning spray, and extra bath towels.

"I'll make sure those items are delivered to room 416. Have a good day, sir," the desk clerk said politely.

His hunger sated and his strength revitalized, Jonas waited for the supplies. It would be at least another hour until Zac rose at sunset. Jonas fantasized about ending Zac's miserable life right now. The simple act of pulling the drapes open and letting sunshine brighten the room would turn the vampire into a heap of ashes.

But Jonas couldn't do that...not as long as there were burning questions that plagued his mind. He needed to know how many other vampires were in the area. And where were their resting places? Zac was the keeper of this vital information, and Jonas intended to get some answers.

While waiting for the supplies to be delivered, Jonas dozed off to sleep with the remote in his hand. Sharp raps on the door jolted him awake. Having no idea how much time had passed, he jumped up and rushed to the door.

He'd opened the door to a mere crack when he heard the closet door sliding open. Jerking around, he saw Zac easing out of his cramped sleeping quarter.

Awakening with a ferocious hunger, it took only milliseconds for Zac to move with lightning speed from the closet to the door. In a swift motion, he yanked the female employee inside the room and locked the door. She made a sound of shock, and the stack of towels and plastic liners fell from her arms.

"Zac, no!" Jonas cried out. Jonas was taken aback by Zac's complexion, which was hauntingly pale from hunger.

Zac placed a white hand around the woman's throat, holding her against the wall. The woman was a petite redhead wearing a hotel-issued uniform: a black skirt and a button down, gray-striped, long-sleeved blouse with the hotel logo imprinted on the left pocket.

Hyperventilating, she took panting breaths. Her eyes bulged wide with shock and fear. Shaking her head, she made an in-coherent, feeble protest.

"Shh!" Zac cautioned, staring into the woman's eyes. "Don't be afraid. It's okay. Shh! Everything's fine and dandy. Do you understand?" He didn't break his intense gaze as he spoke in a low, hypnotizing way.

The woman stood transfixed, nodding her head in a robotic manner.

Zac removed his hand from her neck. "What's your name?"

"Megan," she said in trance-like whisper.

In a gentlemanly fashion, Zac lifted her hand and brought it to his lips. "Nice to make your acquaintance, ma'am."

"Thank you," the woman named Megan replied.

Jonas grabbed Zac by the shoulder, and quickly let go. Zac's shoulder was as cold as a block of ice. "You can't do this, man. Feeding on hotel staff is not an option!" Jonas whisper-shouted.

Zac snarled like a vicious animal and bared fangs that glistened with saliva. Clearly ravenous, Zac's eyes were wild and dangerous.

Jonas was at his wit's end with Zac. Zac's recklessness would bring the police to the door, their guns drawn and eager to open fire on the pair of despicable outlaws. This would be the last day that Jonas spent in the hotel with Zac. Jonas would find his way back to the sugar mill. He'd take refuge there until he made his way to Florida.

"Pull your sleeve up for me, Megan," Zac murmured as seductively as if he were asking her to remove her panties.

Obediently, Megan rolled up her sleeve. With his fingertips, Zac fondled the veined flesh on the inside of her elbow. He bent his head and almost worshipfully, he gently kissed the crook of her arm. Megan let out a soft moan as Zac sank his teeth in the bend of her arm.

Zac withdrew his fangs. Blood flowed freely from the two wounds, running down Megan's arm, and pooling into her slightly cupped hand.

A lingering glance at Megan's bleeding arm caused Jonas's heart to thump with yearning. Unconsciously, he gnashed his teeth and growled deep in his throat. Like a voyeur, Jonas watched with desperate yearning as Zac began leisurely licking the blood that zigzagged down the length of Megan's arm. Megan shivered and moaned as if in ecstasy.

Zac raised her crimson-stained hand to his lips and sipped from the middle of her palm. When the blood stopped flowing, Zac placed blood-rouged lips upon the twin piercings, sucking until Megan's lower lip began to quiver. Her knees buckled as she lost consciousness.

Looking startled, Jonas observed Megan stretched out on the floor with her bottom lip quivering. He mopped nervous perspiration from his forehead. "Is she going to make it?"

Zac lifted Megan effortlessly from the floor and positioned her on the couch. Her limp body slumped to one side. "She'll be fine. A little rest will rejuvenate her."

"But the other hotel staff is going to get suspicious if she stays up here too long. What'll we do if someone comes up here looking for her?"

"We'll tell him that she left."

Jonas wasn't comfortable with the idea. "How long is she going to be unconscious?"

Zac searched the ceiling looking for an answer. "About fifteen minutes or so." Zac bent down and picked up one of the towels that had fallen to the floor. "She'll be a little dizzy at first—staggering somewhat." Zac chuckled and gave a disinterested shrug. He dabbed specks of blood from his lips and then ripped off a piece of the fabric and wrapped it around the woman's injured arm. He carefully pulled her shirtsleeve down over the homemade tourniquet. "Those bites are well hidden. No telltale signs like those others."

"How many humans have you killed, and how many are you keeping alive to feed on?" Jonas inquired.

"I don't keep count."

"Are they all going to turn into vampires...you know, eventually?"

"Only if I decide to turn 'em."

"What's the process for turning someone into a vampire?"

Zac grimaced. "I don't turn people into vampires. There're far too many vampires roaming Frombleton, Georgia, as it is."

"Approximately, how many vampires are in the area?" Jonas prompted.

"Stop prying into matters that don't concern you," Zac snapped.

"I don't understand why you're hanging with me instead of banding together with your own kind."

Zac gestured agitatedly. "They're a new breed of vampires. They prefer hiding in the shadows, keeping up the misconception that vampires are only a myth. During my time, we vampires ruled this town. And I intend to bring back the old ways."

"What do you think happened to the older vampires?"

"They've either died off or left Frombleton."

"Do you think some of the older vampires might be buried... you know...like you were?" Jonas asked, persistently digging for information.

Zac looked at Jonas sneeringly. "Your mind is awfully cluttered with questions about me. Shouldn't you be in Miami by now?"

Moaning miserably, Megan began showing signs of life. Zac and Jonas looked in her direction. "What happened?" she asked groggily. With a befuddled expression, she rubbed her bandaged arm.

"You were partying with me and my friend, over here..." Zac nudged his head toward Jonas.

"Why would I do that?" Megan asked confusedly. She attempted to swing her legs off of the bed, but slumped back, resting her shoulders against the headboard. "Oh, God, what's wrong with me—I feel lightheaded."

Zac laughed. "You had a little too much to drink. But don't worry. What happens in this room stays in this room. We won't speak a word of this to your boss." He winked at Megan.

Jonas shook his head. Zac was a scoundrel of the lowest sort.

Megan pulled her sleeve up and scowled at the makeshift bandage. "Why's my arm bandaged?" Megan looked from Zac's face to Jonas's, waiting for a plausible explanation.

"You had an accident," Zac said in a matter-of-fact tone of voice. "Nothing serious?"

She undid the tourniquet and squinted at the two puncture wounds. "I don't understand how this happened."

"Keep it covered; it shouldn't take long to heal," Zac advised.

Unable to look Megan in the eye, Jonas guiltily shifted his eyes away.

"B-but, how did I get hurt?"

"With one of those little two-pronged forks. You know—the kind used for spearing olives?"

"That makes no sense!" Determinedly, Megan got to her feet. "I'm calling security."

"You're not calling anybody! Now hush up, and stop giving me so much lip!" Zac gripped Megan by her shoulders and gazed into her eyes. Megan's eyelashes fluttered briefly and then her eyes became wide and unblinking.

"You belong to me now, little missy," Zac said contemptuously. "Do you understand?"

"I understand." Megan spoke in a haunted whisper, as if some part of her consciousness objected to Zac's command, but she was without the strength to defy him.

"What time will you finish up with your hotel duties?"

"Eleven o'clock," Megan said in the same whispery voice.

"Okay, then. Go on back to your hotel duties, but when you finish, come on back up here, so I can feed without any distractions."

"I understand. I'll be back."

Robotically, Megan turned around.

"Megan!" Zac barked her name, his harsh tone snapping her out of the trance. "It was mighty nice of you to bring those supplies to our room."

"No problem, sir. Is there anything else I can do for you?" Megan responded in a crisp, professional tone.

"That'll be all for now." Zac ushered Megan to the door.

"Megan will be my eleven o'clock cocktail—a tasty replacement for Phoebe Manning," Zac said, sounding self-satisfied.

"You can hunt anywhere you please. Why risk discovery by feeding on a hotel employee?"

"Because I'm a risk taker. I do as I damn well please. What do you want from me? You asked me to give up your sweetheart's mother, and I'm trying to honor your wishes, but if you keep pushing me, I don't know…" His voice trailed off. "I may end up drinking a double cocktail—your little darling and her dear mother!"

CHAPTER 28

With the shocking revelation that there were vampires living in Frombleton, Holland found herself jumping at shadows as soon as the sun went down. Concerned about Holland's mental well-being, her mother kept knocking on her bedroom door, checking to make sure that she was all right.

It was obvious that her mother had only agreed to disinvite Zac in order to appease Holland's paranoia.

Halfheartedly watching TV while anxiously waiting for Jonas to call, Holland's mind wandered to the people she considered suspect. Zac was a vampire for sure. And Phoebe's client, Rebecca Pullman, had exhibited vampire-ish tendencies. Jarrett, too, now that he was hiding bite marks beneath a Band-Aid. On second thought, Jarrett probably wasn't a full-fledged vampire; he was merely a victim—like her mother.

Holland wondered who had bitten Jarrett: Zac? Rebecca? Or one of the underground swarm?

Holland's phone buzzed with a text from Naomi, stating that she was on her way over and that she had some big news to share.

When Naomi rang the bell, Holland clicked on the porch light and opened the door for her friend. "What brings you out tonight?" Holland arched a brow. Naomi's strict parents didn't allow her to roam around at night, unsupervised. With the news of the vampire situation in Frombleton, Holland looked over Naomi's shoulder, actually hoping to see the family car with one of Naomi's parents waiting behind the wheel.

"Your parents let you walk over here, alone?"

"They don't know I'm here. Holland, I have big, big news, but you have to swear that you won't mention this to a soul," Naomi whispered as she followed Holland to her bedroom.

Holland closed her bedroom door…and locked it, in case her mother felt the need to peek in on her again. "You can trust me, Naomi. Besides, who am I going to tell? You're my only friend?"

I've been bursting to tell you," Naomi said excitedly as she bounced down on Holland's bed. "I'm in love! Head over heels… crazy in love!"

"You can't be serious? How could you keep something like that from me?"

"You were an emotional wreck after your date from hell with Jarrett. The timing didn't seem right."

"Well, I'm completely over him now," Holland pointed out. "So who is this guy, and how'd you meet him?"

Naomi took a deep breath, and began gesturing animatedly. "His name is Ryan Sullivan. We met at my dad's company picnic. Ryan was there with his parents. His mother is on the board of directors at my dad's job. You're not gonna believe this part…"

Holland peered at Naomi, waiting for her to continue.

"Our parents have become good friends, and my mom and dad totally approve of Ryan. They gave me permission to go out with him tonight."

Holland was stunned. "Your dad is breaking his 'you can't date until you're eighteen' rule?"

"Yes! Ryan and I are going to the movies while our parents attend a high society fundraiser." Naomi giggled. "My dad had to rent a tux; he said he hasn't worn one since before I was born."

"So, your parents are rubbing elbows with socialites, huh?" Holland teased.

"Yeah, and they're pretty excited. The Sullivans have this old-fashioned Southern charm, and my folks like them a lot. I'm glad my parents have new, interesting friends that can distract them from hovering over me," Naomi said, laughing.

"I don't remember a kid named Ryan Sullivan; does he go to Frombleton High?"

"Not yet; he'll be enrolling when school starts. He's a senior," Naomi said proudly. "The Sullivans are new in town. They live in one of those big houses on the other side of the highway—in fact, he lives in Jarrett's neighborhood."

So Ryan and his parents were members of the upper crust. Holland wondered what they had in common with Naomi's working-class parents.

Stealthily, Naomi took out a large Ziploc bag that was filled with makeup items. "I figured I'd sneak over here and get beautified for my new man," Naomi said with a wink. She pulled the elastic band from around her ponytail and shook out her curly, light brown hair.

"I told Ryan to pick me up here at your place. I have a half-hour to get my face on." Naomi began smoothing foundation all over her face and neck. Next, she swiped her cheek areas with a bronzer, applied a trio of earth tone eye shadow, mascara, dark eyeliner, and glossy red lips. With her makeup trickery and techniques, Naomi quickly morphed from drab to diva in a matter of minutes!

"You look amazing," Holland said. It was on the tip of her tongue to warn Naomi about the swarm of vampires, but Naomi was a science geek girl; she didn't believe in mythical creatures. She relied on facts.

Do vampires attack couples? Holland wondered. *Probably not. They conduct their bloodsucking activities in secrecy.* After a dreadful struggle with herself, Holland decided that she'd wait until tomorrow to emphatically warn Naomi about the vampires. It was not likely that Naomi would get attacked in a movie theater filled with people.

Ryan arrived and made his presence known by repeatedly honking his horn.

Phoebe called out from the kitchen, "Someone's blowing a car horn outside. Are you expecting someone, Holland?"

"That's Naomi's date. She'll be right out."

"He's usually such a gentleman; I don't know why he's being so rude. I better hurry. I'll introduce you at another time." Naomi gave Holland an apologetic look.

"It's okay. Have fun, Naomi."

Jamming the Ziploc bag filled with makeup inside her handbag, Naomi rushed out of Holland's bedroom.

Through the living room window, Holland watched Naomi get in Ryan's car—a silver Mercedes. *Nice!* Ryan seemed like a total jerk in Holland's opinion. The way he was impatiently honking his horn did not give her a good first impression. But Naomi was happy, and for her friend's sake, she hoped Ryan wasn't as obnoxious as he seemed.

⊕ ⊕ ⊕

Slouched in a chair with one leg dangling over the arm of the chair, Jonas absently ran a finger over the strange markings on the sole of his foot. Clutching his ankle, he examined the scars. They didn't seem as pronounced or as deeply etched into his skin. Was it wishful thinking or were the scars beginning to fade? And what did that mean? Would the evil spell break soon?

Zac was in another room, watching CNN. He enjoyed keeping abreast of current events. He learned modern expressions, educated himself, and had a better understanding of today's world from watching TV in general.

Jonas was bored. Babysitting Zac was inconvenient, but a necessary measure to keep the vampire from getting close to Holland. Until her mother rescinded her invitation, Zac was free to visit the Manning household whenever the mood struck him. And Jonas was sticking to him like glue, making sure that he didn't get anywhere near Holland.

Jonas had promised to call Holland, but he couldn't. There was no privacy when Zac was awake. Not much escaped Zac, with his mind-reading abilities and his superior hearing and vision.

In an attempt to keep Zac from knowing his private thoughts about Holland, Jonas denied himself the pleasure of remembering the taste of her lips...her glorious scent. Instead of thinking about Holland, he focused on Haiti, recalling his mother's face. Imagining her happiness when she received the money he'd sent. But he needed much more. Paying back the interest fees alone for his passage to America would cost well over a thousand dollars. And where would he get that kind of money?

Silent as a cat, Zac crept into the room and seemed to materialize next to the chair where Jonas sat.

Jonas flinched, startled by Zac's sudden presence. "Why can't you enter a room like a normal person?"

"I'm not a normal person." Zac wore a sardonic smile. "I've been listening to your thoughts, and if you're worried about money, we can barter some of my treasures in exchange for cash," Zac said, responding to the question Jonas had posed in his mind.

"I didn't ask for your help," Jonas said with hostility.

"I'm not trying to rile you, fella. Just being helpful. There's places that provide those kinds of services... I believe they're called

pawnshops. As you know, I have an excellent collection of jewelry…
high quality diamonds, gold watches, and all sorts of precious gems.
All locked in the safe." Zac's lips curved into a taunting smile.

"I was raised to be hardworking and honest; I can't accept any
more of your illegal acquisitions."

"To each his own. Meanwhile, your family is being harassed by
ruffians."

"You may have extraordinary vision, but you can't see all the
way to Haiti; you don't know how my family is doing. I sent them
money, and I'm sure they're fine!"

Zac smirked and narrowed his eyes. "I've been around a lot
more years than you have, and I understand the nature of violent
men. Those money lenders will use any means necessary to get
payment—even forcibly take what they want from women."

Outraged that Zac would even suggest that his mother would
be violated, Jonas threw a punch at Zac, but ended up striking at
the thin air.

Pulling a vampire trick, Zac avoided the blow by moving more
rapidly than Jonas's eyes could follow. With lightning-quick
speed, Zac whizzed to the other side of the room and then he was
suddenly standing behind Jonas. Jonas sprang to his feet. Intending
to floor the pompous vampire, he threw a series of punches. Each
one missed the target.

"Temper, temper," Zac taunted, his voice coming from the
dining room. And then in the blink of an eye he stood next to
Jonas again. Jonas threw up his hands, ready to fight.

"Enough!" Zac shouted. "Face it…trying to keep up with me
is a waste of energy," he said in a softened tone. "Listen, the
atmosphere is tense; I believe some fresh night air will lighten
the mood. Care to join me in a drive?" Zac asked.

Breathing hard from anger and physical exertion, Jonas asked wearily, "Do I have a choice? If I don't go with you, you might find an excuse to visit Holland's mother," Jonas said disgustedly.

"I gave you my word, so please stop harping on that subject. I have other donors, you know. By the way, Megan will be tapping on the door at eleven o'clock sharp. You've probably worked up an appetite with all that useless shadowboxing, so it's perfectly understandable if you prefer to regain your strength by feeding on Megan."

"You're despicable," Jonas groused. Slipping on his shoes, he trailed behind Zac and left the suite.

⊕ ⊕ ⊕

Zac's car was an old model, but it ran like a dream. Riding shotgun, Jonas didn't ask any questions when Zac steered in the direction of Burke's Highway. If the crafty vampire had gone even a mile toward the vicinity of Holland's neighborhood, her scent would have alerted Jonas, and he would have pounced on Zac before the vampire could whoosh out of the driver's seat.

Remarkably, Zac kept his word. He drove into a lovely residential area. After parking in front of an attractive stone house on Meadowbrook Lane, he cut the engine.

Jonas looked left and right, questioningly. "Who lives here?"

"A generous donor," Zac retorted. Zac began staring at the house with an unwavering, intense gaze. Jonas had seen that look in Zac's eyes earlier when he'd mesmerized the hotel employee.

The front door opened and a vaguely familiar teenage boy emerged. Walking with no will of his own, the boy took slow steps toward the car. As he grew nearer, Jonas recognized him. It was the boy that Zac had attacked and overpowered inside the arcade. The boy didn't look the same. His once tanned and glowing skin had turned sallow. He was so unhealthily skinny; his eyes were sunken in their sockets.

Jonas shrank back in shame. The boy was a shell of his former, athletic self. And Jonas had had a hand in negatively altering the young man's future.

"You're looking damn near drained," Zac quipped when the boy approached the car. "I don't even know if I should bother with you. You might not have enough blood in your veins to satisfy me."

The boy stood rigidly next to car, waiting for Zac to give a command.

"Should I tap into your skimpy blood supply?" Zac asked sneeringly.

"Yes, I aim to please you, sir," the teen said robotically.

Zac let out a joyous hoot and elbowed Jonas. "Did you hear that? He said he aims to please me. Now, that's power, Jonas. That's the kind of power you'll never realize as long as you're chasing after squirrels and possum."

"Get in the car, Jarrett. There's not much left of you, so tonight I might as well go ahead and drain you." He nodded. "Yeah, you're just skin and bones; it's time to finish you off."

Jonas stole a glance at the miserable teen. There had to be something he could to do to save him. "You're not as smart as I thought," Jonas said to Zac.

"Pardon me?" Offended, Zac scowled.

"Why kill off a willing provider? Let the boy rest for about a month—give him a chance to gain some weight and let his blood supply replenish."

"Hmm. Now you're using your noggin, Jonas." Zac smiled briefly, and then looked off in thought. "Your suggestion will appease my future hunger, but what am I supposed to do right now—pay Phoebe Manning a visit?"

"Absolutely not!" Jonas said in fury.

"Well, I have to feed and I can't wait until Megan comes to see me at eleven o'clock." Zac turned and gazed at Jarrett in the back seat. "Where's that girl you're always cuddled up with?"

"Chaela, sir?"

"Is that your sweetheart's name?"

"Yes."

"Well, where is she?"

"At home, I guess. Or maybe out with her friends."

"Give her a call on that talking piece of yours," Zac instructed.

Zac promptly slid his phone out of his pocket and called Chaela. "She's not picking up," he said without expression.

"She's sneaking around on you, boy," Zac said snidely, trying to get a rise out of Jarrett.

Jarrett merely nodded.

"Don't you want to get even with that lowdown cheat?"

"It doesn't matter much," Jarrett replied in a monotonous, droning tone of voice.

"It should matter!" Zac declared, indignant. "I know you're sickly and all, but that ain't no reason to let a woman walk all over you." He glowered at the boy, but Jarrett didn't change his blank expression.

"We're taking a ride to Chaela's house. I'll deal with that no-good, floozy. Point the way, Jarrett." Zac shifted out of the parking gear.

Sounding more like a computer-generated voice on a GPS navigation system than a human being, Jarrett provided precise directions to Chaela's house.

Feeling powerless, Jonas slumped in his seat. His helpful tip had backfired, and now Zac was going after a new victim.

CHAPTER 29

He'd promised to call, but it was after nine and she still hadn't heard from him. Holland had tried to distract herself by watching a slew of reality shows, but she couldn't shake the feeling that something bad had happened to Jonas. Her state of panic rose as her thoughts raced, *Where could he be, and why doesn't he call me? Is he in trouble?* She thought about calling the police, but what could she tell them? Her concerns would be dismissed as a crank call if she expressed her fear that Jonas was in the clutches of a vampire.

By ten-thirty, Holland was certain that Zac had turned on Jonas and had sucked the life out of him. Sitting up in bed and twisting the coverlet in her hands, Holland was now close to tears. All her fretting and imagining that the worst had happened was a waste of time. She needed to *do* something. Maybe her mom could offer some advice. Holland knocked and then peeked inside her mother's bedroom. She let out a sigh of frustration. Her mother hardly ever went to bed this early, but she was dead to the world.

Forlorn, Holland trekked back to her room and plopped down on her bed. Eyeing her phone, she tried to will it to ring. *Call me, Jonas; I'm so worried.*

Suddenly her phone buzzed, and Holland grabbed it with shaky hands. When she checked the screen, disappointment washed over her. No message from Jonas; it was a text from Naomi. "Super big news! Be over in ten minutes, okay?"

Holland texted back, "Okay," but her heart wasn't in it.

Naomi's life was finally in a good place, and Holland was thrilled for her friend, but she wasn't in the mood for another discussion about Naomi's budding love affair. Holland was far too worried about Jonas to put on a happy face. She mulled it over briefly, and decided that tonight simply wasn't a good time for a visit.

The doorbell chimed before Holland had a chance to tell Naomi that she'd changed her mind. Not wanting the sound of the doorbell to wake her mother, Holland hurried through the darkened living room. Without stopping to turn on a light, she rushed straight to the front door. Snatching it open, she expected to find Naomi standing in the doorframe, but there wasn't a soul in sight.

"Naomi?" Holland murmured, poking her head outside, looking around for her friend. "Naomi!" Holland called again in a sharper voice, and then stepped out on the porch. "Stop being silly! You're too old to play doorbell Dixie."

Where'd she go? Holland wondered fearfully. Was that blood-sucker, Zac, hanging outside of her door? Had he snatched Naomi?

Holland felt a stab of fear. Shadows cast by bushes and trees seemed to loom ominously. "Seriously, Naomi…I'm not in the mood for stupid pranks. You'd better get inside before I call it a night and put the bolt on the door." Holland tried to sound tough, but her voice trembled. She cast her gaze in the direction of the hedges, but Naomi was nowhere to be found. *This is sooo creepy.*

A sudden rush of cold air whisked past Holland as she turned to go inside. Peering around uneasily, she gave the front yard one last glance, and then closed the door and locked it. Intending to send Naomi a harsh text, Holland moved through the dark living room, carefully avoiding bumping into furniture as she headed for her bedroom.

"Hey, Holland." Inside the darkness of Holland's living room, Naomi's singsong voice emerged out of nowhere.

Holland gasped. Her hand flew to her chest. "Oh, shit! Ohmigod, Naomi. You scared the crap of me. Where were you? How'd you get in here?"

Naomi laughed. "I scooted in while you were looking in the other direction. Just kidding around—pulling a prank."

"Some prank! You nearly scared me out of my wits." In the dark, Holland edged her way toward the floor lamp.

"No lights," Naomi said in a stern tone.

"What do you mean, no lights? You're being weird." Holland inched closer to the lamp and reached out, her hand waving around searching for the switch beneath the lampshade.

"Leave it off!" Naomi insisted, her voice cold and menacing.

"Screw you!" Holland retorted and twisted the knob, filling the room with bright light.

One look at Naomi and Holland's legs nearly gave out. Naomi was lounging comfortably on the sofa with an arm outstretched in a glamour pose. But there was nothing glamorous about Naomi. Beneath her badly smeared makeup, her complexion was deathly white. Two grotesque puncture marks decorated her throat and the front of her top was caked with drying blood.

Naomi stood up. Drawing her lips back in a macabre smile, she flashed a set of fangs that dripped saliva.

"Ohmigod, you got bitten! Oh, Naomi...I should have warned you about the vampires."

Grinning demonically, Naomi took steps toward Holland.

"Stay away from me, Naomi," Holland said, her voice quaking with fear.

Naomi laughed mockingly. Her laughter was a coarse and hollow sound. "There's no reason to be afraid, Holland. The change doesn't hurt at all. Ryan was really gentle with me," she said dreamily.

"Ryan did this to you?" Holland said shrilly. Realizing that Ryan was part of the swarm, Holland felt a chill rippling through her. Goose bumps rose on her arms and the back of her neck.

Naomi nodded, a semblance of a smile curving one corner of her mouth. She stared at Holland, and Holland felt instantly drawn into Naomi's hypnotic gaze.

"We've been best friends our whole lives, and I don't want that to change," Naomi said in hypnotizing voice. "I was afraid that going to different schools would put a strain on our friendship, but now we don't have to worry about that, do we? Now we can be best friends forever—literally."

"Oh, no we can't," Holland screamed in her mind, but she nodded dumbly as Naomi glided closer. Holland tried to cry out for her mother, but she couldn't utter a sound. She struggled to move, to run for her life, but for some inexplicable reason, she stood transfixed and immobilized, listening to Naomi making plans for them to be BFF's throughout eternity.

Naomi sniffed deeply. "You smell wonderful, Holland. Delicious in fact. I wish Ryan could experience this with me, but he said I had to learn to hunt on my own. You should be honored that I chose you to be the first of my line."

Naomi's reasoning was totally skewed and irrational, and Holland cautiously backed away from her. With a determined look in her eyes, Naomi advanced toward Holland. When Holland felt Naomi's cold powerful fingers wrap around her wrist, she shrieked as loudly as if she'd been burned.

"Holland, what's wrong? What's going on, hon?" Phoebe called out, awakened by her daughter's sound of distress. Immediately, there was the sound of her slippers, swiftly slapping against the hardwood floor. When she reached the living room, she let out a blood-curdling scream, and then covered her mouth, gawking at Naomi in utter disbelief.

Held in Naomi's icy grasp, Holland shivered noticeably. "Naomi's been turned," Holland whimpered tearfully.

"Turned into what?" Phoebe shrieked, her eyes shifting from Holland's terrified face to the pale hand that was clasped tightly around her daughter's wrist.

"She's been bitten. Naomi's a vampire, Mom." Twisting her wrist, Holland tried to wrench free, but Naomi tightened her grasp.

Naomi glowered at Holland's mother. Furious over the interference, she threw her head back and let out a growl, snarling like an animal that instinctually snaps and bites anything that tries to separate it from its food.

"Let her go, Naomi. Please!" Holland's mother tearfully pleaded, her arms held out for Holland.

Outraged, Naomi shrieked. The sound was ghastly. Inhuman. "Holland has to be with me; she's my best friend!" Naomi wailed, her voice at an unnaturally high pitch.

Naomi suddenly released Holland. Her eyes blazing with hatred, she shot across the across the room with uncanny speed. Exhibiting unusual strength, she lifted Holland's mother off of the floor, with one hand wrapped around her neck. Holland's mother gurgled and tried to scream, but the sound was cut off.

Running at full speed, Holland plowed into Naomi, but her friend didn't budge. With a look of distaste, Naomi tossed Holland's mother aside as if she were a rotting sack of potatoes.

Phoebe Manning lay crumpled on the floor, unconscious, and

unable to protect her daughter from the soulless fiend who'd invaded their home.

"Be with me, Holland," Naomi appealed desperately. "I need you." Her cold hands cupped Holland's face and once again, she mesmerized Holland with her penetrating gaze. "Ryan has lots of friends. You can get a new boyfriend—one who'll never leave you. Let's do this—together. Immortality is better than normal life. Come on, it'll be so much fun."

Holland realized that Naomi was mouthing off a lot of vampire propaganda that she'd gotten from Ryan. But unable to resist Naomi's penetrating gaze and her hypnotic voice, Holland released a sigh and nodded in agreement. Naomi smiled in triumph and threw her head back and opened her mouth wide.

Holland shuddered as she anticipated the death bite. She felt the pressure and heard the crunch of Naomi's oversized canines breaking the skin, but oddly, it didn't hurt. It was more like a tingling sensation as Naomi's sharp teeth slid through neck tissue. Naomi surrounded the fresh, spurting wound with her mouth, her lips tugging on Holland's punctured vein.

Holland felt paralyzed as Naomi greedily sucked the life force from her body. Weakened, her knees buckled. Her arms flailed as she tried vainly to push Naomi away. The room grew dim and she realized she was dying.

Death was speeding toward her. Too soon. She was only sixteen; she wasn't ready to die.

But wait. This wasn't a final death; Naomi was turning her into a vampire.

Nooo! I don't want to be a vampire.

In the midst of slurping hungrily, Naomi suddenly made a painful, gurgling sound. She pushed Holland's weak body away from her and began vomiting blood.

Unable to stand upright, Holland slumped down into a chair, watching with horror as Naomi doubled over, throwing up her guts.

"It's burning," Naomi cried in a mournful voice that sounded like her pre-vampire self.

"What's burning?" Holland asked in a hoarse whisper.

"Your blood!" Naomi shrieked. "Your goddamn blood is like acid, burning me from the inside. What did you do to me?" Naomi writhed and howled in agony as her pale skin turned red and quickly became covered in hideous boils that popped and then oozed yellow pus.

On the floor, Holland's mother stirred.

"Mom!" Holland cried.

Using the arm of the sofa, Holland's mother pulled herself to her feet and then staggered over to her daughter, hugging her and crying, "Are you all right, Holland?"

"I think so. Naomi bit me." Holland pointed to the wounds on her neck. "She bit me the way Zac bit you, only she wasn't going to stop until she turned me into a vampire, too."

On the other side of the room, Naomi let out a long, agonizing wail. Huddled together, Holland and Phoebe gawked at Naomi in revulsion as layers of skin peeled away from her face, her arms, and her legs. They watched in amazement as Naomi's hands became distorted with blisters and then began melting. Resembling candle wax, her skin turned into a thick, white liquid that poured down between her fingers and dripped off the ends of her fingernails.

Loud crackling sounds and the acrid smell of sizzling hair filled the air as Naomi's light brown curls caught fire.

"Help me, help me, Holland." Naomi extended a pleading hand, and attempted to rush toward Holland, but she became stuck in place when the soft flesh of her feet began melting. Bubbling, liquid flesh poured out over her sandals, leaving lava-like, steaming puddles on the floor.

In less than five minutes, Naomi's entire body had turned into a fetid pool in the middle of the living room floor.

Tears fell from Holland's eyes. "Poor Naomi. She couldn't help herself. Her new boyfriend changed her. I told you there were vampires in Frombleton, but you wouldn't believe me, Mom."

"I know, I know. I'm so sorry," her mother soothed, stroking Holland's hair while grimacing at Naomi's remains.

"Zac and Ryan aren't the only ones—there's a horde of blood addicts lurking out there! We have to keep them away from us!"

CHAPTER 30

J arrett's girlfriend wasn't home and she wasn't at any of the places where she usually hung out.

Zac glared at Jonas. "This plan of yours is failing miserably. The hunger is on me, and I can't see any reason why I should spare this here no-account boy." Zac pointed to Jarrett, who sat quietly in the back seat.

Jonas shook his head. "Draining him would be a big mistake. He lives in that big house and his parents must be people of means. They'll alert the police. So far, you've fed without repercussions. But if you continue leaving blood-drained victims, the authorities are going to hunt you down. And in a small town like this, I'm sure they'll find you. They'll find us! We'll both be brought to justice. They'll bury us alive!" Jonas added passionately.

Zac didn't respond, but he winced when Jonas mentioned being buried alive.

"Take the boy home," Jonas appealed to Zac. "We can cruise around and find someone else. But you have to promise me there won't be any killing."

"I promise," Zac said grudgingly. He turned the car around and returned to Meadowbrook Drive. "Where's your ma and pa?" Zac asked Jarrett. "If you invite me into your house, it'll save me a lot of gas and driving around time."

"My parents are out for the evening," Jarrett said dully.

"Dang!" Zac shook his head in frustration. "Listen here, boy, I want you to go in the house and eat yourself a big ol' meal. You need to put on some pounds so you can get your blood flowing right. Your blood used to be sweet and thick as molasses. But here lately, it's gone sour…and it's thin like water." Zac's turned his mouth down in complaint. "Get going, boy," he hissed and hit a button, unlocking the back door.

Jarrett got out of the car and took slow, faltering steps to his front door.

"I thought that big, strapping lad would keep me supplied with blood on a regular basis, but he turned out to be nothing more than a puny weakling," Zac spat as he watched Jarrett moving with a slow, unsteady gait.

As Zac slid the gear into reverse, Jonas noticed a car approaching. The car, a Mercedes sedan, came to a stop next to Zac's car. The tinted window of the Mercedes slid down. The driver was a thirty-something man, dressed in a tuxedo. Though handsome, the man had eerily pale skin, cold blue eyes, and jet-black hair. Seated next to him was a beautiful woman with skin as white as alabaster. She also had raven-colored hair. Her glossy mane streamed down her back. Her strapless evening gown showed off pale, well-toned shoulders. A teenage boy sat in the back of the Mercedes. He had the full lips of the woman and the icy blue eyes of the man.

"Good evening, Zacharias." There wasn't a trace of a Southern accent; in fact, the man spoke in the manner of a refined British nobleman.

Zac did a double take; his astonished expression suggested that he'd seen a ghost. Rendered speechless, Zac's mouth opened and closed wordlessly.

The elegant gentleman chuckled. "I heard that you were back

in town, but assumed it was a baseless rumor. After all, I personally condemned you to spend eternity in the ground."

They're vampires! Jonas thought, his mind racing and panicked.

Zac cleared his throat and said, "You ain't got any jurisdiction over me, Constable Sullivan," Zac hissed. "Not any more. I'm a self-taught man and I've done a heap of learning since we last met. You violated my rights when you had me tossed in that hole in the ground."

"According to whose law?" Constable Sullivan said belligerently. "According to today's laws; now, back off of me!"

"We don't abide by mortal law and order. We live by the vampire code." He waggled his long, white finger. "Now, I don't know how you were able to crawl out of the grave we put you in, but you were sentenced to spend eternity in the earth, and I'm going to see to it that you serve out your sentence. You mark my word, Zacharias Hamilton!" The window of the Mercedes glided upward, and the family of vampires drove off into the night.

"What was that all about?" Jonas asked.

"It ain't any of your concern," Zac said snidely.

Instead of pulling out of his parking space, Zac sat behind the wheel with the motor idling. Jonas noticed that the vampire was shaking and sweating.

"You seem upset, Zac. And from the sounds of things, your fellow vampires are going to be coming after you. Maybe I can help."

Zac looked at Jonas and arched a brow. "Maybe so. If we work together, we might be able to find a way to lure those blasted vampires together in one place."

Jonas nodded. "That's something to consider. I'm surprised that you bumped into someone from the old days. I thought you said that all the vampires here in Frombleton were of a new breed?"

"That's what I thought. But that annoying, uppity constable is still alive and kicking. His wife and son, Ryan, seem to be thriving as well. The Sullivans are one of the oldest and most respected vampire families in the nation. I thought ol' Martin Sullivan was long gone." Zac let out a weary sigh.

"You were buried by your own kind—how come? What was your crime?" Jonas pried.

"Maybe you should ask Mrs. Sullivan that question," Zac said with a telling wink.

"Pretty lady," Jonas acknowledged.

Zac grunted and pulled away from the curb. "So, are you gonna help save my hide?"

"Sure. We don't always get along, but we have to stick together. It wouldn't give me any pleasure for you to get overpowered by an angry, vampire mob." Jonas fought to control his thoughts; keeping his mind off Holland wasn't easy, and so he chattered endlessly.

"We need to hatch a plan, but I can't think on an empty stomach. It's time to go hunting. Are you ready to chow down on some human flesh and blood?"

"No! And I advise you to stick to the agreement. You'll drink enough blood to stave off the hunger, but you won't kill anyone," Jonas ordered, stern-faced. Jonas was feeling the pain of hunger as well, but he refused to hunt down human beings.

Taking unpaved, back roads, Zac drove to the outskirts of Frombleton and made his way to Tulley's Tavern. Rosie's white van was parked in the lot.

"I guess she got her job back," Jonas commented.

"Looks that way." Zac parked and turned off the ignition. "Do you think those drugs are out of her system yet?"

Jonas shrugged.

"Coming in?" Zac asked.

"No, I'll wait in the car," Jonas said.

Zac sauntered toward the bar, and Jonas was relieved to have some space from Zac. With Zac inside the bar, holed up in some dark cubby slurping blood from Rosie's neck, Jonas was free to think about Holland.

Relief turned to pure delight when Jonas spotted a pay phone outside the bar. Digging in his pockets for change, he raced to the phone.

Holland's phone rang only once. "Hello?" she said breathlessly.

"Holland, it's Jonas."

"Where are you? Are you all right?"

"Yes."

"Oh, God, what a relief. I thought you'd been hurt...or killed."

"No, no, nothing as drastic as that," he said with a light chuckle. "I'm fine. Sorry I didn't call earlier, but I've been delayed with Zac."

"You were right, Jonas," Holland said in a hushed voice. "There really is a vampire swarm here in Frombleton. And tonight, something terrible happened."

Jonas felt his heart clench. "What?"

"My friend..." Holland's voice cracked. "My best friend, Naomi, was bitten by some vampire kid named Ryan. She came over here and tried...ohmigod, it was so unreal...I can't bear to talk about it. I wish I could get the image out of my mind."

"What happened?" Jonas asked, his voice raised in panic. The name Ryan rang a bell. Jonas nodded in recollection; Ryan was the teenage son sulking in the back seat of the Mercedes.

"Naomi bit me," Holland blurted. "She wanted to turn me into a vampire so we could be together forever, but she got sick during the process. Right after she drank my blood, her skin started bubbling and peeling, and she was screaming that my blood was like acid." Holland paused. Sniffling and whimpering, she cried softly. "My mom wants to call her parents, but I'm so scared, I don't know what to do. Ryan's parents may have gotten to them."

Jonas recalled the Sullivans sitting smugly in their car. Had they been on their way home after their nightly kill? The wife, Olivia Sullivan, had primly blotted her lips, and now Jonas suspected that it wasn't lipstick that had left a red stain on the tissue.

"Mom wants to call the police, but I begged her not to…I don't think they'll be able to help."

Jonas's heart thundered inside his chest. His worst fear had been realized. A vampire had gotten to Holland's best friend and used her to go after Holland. He thought about what Holland had said about her blood…that it burned like acid. What was that about? Jonas wondered.

"I need to see you, Jonas. I'm so scared. Can you come over?"

He'd been worried about keeping Zac away from Holland, and now he had to worry about an entire swarm. Holland was in danger, and Jonas had no idea how to protect her. But he knew for a fact that he was willing to risk his life to save her.

"Listen to me carefully, Holland. I'm outside the city at the moment, but I'll be back in Frombleton as soon as possible. In the meantime, I want you to stay inside. Don't go out for any reason, and for God's sake, don't invite anyone over—not friends, not Naomi's parents, not the police…no one! According to Zac, you have a special scent that attracts vampires."

Holland gasped and brought her arm up to her nose and began sniffing deeply. "What kind of scent?"

"Very pleasant; makes you irresistible to vampires."

"Oh, God, you're really freaking me out, Jonas. My scent draws vamps like a magnet?"

"Yes, I'm sorry to say. But you need to know. The good news is that a vampire can't cross your threshold without an invitation."

"Other than Naomi, the only invitation I've extended is to you, Jonas," Holland said sincerely.

"Then you have nothing to worry about." From the corner of his eye, Jonas saw Zac emerging from the bar. "Look, I have to go. Don't be afraid, Holland. You're safe as long as you stay inside."

Seeming to possess renewed zest, Zac walked jauntily to the car. Jonas hung up the phone and walked across the gravelly parking lot. He opened the passenger door and slid in.

"Checking in with your sweetheart?" Zac said with a sly grin.

Jonas nodded warily, and instantly began masking his thoughts, exchanging thoughts of Holland with mental pictures of hunting possum in the woods.

"Judging by your thoughts, you didn't catch any critters while you were out here waiting for me."

"No, there's more of a selection in the woods near the hotel."

"All those warm bodies in the bar and you want to hunt possum. Now, that's a daggone shame." Zac shook his head and sneered.

"It's my choice, and I'm okay with it."

Zac rubbed his stomach. "Me, myself…I'm full as a tic. Rosie must have cleaned herself up, because once I got to sucking on her warm blood, it was so dang tasty, I couldn't stop."

Zac backed out of the lot, and zoomed down the road. "I left her for drunk, slumped on a chair in a dark corner with a drink in her hand. By the time someone discovers her bloodless body, I'll be in a deep sleep, dreaming about the sugary taste of your sweetheart's mother's blood."

"You killed Rosie?" Jonas asked, astonished. The wisecrack about Holland's mother didn't go past him, but he chose not to address it.

"Didn't mean to, but hey…shit happens."

"And what about Hugo?"

Zac broke into a wicked grin. "It was a slow night at Tulley's. Hugo seemed bored, so I asked him to neglect his bouncer duties for a minute and join Rosie and me. I had myself a ménage à trois with those two. Rosie's drained dry, but Hugo might have about a half pint of blood left in him." Zac let out a guffaw, slapping the steering wheel as he shook with laughter.

CHAPTER 31

Holland had raced to her bedroom when her phone chirped. She felt let down when Jonas had suddenly ended the call. *My scent attracts vamps. Ew!*

"Was that Naomi's parents calling?" Phoebe inquired, looking worried when Holland returned to the living room.

"No, it was a friend of mine…a boy named Jonas. He's going to come over and help us figure this out."

"We don't need help from a teenage boy. We need a sorcerer, a SWAT team, or a priest!" Holland's mother was shivering and visibly upset.

A sudden popping sound drew Holland and her mother's attention. They crept across the room and gaped down at the heap of fizzing remains that used to be Naomi.

"I should have warned Naomi. I feel so responsible for what happened to her."

"It's not your fault, hon." Phoebe put an arm around her. "You have no reason to feel guilty."

"Yes, I do! I knew there were vampires out there, but I never suspected her new boyfriend was a vamp," Holland uttered in an anguished voice.

"And I never suspected Zac was a vampire. But now that we know, we have to call the police."

"No!" Holland shook her head emphatically. "What can we

tell them? That Naomi bit me and had a bad reaction to my blood? Mom, they'll think we're both psychotic. Or they'll suspect that I killed my best friend. We can't involve the police."

"Well, what do you suggest, Holland? We have to call Naomi's parents; they deserve the truth. As a parent, I know they're probably worried sick, wondering where she is."

"I'm not so sure about that. Naomi's parents were supposed to be attending a formal fundraiser with Ryan's parents—"

"Who's Ryan?"

"The vampire kid that bit Naomi. I'm pretty sure his parents are vamps, too. And that means Naomi's mom and dad have been bitten. We can't reach out to them; they could be as dangerous as Naomi."

No longer bubbling and spitting like hot lava, the pile of sludge on the living room floor seemed to have cooled off.

"We need to clean…uh…clean up Naomi." Her mother's voice cracked with emotion as she gazed at what was left of Holland's best friend.

"I'll take care of it," Holland said, biting her lower lip as she braced herself for the task ahead. "Why don't you check on all the windows, Mom? Make sure they're all locked. We're not safe until dawn."

"And then what?"

"I don't know. My friend, Jonas, sort of hangs around with Zac—"

"I hope Jonas isn't a vampire, too!" Phoebe recoiled in horror.

"No, he's human. He's from Haiti, but he doesn't have his immigration papers. Zac has been leading him to believe he can help him with his citizenship, but Zac's been lying. Anyway, Jonas's association with Zac has made him privy to vampire behavior. Jonas is our only hope at the moment."

Her mother let out a long sigh. "I feel so stupid. Why wasn't I able to see through Zac? I mean…I always thought I read people well, but I absolutely did not detect Zac's diabolical tendencies."

"First off, he's not a person. He's a vampire, and vamps are crafty. By the way, I think your client, Rebecca Pullman, is a vampire, too," Holland added.

Phoebe looked stunned. "But…how can that be? Ms. Pullman is such a lovely person…so dignified and intelligent—so utterly human."

"Vamps are able to disguise themselves pretty well, but the one thing they can't do is walk around while the sun is shining." Holland gave a short, bitter laugh. "We should be doing something useful, Mom. Why don't you look online and find out if there are any spells of protection that'll keep us safe until daybreak?"

"Sure, absolutely," her mother said, eager to help. "I'll also mix together those ingredients I used to heal the mosquito bites…" Phoebe lowered her eyes. "I mean…well, you know what I mean."

Her mother looked at her intently, and then her body jerked in surprise. "Holland, those bites on your neck…they're gone!"

Holland brushed her fingers across her neck. Feeling no punctures—only smooth, unscarred skin, she hurried over to a mirror and scrutinized her neck.

She looked at her mother and held up her hands. She gave a sigh of relief. "I'll get a bucket of water and some disinfectant… and start cleaning up…" Holland became choked up. Swallowing back a hard knot of grief, she uttered, "I'll start cleaning up Naomi."

⊕ ⊕ ⊕

Throughout the remainder of the night, Holland's phone had remained silent. No calls from Naomi's parents and not a word from Jonas. He'd reassured her that he was coming over, but once again, Jonas was a no show. It was Zac! Holland's gut instinct told her that Zac had found some sinister way to detain Jonas.

"The sun's up," Phoebe said, yawning and rubbing her eyes.

"Did you find anything online…you know, instructions on how to keep vamps away?" Holland asked.

"Nothing except the usual folklore: garlic, holy water, a crucifix, a stake in the heart. Oh, and a bullet to the head is supposed to be effective."

"We're both tired; we should try to get some sleep," Holland suggested. "Can I sleep in your bed, Mom?" she asked, her voice tiny like a little girl's.

"Of course, you can, hon." Her mother put her arm around Holland's shoulder as they padded toward her bedroom. "I stumbled on something online—something that I found particularly interesting."

"Oh, yeah?" Holland hopped on Phoebe's big comfy bed.

"I found a Wiccan site. There was an article about witch's blood. Apparently, there's a long-standing belief among the wiccan community that a witch's blood is poisonous to vampires."

Holland looked puzzled. "But I'm not a witch."

"Yes, you are, Holland. I've always suspected it; now I know for sure."

"But Mom, witchcraft is your thing. I don't want any part of that…I just want to be a regular girl."

"You are what you are, Holland. You should embrace your powers. I don't think you can ignore it. Spirit will make its presence known…as it did with the microwave and the Ouija board."

"It's all so creepy. I don't wanna embrace any powers. I'm not the type to sit around chanting and cooking up weird concoctions."

Her mother nodded in understanding. "I've only been dabbling in witchcraft. Finding out whatever I could learn from books and online, but there are schools that can help you perfect your skills."

"Witch-training schools?" Holland sounded appalled.

"They're expensive, but if you demonstrate superior powers, you can get a full scholarship."

"Oh, Mom, that sounds crazy."

"No crazier than what we've been through tonight. And we have no idea what other horror is facing us. You may have the power to help people. To save lives. Sleep on it, hon—okay?"

Holland nodded as she snuggled beneath the soft coverlet, her heart filled with fear for Jonas's safety and grief over the tragic loss of her best friend.

Steering her thoughts to a different topic, witchcraft training school popped in her mind. It was a wacky idea, but also something to consider. She couldn't deny that she needed help, if only to learn how to prevent microwaves from going haywire, and how to keep Ouija boards from spelling out reminders of something she now wished she'd never seen.

Naomi! Holland couldn't get her friend out of her mind. This was the year that Naomi was supposed to live her life free of being bullied. Now she was gone; she'd never get a chance to enjoy a new identity and acceptance at her new school. It was so unfair!

Holland tried to sleep, but she kept hearing Naomi's horrifying wail…seeing her literally melting as if her body were made of wax. Holland shook her head, trying to clear her mind of the horrific images. She wanted to remember Naomi the way she used to be, but the gruesome last encounter played over and over in Holland's mind. The scene was so firmly etched in her memory, Holland realized that she'd never be able to shake it away.

Oh, God…Naomi! Tears flooded her eyes, and then slid down her cheeks, dampening the pillow.

CHAPTER 32

Jonas was exhausted and hungry, but he didn't have time to appease his cravings. He had a job to do. Once again, he'd disappointed Holland, but she'd understand after he explained that during his absence, he was working hard to protect her.

Keeping out the shimmer of the rising sun, the drapes were drawn tightly. While Zac snoozed inside the tomb-like closet, Jonas sat on the edge of the bed, listening to the ticking clock.

Zac had struck a deal with Jonas—a deal that would prevent the vampire constable from having Zac captured and condemned to the earth.

According to Zac's plan, Jonas was to pay Jarrett a visit. Zac figured that Jarrett would know exactly where the new neighbors lived. Acting as a tour guide, Jarrett would be expected to lead Jonas to the front door of the newest residents of the upscale housing development.

And while Constable Sullivan and his lovely wife and son were vulnerable and resting in their lair, Jonas was expected to fling open the shutters, then roll up the shades. It was his responsibility to expose the vampire family to lethal rays of sunlight.

Jonas had no way of knowing if a human guard watched over the Sullivans as they slept. It was a dangerous mission, and Zac fully expected a successful outcome.

Zac had offered Jonas a large portion of his treasure—more

than enough money to pay off the money lenders in Haiti, and there'd be enough left to pay the voodoo woman a hefty sum to remove the debilitating spell.

Jonas watched as the hands on the clock moved slowly. The sun was brightest at high noon, but Jonas didn't have the patience to wait until the afternoon.

Jonas rose to his feet at seven o'clock sharp. Grim-faced, he took strides to Zac's bedroom and opened the door. He drew back the heavy drapes, filling the darkened room with sunlight. When he heard anxious rustling inside the closet, he raced across the room and yanked open the closet door.

The closet was flooded with light. Zac hissed and shielded his face with his arm. Grimacing, the vampire tried to scamper to the dark end of the closet, but he didn't possess his usual speed—his movements were awkward and sluggish.

Capturing Zac by an ankle, Jonas used all his strength to pull the struggling vampire out of the closet and into the sun-filled bedroom.

Zac fought frantically, swinging his hands and trying to twist himself out of Jonas's grasp. All to no avail. Holding both of Zac's ankles now, Jonas dragged the vampire to the center of the room where the sun shone brightest.

Panting with exertion, Jonas pressed his foot on Zac's chest, pinning him to the floor. Reflexively, Zac balled up into a writhing knot, hissing like a cornered snake as the sun baked his skin.

Jonas hadn't known what to expect, but he was hardly prepared for the vampire's white feet and legs to darken like charcoal and burn so rapidly. An unpleasant smell of smoldering flesh was thick in Jonas's nostrils. The sensation of Zac's ankles changing from soft, cold flesh to a hot, crumbling shell of crust was disturbing.

Crusted layers of skin on Zac's face and arms began to slough off. Thankfully, Zac's lips were charred and cracked, preventing him from discharging an alarming scream. In what seemed like a matter of seconds, all that was left of Zacharias Hamilton was a mound of ashes.

Clearing away evidence and saving the housekeeper extra work, Jonas scooped up the ashes and dumped them inside the plastic liner of a waste bin.

One vampire down and an entire swarm to go. Now Jonas had to figure out the combination to the safe. He tried to think like Zac. What numbers were important to the vampire? Seventeen-ninety-two, the year Zac was turned into a vampire came to mind.

Jonas pressed the numbers and like magic, the safe popped open. Inside were the keys and the title to the Saab, stacks of cash, and a jewelry collection that was all neatly organized. Gold, silver, and an assortment of diamonds gleamed as brightly as the beams of sunlight that had caused Zac's demise.

⊕ ⊕ ⊕

Along with the money, jewelry, the keys to the Saab, and the plastic liner filled with Zac's ashes, Jonas stuffed his remaining meager possessions into a bag, and left the hotel. Having access to transportation was convenient. Jonas wasn't an inexperienced driver, but as long as he steered clear of the busy thoroughfare, he believed he was capable of handling the car.

Traveling slowly and carefully, Jonas drove to a pawnshop that was in the vicinity of the hotel. After exchanging the final piece of jewelry for cash, he felt a surge of relief. The nightmare he'd been living was almost over. The compulsion to eat living flesh and drink blood was sickening, and now he finally had enough money to pay Madame Collette to break the spell.

But he couldn't go to Miami just yet. There was Holland to consider. She was depending on him for support and protection, yet once again, he was unable to go to her…at least not in his current condition.

. Bone tired and weary, Jonas yearned to sleep, yet the nagging hunger denied him the possibility of even a brief rest. With his pockets stuffed with more cash than he could have ever earned from a menial job, he made what he prayed would be his final visit to the poultry market.

This time, he purchased an entire crate of chickens and carted them off to the deserted woods—the site of his former burial place. The first thing he did in the solitude of the woods was to scatter Zac's ashes. Carried on a breeze, the vampire's ashes began to spread. Airborne, Zac's remains were dispersed in different directions. Jonas was satisfied that the crafty vampire would not be able to easily reassemble himself to wreak havoc once again.

The chickens' squawks echoed through the trees. Ravenous, Jonas stomach knotted and cramped so violently, he bent over in pain. He snatched a bird from the cage and tore into it, spitting out mouthfuls of feathers. Jonas was concealed by foliage and low-hanging tree branches as he feasted in private, feeding until his voracious appetite was satisfied.

A running stream in the woods efficiently washed away the blood and feathers, and with a change of clothes in the trunk, Jonas made himself presentable.

Back in the car, he didn't need a GPS to direct him to Holland's address. Her enthralling scent guided him, taking him straight to her door.

CHAPTER 33

"**S**till no answer," Phoebe said with a sigh after calling Naomi's parents for the tenth time. Her tired eyes had dark circles underneath.

"They're not going to answer, Mom," Holland said gloomily. "They've probably been changed, and they're hiding out somewhere with the vampire swarm."

"Right here in Frombleton?" her mother said incredulously.

Holland nodded grimly.

"There's also the possibility that they're worried sick about Naomi. For all we know, they could be at the police station or the hospital…they could be driving around, frantically searching for their daughter."

"If that's the case, they would have checked with us. If they're alive and cognizant, don't you think they would have called *me*, Naomi's best friend?"

"You have a point, but I'm not comfortable sitting around, doing nothing. It can't hurt to take a walk to their house…check on them while it's still daylight."

"And suppose they're home and unharmed? Suppose they're in the midst of organizing a search party for Naomi? What'll we do, Mom…grab some flyers and join the search team?" Nibbling on her bottom lip, Holland shook her head.

Worry lines etched Phoebe's face. "I don't know, hon, but we have to do something.

⊕ ⊕ ⊕

Half an hour later, Holland and Phoebe stood outside Naomi's house. They were mixed in with a cluster of people from the neighborhood, watching with wide-eyed horror as an emergency rescue team brought Naomi's parents out on stretchers. They were both zipped into body bags.

"Probably a murder-suicide," one neighbor speculated.

"There's talk that the daughter's on drugs. They say she went wild and slaughtered her own parents," said another neighbor.

Hugging each other, Holland and her mother backed away. They turned around and eased out of the crowd.

"Well, you have your answer now, Mom. Those bloodsuckers killed them," Holland murmured harshly as she and her mother headed down the path that led home.

Phoebe pressed her lips together tightly. "Maybe it's for the best. Personally, I'd rather die than roam the night thirsting for blood."

"You're not looking at the big picture. Naomi is dead, and so are her parents…no one in town in safe until every one of those vamps has a stake in its heart!"

"The police will think we're nuts if we report what we know, but an anonymous tip might be good idea. Seriously, hon, taking on vampires is out of our league," her mother said, her expression fearful.

Holland didn't respond. She thought about Naomi's violent reaction after drinking her blood. Maybe her blood actually had some type of anti-vampire properties. No, that wasn't possible. Naomi was a new and inexperienced vampire; she probably drank too quickly and choked. She could have made any number of fatal mistakes.

"Our best defense is to stay in at night, and to not extend an invitation to anyone," Holland said firmly. Regretfully, that rule now applied to Jonas, too. The last time she'd spoken to him, he was with Zac. Though it clenched her heart to think that Jonas may have been turned, she had to be realistic…Jonas had been in the company of a vampire last night. He'd promised to come over, but hadn't shown up. Holland couldn't help from thinking the worst.

"Shouldn't we at least alert the neighbors…you know, make them aware that there're vampires in our midst?" Phoebe asked.

Holland shook her head. "They'll think we're crazy."

Holland and Phoebe made the rest of the trek home in silence. Both dreaded nightfall, and neither had the vaguest idea of what to do next.

When they reached their street, her mother's stride slowed and then came to a complete stop. "Ohmigod!"

"What's wrong, Mom?" Holland looked at Phoebe and then followed her shocked gaze. Astonishingly, her mother's old Saab was parked in their driveway.

"Zac is visiting in the daylight; how is that possible?" Holland blurted, her voice tinged with fear.

Mother and daughter grasped hands and took two timid steps forward. When the car door opened and Jonas emerged, Holland's heart soared; she let out a shriek of joy.

Unclasping her mother's hand, Holland raced ahead; her breath came out in hot gasps as she fell into Jonas's embrace.

"Jonas! Jonas! You're alive," she said, touching his face in disbelief. "When you didn't show up last night, I thought Zac had turned you." Feeling extraordinarily relieved, Holland took a step back and grinned at Jonas, and then furrowed her brow. "You look tired; are you okay?"

"Other than a lack of sleep, I'm fine," he said, leaning in and giving Holland a quick kiss on the lips.

When Phoebe caught up to Holland and Jonas, she stroked the Saab affectionately, and said, "You must be Jonas. I'm Phoebe Manning, Holland's mother."

"Hello, Mrs. Manning. It's a pleasure to meet you," Jonas said.

"Is something wrong with the car? Does Zac want his money back?" Holland asked.

"No. I'm returning your mother's car, along with the title. Zac won't need a vehicle any longer." Jonas reached in his pocket, withdrew the folded document, and handed it to Phoebe.

"This is a pleasant surprise, but with all that's going on, I hope Zac doesn't come around tonight, trying to get the car back."

"He's not going to bother you ever again," Jonas said with conviction.

Holland broke into a grin. "Thank goodness. How'd you get rid of him? Did you put a stake in his heart?"

Jonas looked around embarrassedly. "No, uh—"

"Let's go inside and talk," Holland interjected.

In the living room, Jonas took a seat next to Holland on the sofa. Phoebe sat in the chair across from Holland and Jonas. Leaning forward anxiously, she said, "Please tell me Zac's dead. Holland and I are absolutely terrified of him."

"Yes, he's dead." Jonas winced at the memory of battling the vampire.

Holland leaned in and searched Jonas's face. "Did you kill him?"

Jonas flinched and then nodded. "I exposed him to sunlight." In a nervous gesture, Jonas rubbed his forehead.

Holland massaged his forearm. "What about the other vamps?"

"They're still out there…at the moment, they're asleep in their lair."

"Do all the vampires live together?" Holland's mother inquired.

"I'm not sure. But there's a family of vampires—the Sullivans—they live in the housing development on the other side of Burke's Highway."

"The Sullivans killed Naomi's parents, and their son turned Naomi into a vampire," Holland said bitterly. "How dare they rest peacefully while my best friend is dead? We should drive over there right now and flood the place with sunshine!"

"Oh, I'm not sure about that idea, hon," Phoebe said uneasily.

"Going to their house may unwise," Jonas said gently. "The Sullivans are well-respected leaders in the vampire community. They probably have humans guarding them while they sleep."

"Well, what do you suggest, Jonas? We can't sit here like bait! You said yourself that I have a special smell…a scent that attracts those bloodsuckers."

Phoebe did a double take, and then gaped at Jonas. "What kind of special scent?"

"That's what Zac told me. He said that Holland's scent is irresistible to vampires. It was only a matter of time before he attacked Holland, and that's why I had to destroy him." Jonas's voice grew weary.

"You must be exhausted." There was gratitude in Phoebe's eyes.

"Yeah, I've been up all night…I'm pretty tired," Jonas admitted. "If I can get some rest for a few hours, I'll be able to think clearer—come up with a plan when the sun goes down."

"Is it okay for Jonas to sleep in my room?" Holland asked her mother.

"Absolutely." Phoebe rose to her feet. "Are you hungry, Jonas? I can make you a sandwich."

"No thanks."

"A cold drink? Apple juice or iced tea?" she inquired, fidgeting with her hands.

"You're very kind, but no thank you—maybe later," Jonas replied.

Holland gestured to Jonas. "Follow me. My room is right down the hall."

CHAPTER 34

Holland closed the door to her bedroom. "Sorry I can't offer you a pair of PJs or something."

"Don't worry about it. I'm fine sleeping in my clothes." Jonas sat on the side of Holland's bed and slipped off his shoes.

"Was it gross?" she asked, wrinkling her nose.

"What do you mean?" Jonas leaned back and rested his head on the pillow.

"Killing Zac—did he melt and turn all gross and sticky?"

Jonas heaved a sigh and pulled his legs up on the bed. Lying curled, he let out a sigh and closed his eyes briefly. "He didn't melt; he burned and sort of turned into ashes. It was terrible, but I'm glad he's no longer a threat to you or anyone else."

Holland sat in the curve of Jonas's body. "Thank you for protecting me," she said, and then leaned over and kissed him. He wrapped his arms around her waist, pulling her close to him. Holland lay snuggled in his arms briefly, and then pulled away.

Jonas looked at her questioningly.

"Lying next to you feels good—too good," she explained. "I'd better let you get some rest before things get out of hand." She gave a little, nervous giggle.

Jonas smiled at her. "Wake me up in a couple of hours, okay?"

She nodded and stood up. Reluctant to leave, she leaned over and caressed his face. "See you later," she said and turned to leave. From the corner of her eye, something caught her attention.

"Jonas, those marks…on the bottoms of your feet—I've seen them before!" She stared at him with her mouth open, her eyes roving incredulously from his face to the soles of his feet.

"They're burns," he said with a tinge of embarrassment as he sat up.

"Looks like some kind of design…like intricate patterns. I saw footprints like those on a path near the woods—the shortcut route that I used to take to Naomi's house."

Holland thought of the message spelled out on the Ouija board, and the hairs stood up on the back of her neck. "Jonas," she said in a frightened whisper. "Are you dangerous…should I be afraid of you?"

"No." He shook his head. "I care about you; I'd never hurt you."

"But that's not normal." She pointed to his feet. "And I had a strange warning from my mom's Ouija board."

"Those marks—I don't understand what they mean, but they're symbols of a voodoo curse that's on me. Please trust me…I'd never hurt you." Jonas reached out his hand to Holland. "Sit down…please. I want to tell you what happened."

Holland hesitated for a few moments and then took his hand and sat down next to him. Jonas took in a shuddering breath and then started his story, beginning with the ceremony the night before the boat departed. Jonas wanted so badly to unburden himself and tell her everything. But he was afraid that if she knew the whole truth—if she knew that he'd actually devoured a human being, she'd condemn and shun him, and fearfully flee from him.

And so he left out the crimes he'd committed while out of his mind with hunger, and admitted only to feeding on animals and fowl. He concluded his haunting tale by showing her the bullet wound in his chest, and telling her how he'd been mysteriously pulled from the grave, as was Zac.

"Zac promised to help me get back to Miami, but he was a deceptive vampire. Still, I believe that the woman, Madame Collette, has the power to remove this horrible curse that's upon me. And I have Zac's money—more than enough to pay the voodoo woman."

"But, Jonas…Madame Collette was involved in enslaving the other cursed people. What makes you think she'd help you?"

"I believe the proper amount of money will convince her."

Holland shook her head. "Her magic is dark and harmful. You need someone that is well-skilled in healing magic. My mother knows a little bit about magic…I could ask her to try, but I'm not sure—"

"No, don't involve your mother. Only powerful magic will help me."

"You're right, and I'm going to help you."

"You?" Jonas pointed at Holland, looking surprised.

"Yes, me! I saw the footprints and I received the message. Now I understand what spirit was trying to tell me. Up until now, I've been suppressing my power…afraid of it, actually. Knowing the harm that's been done to you, I'm ready to embrace my gifts and learn how to use them properly. It may take a while, but I promise that I'm going to do everything in my power to break the spell that you're under."

"I believe you," Jonas said in a quiet voice. "I'll also understand if you've had a change of heart about me."

"What do you mean?"

"When the hunger comes over me…when I'm feeding…I'm not myself. I behave like a barbarian. It's not something I'd want you to see."

"I won't intrude on your privacy, but I want you to know that my feelings haven't changed. I still care deeply about you."

A visible wave of relief washed over Jonas. "I feel the same, but I wasn't sure about you."

"We'll work it out," she said, her brown eyes conveying sincerity.

"I hope so," he said with a pained expression.

"Get some rest, Jonas." Holland brushed her lips against his, and skimmed her fingers through his tightly coiled hair.

Jonas reached up and brought her palm to his lips and kissed it, giving Holland a ripple of chills. Holland's eyes grew dreamy. "I'd better get out of this room while I still have a chance, Mr. Suave," she said, laughing.

"There's nothing suave about me; I'm just a boy in love," Jonas clarified.

CHAPTER 35

Holland found Phoebe in the kitchen, her eyes glued to the computer screen.

"It didn't seem right to know about this vampire crisis and not make our neighbors aware, so I posted an anonymous warning on some local message boards."

"Good idea, Mom."

Holland looked over her mother's shoulder and squinted at the screen:

Strange things have been happening in Frombleton, and there's evidence that there are vampires living among us. This is not a joke. Please don't go out alone at night, and don't invite anyone to your home after the sun goes down.

"You got the point across; I hope people take the message seriously," Holland said. "Can you put together a list of witch-training schools? I want to start applying as soon as possible."

Phoebe's face lit up. "Sure, hon. I'll print a list right away."

"Oh, and I have a favor to ask."

"What is it, hon?"

"Can I borrow your car? I wanna pick up some wood from Home Depot, and have it chiseled into stakes. You know, just to be on the safe side."

"But your blood is a repellant, isn't it?"

"I'm not sure; it may not be poisonous to older vampires.

Besides, we need some weapons. I don't want to get bitten in order to kill a vampire."

"You have a point." Phoebe handed Holland the set of car keys.

⊕ ⊕ ⊕

She circled around three times before finding a parking spot. She got out and armed the car and a few moments later, the Durango pulled up beside her. In a small town like Frombleton, you could never go to the mall without bumping into someone you knew, but bumping into Jarrett Sloan was becoming a regular habit.

"Holland!" Jarrett said with surprise in his voice. "I thought you were someone else."

"Judging by your weight loss and those bites on your neck, I assume you've been spending a lot of time with Zac, the vampire."

Jarrett's eyes bulged. "You know about him? You're the first person that believes he exists. My parents think I'm crazy; they want me to see a psychiatrist."

"I can see why they'd be concerned," she said, observing his frail body. "After what you've been through, counseling might not be a bad idea."

"No, I'm sane. And for some strange reason, I feel a lot better today. But when I saw the Saab, I thought Zac was coming for more blood." Jarrett shook his head. "I should have known that Zac wouldn't be out in broad daylight."

"You don't have to worry about Zac anymore. He left town… for good."

"Really?" Jarrett broke into a huge smile. "Do you mean I can actually get my life back to the way it was?"

"I hope so, but you need to know that there are others. A large swarm…and there's a vicious family of vampires living in your neighborhood."

"In *my* neighborhood?" Jarrett's face turned a shade paler.

"Be careful, Jarrett. Stay in the house at night and don't invite anyone in your home after dark. And warn your family and friends."

"I've already told a ton of people, but everyone acts like I'm a mental case." He looked briefly troubled, and then he broke into a broad smile. "Wow, Holland, you look awesome as usual. I feel like such a jerk for the way I treated you that night..." He shook his head. "I'm sorry; will you accept my apology?"

"You were pretty heartless, and I was devastated, but I'm over it now."

"Think we could try it again? Chaela's out of the picture. I'm not kidding. I'm through with her for good." Jarrett gazed at Holland, his eyes hopeful.

Holland shook her head. "Sorry, I'm seeing someone." Clutching her handbag, she walked away from Jarrett and made strides toward Home Depot.

After purchasing three sharpened sticks of wood, she stopped by Petco, and left the store carrying two fat rabbits in a cage. Feeling sorry for the bunnies, she couldn't look them in their large, soulful eyes. Along with the stakes, she set the cage in the back seat, and then headed home.

The garage in the back of the house was crammed with so much junk there was no room for the car. Luckily, Phoebe hardly ever went inside, and so Holland secretly stashed the rabbit cage in the garage, grateful that the animals were quiet, docile creatures.

⊕ ⊕ ⊕

Holland stood over Jonas and called his name softly. "It's five o'clock...time to get up."

Jonas stretched and yawned, and when he came fully to his senses, he was dismayed to find Holland leaning over him, kissing him on the cheek. In her presence, he always steeled himself against his urges, but he was taken off-guard by her closeness—by her overpowering sweet scent. Determinedly, he fought the urge to sink his teeth into her fragrant flesh.

"Hungry?" she asked sitting next to his prone body.

"Sort of," he replied with a frown, wanting to move far away from her delicious smell.

"I picked up something for you to eat—it's stashed in the garage. My mom's in her room, busy on the computer. You can sneak through the kitchen to get to the garage."

"Thanks." Jonas lowered his eyes, feeling vulnerable and ashamed.

His unhappy expression didn't escape Holland, but she went on chatting in a perky manner. "It's pretty junky in the garage, but I cleared out a space. And I left some plastic bags for cleanup. There's a hose that's hooked onto a spigot, and you can't miss the drain…it's in the center of the floor…you know…to get rid of the blood."

Jonas put on his shoes and stealthily crept to the back door. Inside the garage, the rabbits observed him with curiosity and trust. Starving, Jonas felt saddened and excited at the same time.

At dusk, Holland, Phoebe, and Jonas sat in the living room. The sharpened stakes were propped in a corner near the front door.

"Several people responded to the vampire piece that I posted on the 'Happenings in Frombleton' message board," Phoebe announced. "One woman said that mysterious puncture wounds turned up on the neck of one of her coworkers at a downtown hotel where she works. She said that the woman with the wounds has no idea how she got the injuries."

Megan! Guiltily, Jonas looked down at his sneakers.

"Also, the mother of a teenage boy wrote that her son has bruises and peculiar pricks on his neck. The boy's pale and has been losing weight at an alarming rate. She said that his doctor can't find any cause for his condition."

Sounds like Jarrett, Holland thought, but didn't say anything. She hoped Jarrett had taken her advice and stayed in after the sun had gone down.

Phoebe Manning continued, "A bartender claimed that two people were found dead at a local bar, their bodies completely drained of blood."

Rosie and Hugo. Jonas shook his head solemnly.

"And the last reply was from a guy that works at the city morgue. He said that a married couple was brought in today and every ounce of their blood had been siphoned."

"Naomi's parents," Holland blurted. She squeezed her eyes shut, trying to block out the appalling reminder that her best friend and her parents were all wiped out by vampires.

"I hope your post raises awareness in this town," Holland went on. "There's no telling how many unsolved deaths were actually caused by those bloodsuckers, and it's time for people to start fighting back."

Holland's mother glanced worriedly at the stakes. "It's good to be prepared, but with Zac gone, maybe we won't need those. Perhaps life here in Frombleton will go back to normal."

"Zac wasn't the only vampire that bites people, Mom. He was only a small part of the problem.

"Holland's right," Jonas piped in. "The other vampires are as malicious and as dangerous as Zac.

Holland nodded vigorously. "And don't forget that Naomi had a date with a vampire; he picked her up here at our home. If my scent is as potent as Zac claimed it to be, then I'm sure Ryan, his parents, and all the other vamps are gonna try to figure out a way to cross our threshold."

Phoebe shuddered visibly, and then stood up. Raking her fingers through her hair, she began anxiously pacing in a tight circle around the coffee table. "This is outlandish! We're not capable of battling vampires; we need help." She nudged her head toward the stakes that were propped near the door. "It's foolish to think those sticks are going to protect us."

"I wish I knew the perfect solution, but I don't," Jonas replied apologetically.

Holland sprang to her feet and put an arm around Phoebe. "Don't fall apart, Mom. We're going to get through this. There's no guarantee that any vamps are coming here tonight, but in case they do, at least we won't be defenseless."

"She's right," Jonas added. "Tomorrow, I'll try to find out if anyone is guarding the Sullivans during the day. If not, they'll meet the same fate as Zac."

CHAPTER 36

From the back of the house there was a loud crash and the sound of shattering glass. Holland jerked around with a violent start.

"What was that?" Phoebe trembled violently, her eyes bulging in terror.

"I don't know." Jonas crept to the door and grabbed the stakes. He tossed one to Holland, and then forced a wooden stake into Phoebe's quivering hand.

Holland's eyes darted around. "Someone or some *thing* just crashed through the bathroom window." Holland searched Jonas's face. "We didn't invite them; how can they barge in like that?"

"The constable doesn't need an invitation to investigate a crime scene," Martin Sullivan announced, his voice filled with arrogance as he emerged from the shadows, flanked by his wife and son. Approximately six feet-seven, Sullivan towered over his family.

"My son is distressed over the loss of his mate," the tall vampire explained, his voice straining with anger.

"And someone is going to pay dearly for that loss," the woman declared as she floated upward, absurdly rising a few inches from the floor and then giving the constable several reassuring pats on the back.

Constable Sullivan nodded. "Indeed, that payment will be extracted in blood."

Phoebe gasped at the vampire's threat. With both arms wrapped around Holland's waist, she drew her daughter near.

Her feet back on the ground, Andrea Sullivan placed a slender arm around her son's shoulder. A delicate white hand with pointed, red-painted fingernails smoothed back the boy's hair and dotingly caressed his face.

With a mass of black curls framing his face, Ryan had the angular-shaped face of his father, and the full sensual lips of his mother. He was unusually good looking, and so were his parents.

Holland found herself staring at the Sullivans in fascination. The unearthly beauty of this vampire family was breathtaking. No wonder Naomi and her parents had been lured into their clutches.

The boy's thick eyebrows drew together in a curious frown. His nostrils flared as he inhaled sharply. "There's that uncanny odor again. Do you detect it, Mother?" His eyes settled on Holland.

"Yes, I do. The air is thick with the scent." Through the veil of dark, long lashes, the female vampire squinted at Holland and sniffed. "You have a very appealing odor," she said to Holland, and released a long sigh of yearning.

Holland shrank back and unconsciously placed a hand over her rapidly beating heart.

Jonas raised his stake defensively.

Constable Sullivan angled his head and regarded Jonas contemptuously. "I've seen you before, haven't I? You were riding in the car with that no-account scoundrel, Zacharias Hamilton."

Jonas didn't deny the claim. He raised the stake higher, indicating that he had no intention of backing down.

An amused expression crossed the vampire's face. "What do you plan on doing with that stick, boy?"

"Don't come any closer," Jonas warned.

The three vampires inched forward menacingly. Looks of hunger inhabited their dark eyes.

Holland wrenched free from her mother's embrace and joined Jonas, trying to ward off the vampire family by stabbing at the air with the pointed end of the stake.

In a swirl of movements that were faster than the eye could see, the constable whizzed across the room. Before Holland and Jonas had time to aim their weapons at the target's heart, the eerily fast vampire had ripped the stakes from their hands.

In horrorstruck surrender, Phoebe let the stake she was holding fall from her hand.

Ryan and his mother applauded. "Bravo, Father," Ryan said.

"Well done, darling," said the vampire wife.

Showing off his unnatural strength, the constable snapped each stake in two and sent the broken pieces of wood scattering about the room.

Wearing a triumphant smile, the vampire wife strutted toward Holland's mother and yanked her by the arm. "We'll take this one. Come, my son…give her the dark kiss. We'll feed together."

Phoebe let out a frightful shriek.

"Get your hands off of her; leave my mother alone!" Holland shouted.

"I don't want to merely feed, Mother," Ryan objected, folding his arms in defiance. "You promised me a mate. And I choose the strange-smelling girl." He pointed to Holland.

The woman smiled at Holland. "My son's smitten. What's your name, my dear?"

Face twisted in sneer, Holland responded by holding up her middle finger.

"Vulgar manners for such a pretty girl." The female vampire gazed at her son.

"Your mother's right," the constable agreed, "She's not the one for you."

"You don't get to choose my mate. Not anymore," Ryan bellowed. "I want her, and by all that's unholy, I swear that I'll have her." Ryan made purposeful strides toward Holland.

Seething, Jonas glared at Ryan. "Stay away from her." Jonas's voice was barely recognizable as a deep, throaty growl distorted the sound of his voice. Without warning, and using all of his strength and speed, he charged into Ryan. Jaws open, his teeth sank into the boy's neck. Taking a massive bite, he ripped out a chunk of the boy's throat.

At the sight of such savagery, Holland's mother released a strident scream.

Taking a flying leap, the constable shoved Jonas off of his son, and flung him across the room.

With his hands on his throat, the boy held his wound closed. The vampire couple rushed to their child's aid.

"Mother," the boy gurgled, his eyes wide and desperate.

"Shh, shh. Calm down," she cooed. "You're immortal; the wound will heal."

The doorbell rang suddenly and insistently, while at the same time, there was a hard hammering on the door.

"The police!" Holland uttered with a look of relief in her eyes.

"Stay where you are; don't move," the constable warned. "I know how to handle the police." Intending to bedevil the enforcers of the law with his mesmerizing eyes, the constable took purposeful steps toward the door.

But before he reached it, the doorknob began turning and there was the sound of locks disengaging.

Magically, the door opened on its own. And standing in the doorframe was Rebecca Pullman. She wore a vibrant blue Kimono jacket and wide-legged pants. "Good evening, Constable," she greeted with a pleasant smile.

"You have no business here, witch," the vampire spat and then drew back his lips, revealing fangs.

"I beg to differ." Rebecca slid a hand inside her Kimono pocket and retrieved a shiny, silver blade. In a swift motion, she sliced the constable across the throat. The tall vampire's legs buckled, and he stumbled backward as a fountain of blood gushed from the open wound.

"You'll heal, father. We're immortal," the son called out, his neck miraculously healed and unscarred.

"He won't heal; that blade is made of silver." Rebecca held up the thin blade.

The constable fell, causing a thud when his lifeless body hit the floor.

Andrea Sullivan looked at her husband in horror. "You'll pay for this, witch!" she cried, pointing a finger at Rebecca Pullman.

Andrea and Ryan both leapt to their feet, preparing to retreat through the window they'd crashed through when they'd entered the house.

"Stop!" Rebecca bellowed in a voice that echoed. The two vampires stood frozen in place as if surrounded by a force field.

Rebecca stared at the broken stakes and mumbled an incantation that enlivened the pieces of wood, causing them to elevate and soar through the air, staking both Andrea and Ryan through their hearts.

Mother and son struggled to pull the stakes out of their chests. "I'm dying, Mother, help me," Ryan wailed.

With the stake jutting out from her chest, Andrea fought through the force field until she reached her son. She yanked and tugged on the broken piece of wood, to no avail. When Ryan began to lose consciousness, Andrea screamed, "Don't leave me, Ryan. You're my son; you can't die!"

Standing upright, Ryan's head fell forward. His eyes closed in death.

Andrea covered her face, and dropped to her knees. From her lips came a low, sustained moan that sounded very much like a wounded animal.

CHAPTER 37

Three dead vampires lay stretched out on the Mannings' living room floor.

"They'll disintegrate when the sun rises," Rebecca said.

"I'm still in awe over the way you used your powers. I've been afraid of you, thinking that you were a vamp, too," Holland confessed, gazing at the witch in gratitude.

Rebecca shook her head. "Ever since your mother awakened your dormant powers, I've had the singular urgent goal to protect you. I pretended that I needed financial advice so that I could make contact with you."

Phoebe's cheeks were flushed pink. "It's embarrassing that I had the gall to try to assist a seasoned witch."

"The drum healing session was somewhat soothing. I apologize for being deceptive, but I must advise you that dabbling in the unknown often has adverse effects."

Phoebe held up her hands in surrender. "Believe me, I'm through experimenting with the occult. I'm proud that Holland is a real witch, but I'm extremely curious about something...I don't understand how, with my limited knowledge, I was able to awaken my daughter's power?"

Rebecca gave her a patient smile. "Didn't you cast a spell on your daughter's behalf?"

Phoebe looked perplexed for a few moments. "Yes, I did, but

that was quite a while back. She was upset over a bad haircut and wanted her hair to grow back."

"That spell was more powerful than you realized. It was cast with an immense amount of love and caring. Your desire, coupled with your daughter's desire, unleashed the magic in her."

"Will I be able to make objects move and…and…you know… kill vampires?" Holland asked.

"Absolutely. You're much more powerful than I am. I'm a witch of the Second Order; you're one of the rare witches of the First Order."

"What does that mean and how do you know so much about me?"

"I've always known about you. I've been assigned to watch over you since the day you were born."

Holland's mother frowned. "I appreciate what you've done for us, but I never assigned you or anyone to act as Holland's guardian."

"No offense to you, Mrs. Manning, but I was assigned by the Highest Order. Holland has been relatively safe up until the time she began emitting pheromones. But vampires being even vaguely aware of her puts her life in jeopardy."

Holland and Phoebe exchanged an anxious look.

"But now that the head honcho vamp is dead, I should be okay, right?" Holland spoke up.

Rebecca shook her head. "I wish it were that simple. You're a threat to vampires; your blood is poisonous…it can kill them."

Feeling guilty, Holland winced and was briefly pensive. "So that's what happened to Naomi. My blood killed her." Holland winced.

"You must release that guilt, my dear. Your friend was already dead."

"So, in a way, it's like I kind of did her favor? You know, sparing her from being eternally damned."

Rebecca smiled patiently. "I suppose you could put it that way. Thankfully, none of the remaining vampires in this town know about your blood, at least not yet, but it's only a matter of time before they detect your scent. If the vampires discover that they can die from biting you, there'll be a witch hunt of monumental proportions."

Holland scratched her head in confusion. "You're a powerful witch, Ms. Pullman; don't you have the scent, too?"

"Call me Rebecca. Yes, I have the witch's scent, but it's faint, and my blood is not lethal."

Phoebe cleared her throat. "Holland and I were looking at witch-training schools online, but the costs are astronomical. We were hoping she could get a scholarship."

Rebecca pursed her lips. "Our school doesn't advertise. Our scouts select the best candidates from all over the world. There's no tuition, and Holland would be in a learning environment with girls her age who have similar abilities."

"I'm very interested in the school, but I can't commit. Not right now; I'm worried about Jonas's...uh...his problem." Holland reached for Jonas's hand.

Jonas squeezed her hand reassuringly. "I'll be okay. I have the funds to get to Miami...to get the cure."

"What kind of cure?" Phoebe's voice rose with concern. "What are you, Jonas?" she asked, recalling the way he'd bitten into Ryan Sullivan's throat.

Jonas took a deep breath and once again told his story, beginning with his harrowing voyage to America. While admitting to unusual strength and a propensity toward violence when offended, he intentionally avoided mentioning his desperate craving for living flesh and blood.

"But I don't trust the voodoo woman in Miami," Holland

blurted at the conclusion of Jonas's account. "Jonas believes that she'll remove the spell for the right price, but I think it's a big mistake for him to put any trust in a woman that was involved in a conspiracy to sell human beings for free labor."

"I have no one else to turn to," Jonas said, and then sighed in defeat.

"Can you use your magic to help him, Rebecca?" Holland pleaded.

Rebecca lips tightened into a sad smile. "Unfortunately, my powers don't extend to voodoo magic, but I do know of someone that can help you, Jonas."

"Who?" Jonas asked eagerly.

Rebecca fixed a serious gaze on him. "Young man, I'm aware of the extent of the troubles that plague you, but the relief you seek...the freedom from this curse can only be found in your native land."

Jonas looked appalled. "You expect me to go back to Haiti— like this?"

"Yes, that's where it all began and that is where the spell will be broken."

"But how can I return to my island with this vile curse upon me?"

"A mother's love endures all things—even a wicked curse. There's good and bad voodoo, and the remedy you seek can only be found with one who practices good voodoo. I know such a person. She lives in Haiti, and her name is Mamba Mathilde. Go to her, she'll help you."

Jonas looked doubtful. Rebecca placed a gentle hand on his shoulder. "You must return home, Jonas. You have the ability to accomplish great things one day. Go home; the mamba will be expecting you."

"But I don't have the proper documents to return to Haiti."

"Leave that to me. Manifesting documents is much easier than slaying vampires."

⊕ ⊕ ⊕

The next day, while the sun glowed brightly, Holland drove Jonas to the airport.

Rebecca had whipped up a cocktail made of pulverized animal skin, inner organs, and blood to stave off the craving during Jonas's journey home. The mixture was a tidier way of managing his hunger, and he was enormously grateful.

Still, nothing could compare to the glorious taste of human flesh. He hadn't derived any enjoyment when he'd bitten into Ryan Sullivan's cold, dead, and tasteless neck. He wanted to share all of his inner thoughts with Holland, but he couldn't bear the idea of her fearing or being repelled by him.

Looking on the bright side, Jonas held up the documents that Rebecca had acquired for him. "Now that I can travel freely, I hope we won't become strangers."

"Never!" Holland vowed. "You have my email address, and until we can plan an actual visit, we can always communicate with each other online."

"Oh." There was sadness in his tone, and he glanced downward. "I don't have a computer, but who knows, I may find a way to access the Internet." His pockets were bulging with American dollars, but he couldn't worry about purchasing a computer when he had to take care of his family and pay off the big debt that he owed the moneylenders.

"We can write letters," Holland said optimistically. "I have your home address; I'll write you every day, Jonas. Of course, with the school being in a secret location, you'll have to send your letters to my home address."

"Of course," he said gloomily.

"Don't be so glum; my mom will make sure that I get your letters."

"I know, but I can't help it if I'm starting to miss you already. Teenage love affairs are supposedly doomed from the start." Jonas laughed sardonically. "And with the distance between us...well, the odds are terribly stacked against us."

"Hey, stop being so pessimistic. Don't you believe in destiny?"

A slight smile formed on his face. "Destiny led me to you."

"And destiny will reunite us again," Holland said, nodding.

Their farewell kiss was the sweetest ever, and for the first time, Jonas was sated and calm, with no overwhelming urges to tear into Holland's supple flesh.

⊕ ⊕ ⊕

Parked at the curb, Holland watched Jonas exit her life. She touched her chest, aware of the perceptible sensation of her heart breaking in two. Tears that she'd bravely held back while Jonas was in the car now fell freely.

Oh, Jonas, I miss you already, too!

CHAPTER 38

S toneham Academy was nothing like Holland had expected. She'd imagined it would look like a castle or a stately old structure that was covered in ivy. Stoneham was thoroughly modern—a magnificent glass, metal, and mirrored architecture that required no artificial lighting during the day.

There were no stern-faced portraits of the school's founders lining the walls. Inside the hallowed halls was an interesting collection of abstract art and crystal sculptures.

The dress code was relaxed, and with only ninety-eight students enrolled, the girls were treated as individuals and were not required to wear the traditional private school tartan skirt and white blouse.

During the tour given by Miss Livingston, the head mistress, Holland marveled at how normal all the girls looked. Never in a million years would she have guessed they were witches possessing special powers.

And the perks were plentiful: dozens of computers, PC tablets, netbooks, e-Readers, iPads, and iPods. The state of the art facilities included Jacuzzis, two heated swimming pools, a five-star fitness center, and en suite bedrooms took the place of drafty dorms and dreary common areas.

"You have a choice of eating in the school's dining room area or having your meal delivered to your room," Miss Livingston said with a radiant smile.

"If you don't mind, I'd like to eat in my room," Holland responded, needing a few moments of privacy to take in her new environment. She also wanted to call her mother and give her the scoop on her cool, new school.

Holland's accommodations were spacious, airy, and elegant and seemed more suited for a member of the royal family than for a lowly student. Never in her life had she been surrounded in so much luxury.

She thought of the devastated island that Jonas had returned to, and felt a pang of guilt. Weeks had passed since she'd dropped him off at the airport, and there hadn't been a word. Hopefully, she'd get a letter or an email from him soon.

As a favor to Holland, Rebecca Pullman had placed an energy field around her house in Frombleton. It was comforting to know that her mother was safe when the vampires roamed at night.

Holland picked up the thick leather-bound menu from the desk. It was hard to make a selection from the numerous, yummy-looking selections. She finally settled on a simple grilled cheese sandwich and a cup of tea, which reminded her of dinner at home.

While waiting for her food, she picked up the phone and called home. She smiled the moment she heard Phoebe's voice. "Hi, Mom, I'm here."

"How do you like it? Are the girls nice? Are you settled in, hon?"

"It's amazing, Mom. I'm kind of in a daze…you know, it's all so ritzy. I'm sort of overwhelmed."

"You'll get used to it. I'm already checking off the days until Thanksgiving break. I miss you, hon."

"I miss you, too, Mom. Did I get any mail from Jonas?"

"No, not yet," Phoebe said solemnly. "But I'm sure you'll hear from him soon."

"Yeah, I'm sure I will," Holland agreed, but in her heart she was worried that she'd never see Jonas again. "So what's new in Frombleton?"

"Nothing new here. There haven't been any recent posts about puncture marks or blood-drained bodies turning up. But there is something strange going on in Willow Hill, the farming community twenty miles north of here."

"What's happening there?" Holland asked, without much interest. Her mind was on Jonas.

"It's been reported in the news that human carcasses have been turning up on the side of the road and in wooded areas. They suspect that the majority of the bodies are undocumented migrant workers because they haven't been able to identify them. They were able to identify one victim—a female college student who'd gone out for a morning jog and never returned home. That poor girl's body was ripped to shreds. Investigators think that these people were attacked by wild animals, but there's a rumor going around that there's a plague of zombies in that area."

"Zombies!" Holland repeated in a shocked voice.

"It's an outlandish notion, but I plan to avoid that area to be on the safe side."

"Good idea," Holland mumbled, her thoughts on Jonas and the curse.

There was a knock on the door. "I have to go, Mom. My food is here."

"Fancy, shmancy," Phoebe kidded. "Room service, huh? Sounds like you're getting the royal treatment."

"Yeah, it looks that way," Holland said distractedly. "I'll call you tomorrow. Love you, Mom."

Sitting on her bed, eating a gourmet grilled cheese made with Mediterranean cheddar, pesto, black olives, and shiitake mushrooms on marble rye, she wondered if Jonas had found Mamba Mathilde.

And she also wondered if there was any connection between Jonas's affliction and the killings in Willow Hill.

No! How could there be? From her knowledge, Jonas had never traveled to Willow Hill or anywhere north of Frombleton.

But something nagged at Holland. A vague knowing that whatever was going on in Willow Hill was more than a mere rumor—something was horribly amiss.

And though she was hundreds of miles away from home, and living in the loveliest and most peaceful environment that she could have ever imagined, Holland had an ominous feeling that she'd be battling zombies in her foreseeable future.

CHAPTER 39

HAITI

A white candle, a clear glass of water, and a pot of flowers were set on a table in honor of the spirits. The mamba clasped both his hands and closed her eyes as if in prayer. Jonas had expected a more elaborate ceremony—a complicated ritual with drumming, song, and dance, but Mamba Mathilde was conducting a very simple ritual.

With bated breath, Jonas waited for her to open her eyes and give him the good news. Minutes passed and still her eyes remained closed.

Finally she lifted her eyelids and unclasped his hands. She looked at him for an uncomfortably long time. Finally, she spoke. "Your hands are cold. Your soul is lost in the wind. I'm sorry, you are too far gone; there's nothing I can do."

Surely his ears deceived him. "Wh…what do you mean? I was told that your magic is the best—that you can help me."

"I cannot reach your soul."

"Please. You must help me. I can't go on like this." Jonas abruptly stood and stuck his hand in his pocket, pulling out money. "I'll pay you! I'll give you everything I have."

"Your soul has fled; I can't bring it back. You are dead."

"No! Don't say that. I'm alive." He strode to her side. Anguish stooped his shoulders and lowered his head. "I stand here before you with breath in my body; with a heart that beats. Is that not proof that I'm alive?"

Mamba Mathilde shook her head. Jonas dropped to his knees and wailed. "I beg you, find my soul…return it to me."

She touched the top of his head. "You must accept it—accept your death. The person you once were is gone."

Jonas shook his head. "That's not true."

"The sprits tell me otherwise."

He dropped his head in Mamba Mathilde's lap. Grief that he was unable to contain any longer poured out in tears and choking gasps. And when he could cry no more, he stood.

"I'm alive," Jonas insisted for the final time, and then departed the mamba's house.

⊕ ⊕ ⊕

Blending with the night, Jonas crept toward a crumbling hut and slipped silently inside. In a tiny room, his mother and two sisters slept.

"Mother, I'm here," Jonas whispered. His little sister, Racine, woke up first. The smile he expected did not appear on her face. Her cry of fear awakened his mother and sister, Desiree.

They also emitted shouts of alarm and wept in despair. Desiree reached under a pillow, and brought out a large crucifix, which she clutched in horror.

"No one greets me with smiles…only tears and shouts. Why?" Jonas's face was contorted in pain.

"You died in the water—you were buried at sea. I received word that you drowned," his mother said, both arms stretched protectively around her two daughters.

"But I live. You see me."

"Yes, my son, I see you. And your appearance in my home is something I've dreaded since I received your letter that contained

American money. My son is dead, I told myself. Was this money sent from the grave?"

Desiree and Racine cried harder.

"I figured it out. I realized that you were involved in dark magic—a spell was cast on your unholy soul. And now you have returned." His mother shook her head; tears filled her eyes. "There's no place for you in this house."

"Mother..." His voice broke off. It was hopeless.

"You must go before someone sees you. I no longer care what happens to me, but your sisters will suffer unendurably if word gets around that their dead brother makes visits in the night."

Jonas nodded solemnly. Resolute, he dug in his pocket and withdrew money and placed the bills on the bed. "It's for the lenders. To keep them from harassing you."

"They're wicked men. No amount of money will ever satisfy them." Jonas's mother removed her arms from around her weeping daughters and pulled down the sleeve of her nightgown, revealing a deep gash that was in the process of healing.

Tears pooled in Jonas's eyes.

"They promised that it will be my face the next time the payment is late."

"Oh, Mother..."

"Go to Verrettes. No one knows you there. No one will suspect that you are not a living person. Get an education. Make a life, where there is no life. Go now, Jonas. You must leave."

He took brisk steps toward the small bed and threw his arms around his family, and kissed them goodbye. He touched his mother's face one last time before returning to the darkness of the night.

⊕ ⊕ ⊕

Jonas watched in the shadows as Francois banged on the door. The pockets of Francois's trousers bulged with his collections of the day. Jonas watched as Desiree opened the door with a trembling hand, and admitted the well-dressed moneylender into the old, rundown ramshackle hut.

And when the moneylender exited, Jonas followed, hands clawed and grinding his teeth as he quietly stalked his prey.

ABOUT THE AUTHOR

After nearly a decade of penning erotic bestsellers, Allison Hobbs was ready to embrace her passion for writing paranormal novels. Using the pseudonym Joelle Sterling presented the perfect opportunity for Allison to share her fascination with the supernatural and broaden the scope of her readership.

Joelle Sterling is a full-time writer living in Philadelphia, PA.